Written in Stone

Cobble Cove Mystery #3

Debbie De Louise

Written in Stone

Third in the Cobble Cove Mystery Series

By Debbie De Louise

Dedication:

To writers everywhere who may not kill for a good story but would die for a bestseller and to those fans and friends who have supported me in my writing journey and traveled with me to Cobble Cove for three adventures.

Chapter One

The scream echoed through the library. Patrons looked up from their books and computer screens. Those browsing nearest the outburst made their way toward the sound. Questioning exclamations and puzzled whispers mingled with footsteps. "What was that?"

Alicia, Gerry, Donald, Bonnie, and Gladys rushed from different areas and converged into the 364 section. Gilly stood there shaking, her finger pointing at the ground where a body lay face down. "Oh, my God! It's Mary Beth!" she exclaimed.

After the initial shock of numbness flooded her body keeping her distanced from the horror in front of her, the first thing Alicia noticed besides the blood and the gaping hole in the back of the woman's head was the light purple blouse the victim wore. It was the same one she'd admired in the window of Chloe's Closet and bought on sale a few days ago. It was the same blouse she wore to work this morning and the one she'd mentioned to her editor the night before.

Gerry took his cell phone out of his pocket. "Don't touch anything," he instructed. "I'm calling 911."

As a bunch of onlookers gathered on both sides of the aisle, Alicia tried to keep things calm. There were gasps and murmurs. Adele Wexler, at the front of the crowd, was observing the event with excitement as if she were happy to be present for a real-life murder.

"Looks like 911 can't do anything for her. We should call Ramsay," said Donald. "We also have to close the library. I'll go lock the doors and put up a sign, but I don't think we should let people leave."

Patrons reacted to that with raised voices, and Alicia tried again to quiet them. "Please, keep it down. We are trying to get things under control here." Turning back to her co-workers, she said, "We need to contact Sheila immediately."

"You should do that," Donald told her. "You're the librarian in charge."

"But what if the killer is still in the library?" Gilly asked, her voice as shaky as her body. Her words caused the onlookers to become more agitated.

"We all need to stay together," Gerry said. "I'll call the sheriff as Donald suggested. We might have an active shooter scenario on our hands."

"How come we didn't hear the gun go off?" Donald asked.

"Haven't you heard of a silencer?" Gilly said. Her voice was still shaky, but she seemed to be making an effort to get herself under control. "I'd say this was planned. Didn't you all notice we're by the crime books?"

"What does that have to do with anything?" asked Donald.

"A murder near the murder books. Isn't that ironic?"

"That is strange, Gilly, but if the shooter is around, we need to get out of here but keep everyone together." Alicia tried to recall the video the staff had been shown on what to do in a situation where a gunman was on the premises.

"First, we have to be quiet," Donald said. He glanced behind him. "There are plenty of places to hide in the library. He could be anywhere ready to spring out at us."

"Thanks for helping me calm down." Gilly frowned at Donald, but Alicia felt relieved her friend's shaking seemed to have stopped. Throughout all of this, Bonnie and

Gladys hovered by Gerry's side as if hoping the unarmed security guard could protect them.

Gerry spoke into his phone. "Ron, it's Gerry. There's some trouble at the library. We have a shooting. We don't know if the shooter is still here. The staff and patrons are in the building. We're closing the doors and keeping everyone contained." He paused listening to the sheriff's reply. "Yes, we aren't far from the back exit. We'll head there and wait for you. Yes, we'll lie low. Over and out."

Chapter Two
Two Months Earlier

Alicia glanced out the front window for the tenth time. Her friend Gilly was on her way to Cobble Cove, not just to visit as she had during her kids' spring vacation in April, but to move in and take over the Cobble Inn. She couldn't contain her excitement.

"Calm down, Ali," John said from behind her as he placed some toys in the playpen where their twin toddlers were playing. "You've been watching for Gilly's arrival for the past hour. It's Monday morning. She probably got caught up in rush hour traffic driving through the city."

"I can't help it, John. It's hard to believe she's finally coming."

The sky was a clear powder blue with high fluffy clouds that still allowed the July sun to shine through. It was a perfect summer day in the small town of Cobble Cove, New York. Dora had invited them to a barbecue that afternoon to celebrate her and Charlie's upcoming departure to a retirement complex in Florida while welcoming Gilly and her sons to their new home.

Just as Alicia was about to abandon her watch, a minivan pulled up. Alicia ran out before it was even parked. Gilly, her three boys, and their dog exited the car.

Gilly wore the "Mom of Boys" sweatshirt Alicia had gifted her at Christmas. Her dark hair was neatly brushed back with just a few stray strands forming bangs on her round forehead. Her face broke out into a huge smile and she threw herself into Alicia's waiting arms.

"Oh, honey. It's so good to see you."

"Gilly, I'm so happy you're here."

The boys looked on behind their mother as John joined them. The beagle ran around the group yapping for attention.

"And who are these young men?" John asked. "I briefly recall meeting them when they came down for Ali's baby shower, but they've grown so much since then I hardly recognize them."

Gilly introduced the boys as they stood in a line one head higher than the other. "That's Danny, my 12-year old." She introduced the tallest, who had dark curly hair and a few freckles on his cheeks. Next was Joey, her 10-year old, who had lighter hair and eyes. Last was her "baby," eight-year old Billy, who looked like a mix of his two brothers. They wore sports-themed t-shirts. Alicia could see Gilly in all of them, but she recalled that Gilly said Danny took most after her ex-husband. After Gilly had introduced them, she glanced at her dog who had quieted down and come to stand by her side. "And this is my fourth child. Her name is Ruby."

John laughed. "Why don't you all go inside? There's plenty of time before the barbecue, and I know you're eager to see our twins. They've just started to walk, so we have gates everywhere in the house. They're in their playpen now, but we shouldn't leave them alone for long."

"I remember those days." Gilly smiled. "C'mon boys, let's go inside with the McKinneys. Do you mind if Ruby comes along too?"

"Of course not," John said. "Fido always makes himself at home in our house when Dad visits, and he'll be at the picnic to keep Ruby company."

***

After Gilly had been formally introduced to Carol and Johnny and had oohed and aahed over how big they were and how much cuter than their photos, John took the boys into the kitchen for some snacks Alicia had picked up for them from Duncan's grocery store. When she'd asked for suggestions, Gary had directed her toward a shelf of goldfish crackers, potato chips, and pretzels. He then added a 10-pack of Capri Sun to her shopping cart. Even though he only had a daughter, Gary seemed pretty knowledgeable about boys. He said he grew up with two younger brothers.

When the women were alone with the twins and Alicia finally was able to tear Gilly away from them, the topic turned to Gilly's takeover of the inn and her new position as part-time clerk at the library. Gilly sat on the couch with Alicia as Ruby obediently lay next to her, eyeing the twins who had briefly been allowed to pet her from their playpens.

"So, do you think you'll enjoy your new jobs?" Alicia asked as she and Gilly sat on the couch watching the babies walk around stumbling into one another every so often but giggling as they did so. Most of the laughing was done by Carol. Johnny was still the shy one. Alicia knew he'd inherited the serious side of John along with his father and grandfather's dimples.

"I think I'll love both of them," Gilly replied. "I'm a little nervous about running the inn because I've never done anything like that before, but I'm sure the library position will be a piece of cake for me after my experience at our library on Long Island." She laughed. "I just hope there are some nice-looking men around town. You said a lot of new people have moved here and that more are arriving to teach at the new high school."

"I don't know, Gilly. Most of the newcomers are couples or women, and the high school won't open until next year." Alicia thought of Chloe Gibbons who ran Chloe's Closet, a boutique in Cobble Corner; Gary and Patty Millburn and their sweet daughter Angelina who was still on a waiting list for a bone marrow donor; Dr. Donna Clark, the veterinarian who'd opened a much-needed animal care center in her home; Andy Phillips, the young college student who now ran the *Cobble Cove Courier* newspaper with John's occasional help; Kim Pierce, Andy's girlfriend and Alicia's babysitter; and some of the staff of the Fairmont Elementary School. With Casey gone, there was no one left as a possible match for Gilly that Alicia could imagine. Even the new employees at the library—including the public relations director and guard—were not likely candidates for a romantic partner for her friend.

"Just my luck. You grabbed the last eligible bachelor in Cobble Cove."

"That she did," John said as he walked into the room.

"What have you done with my sons?"

"I gave them a job. They're testing Alicia's new computer in her office."

"What?" Alicia jumped off the couch.

"Don't worry, honey. I set them up with some cool games. It'll keep them busy while you ladies chat before we have to leave for the barbecue. I can watch the babies if you want."

"I'd rather you watch Gilly's boys." Alicia could picture what the kids could be up to unsupervised with her brand new PC.

"I'll go check on them," Gilly offered. "You and John can stay here. I've already lectured them about being on their best behavior in this house and at the inn once we move in."

Alicia marveled at how Gilly managed being a single mom.

Alicia followed Gilly down the hall despite her friend's protests that she could handle her boys. John stayed behind to keep an eye on the twins and Ruby who seemed content to remain by the couch.

When they entered the office, Alicia was shocked to see a trail of crumbs spread across the beige carpet while the three boys gathered, heads bent together, staring at the computer screen. Danny had his hand on her mouse roughly pressing and rolling it, while Billy was swiveling in her desk chair. Joey was making sounds to mimic those of the cartoon-like characters on the monitor. All of them were munching ripped open bags of goldfish crackers, chips, and pretzels. A combination of messy fingerprints was smeared across her screen and desktop. Her mousepad was covered with a layer of cheese powder and salt.

"Oh, my God!" Alicia stood in the doorway, dazed.

Gilly immediately took control. "Excuse me, boys. What are you doing?" Her voice had deepened to one of absolute authority. It threatened instant death to any child who backtalked her.

Joey shut up. Billy jumped off the desk chair. Danny let the mouse go. They all looked toward their mother with an expression of being caught with their hand in the cookie jar. Danny, the elder spokesperson for the group, answered for his brothers. "We were just playing, Mom. Mr. McKinney said we could. This is a real cool machine. The screen is huge."

Alicia had been so happy when John brought home the Dell computer with the 27-inch monitor. He said it would help reduce her eyestrain when she edited their mystery novels. Now the beautiful screen was caked with crumbs.

"I'm sure Mr. McKinney did not tell you that you could eat in here or make a mess of Mrs. McKinney's desk." Gilly still spoke calmly, but there was that sharp edge in her voice that warned her kids that she meant business.

Danny continued to explain in his brothers' behalf as they looked on with terror in their eyes. "We didn't mean to make a mess. We'll clean it up. We promise," he implored.

"You'd better." As Gilly took a step into the room, the boys walked away from the computer. A few stray crumbs fell off Joey's shirt.

"We are going to the inn soon. I expect you to have everything back in the condition it was when you started playing in here. If it isn't, you will all be punished. Is that clear?"

"Yes, Mom," Danny said. His brothers nodded.

Gilly turned to Alicia. "I'm so sorry about this. Show me where you keep your cleaners and vacuum. The boys are going to fix everything before we leave."

"No, please, Gilly. It's okay. Boys do things like this. I was just not expecting it. John should've known better than to let them bring snacks in here, so it's partly our fault. I'll clean it up. You are our guest and so are the boys."

"I can't let you do that, Alicia. They have to learn from their mistakes. They're not babies anymore. Besides, they're going to be living at the inn and helping me out there. If they make a mess, we'll lose guests."

Alicia relented. She knew Gilly had a point. "Okay, I'll go get the vacuum and some of the wood cleaner for the desk. John also has a cleaner for the computer."

***

The adults ended up assisting the boys in cleaning Alicia's office while Ruby, alert to the commotion, raced around them emitting short barks. Alicia imagined John was a bit guilty about allowing them in her sanctum with food, but he only grinned when she told him what happened and said no damage was done. Nothing that a little elbow grease won't clear up.

"You're getting more like your father every day," Alicia commented. "With all your sayings and euphemisms."

"I take that as a compliment." He grinned, and she couldn't stay angry with him. Just as Gilly had been tough on her boys, underneath, she adored them and her disappointment in them dissipated as quickly as Alicia's at John's misjudgment.

***

Once the office was clean, Alicia prepared to gather up the twins for the trip to the inn. Gilly gave her a hand folding up the playpen, packing the diaper bag and other accoutrements of motherhood, while John strapped the twins in the two car seats in his pickup.

"I'm happy you're here, but I'm also sad," Alicia told Gilly as they left the house. "I'm going to miss Dora and Charlie."

"That's only natural, hon, but I'm sure they'll keep in touch."

Alicia got into the passenger side of John's truck, and Gilly, her boys, and Ruby piled into their car. They planned to follow Alicia and John up the road to the inn. It was a short drive and they could've walked on such a nice day, but with the babies and all their supplies, it was easier to drive.

It took all of five minutes to pull up to the Cobble Inn. The sun shone on the newly painted and renovated building. The flower boxes were resplendent, their pansies and marigolds in full bloom. Dora came outside as soon as they drove up. She walked to the car and assisted Alicia and John in unbuckling the babies, bending down and kissing both on their cheeks. John took Johnny while Dora picked up Carol. Alicia strung her diaper bag over her shoulder and toted the folded-up playpen in her other hand.

"Here, let me help you," Gilly offered. "I'll take Carol. Danny, why don't you bring the playpen and Ruby to the backyard? Joey, you can carry Alicia's bag. Billy, please take the container of cookies I baked inside."

"Thanks, Gilly," Alicia said, handing the playpen and diaper bag over to the boys her friend had assigned them to as Dora gave a sleepy Carol to Gilly. Car travel, no matter how short, always seemed to make the twins drowsy.

She turned to Dora. Now that her arms were empty, Alicia could embrace the woman who was instrumental in her and John's introduction.

"It's so good to see you, Dora. I can't believe you're leaving tomorrow."

Dora's eyes glistened, but no tears fell from them. "I'll miss you and John and everyone in Cobble Cove, but I'll be back to visit. I promise." Dora paused and looked back at Gilly. "Excuse me, where are my manners? It's nice to see you again, Gilly, and your boys. We had such a pleasant visit in April and now you're moving in already."

Gilly smiled. "I would give you a hug, Dora, but this little girl is an armful."

"You can put her down," Alicia said. "She's walking now, but you might want to hold her hand. She's quick when she wants to be, so don't be deceived by her snoozing act."

Gilly lowered Carol to the ground and took her hand as Alicia instructed. The girl wiped her eyes and blinked.

"Maybe John and I should take the kids inside while you two catch up," she told Alicia. "Joey and Billy have already brought in the supplies."

"That would be great." Dora looked over at John who had also put Johnny down and was holding his hand. "Why don't you bring the little ones out back, John? Charlie's there setting up the barbecue with your dad. He can help you put out the playpen, and maybe you can assist them with the cooking?"

John grinned. "Sounds like a plan. You ladies go inside and do your lady stuff." He came to Gilly and took

Carol by his free hand. Alicia loved the sight of John walking both his kids to the backyard gate. It was slow going as Johnny and Carol were taking wobbly steps, but he was patient with them.

"What a great dad," Gilly said, reading Alicia's thoughts.

"Alicia and John are both wonderful parents," Dora added. She looked toward Gilly's car that was parked at the curb behind John's. "I can ask John and Charlie to help you with your suitcases later, Gilly. You don't have to unpack everything right away. Edith and Rose will also help. I've invited them to the barbecue today. There's plenty of room for you at the inn tonight. We have a few guests, but they're out most of the day, and we'll be gone early tomorrow. You and the boys can stay in the new wing upstairs, and I'm glad you brought your dog. It's about time the Cobble Inn had a watchdog."

***

After John set up the playpen under a shady tree, Alicia helped Dora bring out the salads, rolls, and Gilly's chocolate chip cookies. Gilly lent a hand with the pitchers of iced tea and lemonade.

Charlie, wearing an apron that was a bit snug around his ample middle, and Mac, overseeing the grill, his cane propped against a nearby tree, greeted them. Fido was romping around the yard and dashed over to Ruby when he saw her. The two dogs sniffed one another and then began playing like old chums. Betty sat on a swing, where she offered to rock the babies.

"I know this is a barbecue," Mac said, "but I made a few of my special PB&J sandwiches if anyone wants a break from burgers and hotdogs." He indicated a platter on the picnic table covered with aluminum foil.

John laughed. "No lunch would be complete without one of your PB&J sandwiches, Dad."

Edith and Rose showed up just as Charlie was starting to flip the burgers. Edith held a cake carrier while Rose hefted a fruit bowl and a plastic grocery bag that brimmed over with decorations.

"Good day, ladies," Charlie said. "I've put out some folding chairs in that shady spot by the swing or you can sit at the picnic table if you'd like."

Edith brought the cake to the table, while her younger sister placed the fruit next to it. "Would you mind introducing us to all these nice new folks?" Edith asked.

Dora made the introductions. Edith and Rose had been away on a cruise to celebrate Edith's seventieth birthday when Gilly had visited the inn in the spring.

While Charlie barbecued, John played catch with the boys and dogs at the far end of the yard. Fido tired out sooner than Ruby, who was several years younger. He lay in the shade of the swing panting, his flanks rising and falling quickly as his tongue lolled out of his mouth. Alicia, worried about the old dog, refilled his water bowl that Mac had brought over. Fido drank thirstily and seemed more alert but didn't go back to play.

Betty rocked Carol and Johnny on the swing, and they dozed from the motion. Alicia, Gilly, and Dora chatted about Cobble Cove, the beautiful weather, and the inn. Edith and Rose busied themselves adorning the table with cut-out welcome signs, napkins, and paper plates. When Rose took out two balloons from the bag, Alicia was amazed that she could blow them up effortlessly. Singing in the church choir must've strengthened her lung power. One balloon featured a welcome message for Gilly, while the other, meant for Dora and Charlie, read, "Happy Retirement."

***

The barbecue was in full swing when one last guest came through the white picket gate. Alicia was surprised to see the town's new sheriff, Ron Ramsay, enter the yard. He carried a bottle of champagne.

"Hi, there," he said. "Sorry I'm late, Dora, but I had to check out a stolen bicycle. It's been recovered, and the thirteen-year old thief has been given a warning. It turns out he's the victim's brother and just borrowed the bike without asking." He smiled. Alicia couldn't help but admire the fact that the change in the man from his previous incarnation seemed to be sticking.

"No problem at all," Dora said. "Have a seat and something to eat, Sheriff Ramsay. Charlie just put on another batch of hotdogs and burgers to replenish the ones the boys and men devoured."

Ramsay handed Dora the champagne bottle that she placed near the cake and walked over to the vacant chair next to Gilly. "Is this seat taken?" he asked.

Alicia noticed her friend eyeing the sheriff in the way she did most men and couldn't help but realize that Ramsay was now one of the few eligible bachelors in town.

Gilly stood up from her own chair that was on the other side of the swing under the weeping willow. It was very close to Dora's herb garden that Alicia hoped Gilly would be able to maintain, although she knew Edith had a green thumb and would probably nurture the plants.

"Only you, Sheriff. You're looking wonderful these days," Gilly said, her voice raised an octave into what Alicia considered a lilt, one she reserved especially for greeting men. "If you don't recall our brief meetings, I'm Abigail Nostran, but you can call me Gilly." She extended her hand.

"My pleasure, Gilly. I do remember you. Please call me Ron. You needn't have gotten up." Alicia saw a light come into the sheriff's face, or was it just the sun shining on him?

"The three boys playing ball over there with John and the dog are my sons. When they come back for food, I'll introduce you."

As Alicia saw Ramsay's face darken at Gilly's words, she knew what she'd seen hadn't been a trick of the sun.

When Gilly added, "It's hard being a single mother, but friends like Alicia have been so helpful," Ramsay's face lightened again, and Alicia observed Gilly glance down at his left hand. She shouldn't have been surprised her friend was flirting with the single sheriff.

It was then that John and the boys, sweating and hungry, returned to the table, with Ruby and Fido at their heels, ready for more food scraps.

It's going to be interesting and fun having Gilly living nearby and working with me again at the library, Alicia thought. She only hoped the dark events of the past that had cast a shadow on the town would not return.

Chapter Three
Two Months Later

Alicia was nervous and excited at the same time. The new public relations director at the library, Nancy Haines, had arranged, along with Sheila, for a party in honor of her and John's release of their second Groucho Marks mystery.

Browsing through the outfits in her closet, she couldn't decide what to wear. She envied John who just had to grab his one multi-purpose suit, shave, and brush his hair. For her, it was selecting a matching dress or pants set with shoes and jewelry, and then applying the right touch of makeup – not too heavy, not too light. More decisions would follow. Should she wear her hair up or down? Curled or straight? She sighed. As her friend Gilly would say, "Men have it easy. Maybe that's why they're so screwed up." Alicia laughed to herself. Gilly, a divorcee, was not the best one to judge men. Even though some men were screwed up, so were some women. Tina and Gloria Langley came to mind. She pushed thoughts of them aside to focus on the happy upcoming events of the night.

"Alicia, are you ready yet?" John called from the nursery next door. He was getting the twins ready for Kim who would be watching them while they attended the party. Since Gilly moved to town, she babysat Carol and Johnny occasionally at the inn with her boys, but tonight she wanted to attend the library event. Danny, Billy, and Joey would be there with her, too.

"Not quite, John," Alicia replied. "Can you help me choose between two outfits?" She took a dress and pants set from the closet and laid them next to one another on her and John's bed. She'd worn the red dress in New York to dine out with John and see the Radio City Christmas

Spectacular last year. Her new blue blouse and slacks were from Chloe's Closet, a local shop that had just celebrated its first anniversary with a sale she couldn't resist.

John entered the room, and his blue eyes zeroed in on the bed. "Definitely the blue outfit, Ali. The dress is too fancy, and it might bring back some bad memories."

Even though she agreed, she said, "The dress had nothing to do what happened last year, John, but I haven't worn the blue set, so I think that'll work for tonight. Thanks."

John grinned, showing the dimple she found so attractive. He looked especially handsome in his gray suit, and she couldn't help but notice the engraved pen she gave him clipped to his breast pocket. The memory of how the original gift, the one Gilly gave John, had saved his life brought back another memory she had to suppress. John was likely wearing it tonight to have it handy to sign books.

"Okay then. I'll wait downstairs for Kim. I already gave Carol and Johnny kisses."

***

Although the Cobble Cove Library was within walking distance of their house on Stone Throw Road, they decided to drive to the party. They used Alicia's car because John's truck didn't seem the right vehicle to use for authors to arrive in at a book launch. John had initially argued that they could fit the boxes of their hot-off-the-presses books more easily in the pickup, but Alicia simply removed the extra car seats in the back of her car and placed the boxes there. John had to be content with being the driver.

Since the September night was mild, Alicia didn't have to worry about wearing a coat. Her blouse was long-sleeved, anyway, and fit comfortably over her pants. She hoped there wouldn't be too many fattening desserts at the party because, despite a regular fitness routine after the babies were born sixteen months ago, she had to watch every calorie to keep the pounds off.

When they parked in the library lot behind the building, John said, "You were quiet on our drive, Alicia. I know you must be nervous, but all your friends and co-workers and probably some patrons, too, will be here to congratulate us on our new book. Just relax and enjoy the limelight."

Alicia laughed, but it sounded strained. "You forget the press will be there, as well as Mary Beth." Mary Beth Simmons was Alicia and John's editor. John considered her a thorn in his side. She was a female version of Sheriff Ron Ramsay before he reformed himself, a fast talker who was rude in a more social way and persistent to the point of aggravation.

John winced at the name. "I know she'll be here, but I'll survive. As far as the press, Alicia, I *am* the press. Actually, I know Andy's handling the story as he is most of the *Courier* news nowadays."

Alicia took a breath. "Okay, John. Let's go."

As they got out of the car and were taking their books from the back seat, Gilly and her sons pulled up in the spot next to them.

"Hello there, famous authors," Gilly said smiling. Alicia was surprised to see her in a dress, but it was a simple black one offset with a white belt and low heels. The neckline was high, but Gilly never bothered with jewelry. Alicia couldn't help feel that a pearl necklace would've added a nice touch.

"Looks like we're just in time." Gilly turned to her boys who were starting to argue in brotherly fashion. "Stop fighting, guys, and help the McKinneys with those boxes."

The boys complied immediately, each one taking a box. Alicia admired the way her friend handled her twelve, ten, and eight-year-old boys without a father. She was thankful she had John and that he had decided not to pursue the job at Columbia that had opened for a Journalism professor last year. If he had been accepted for the position, it would mean his being away from home five days a week. As the twins were walking now, it was even harder to keep an eye on them. She also had to find the time to write and wasn't ready to give up her full-time job at the library. Their books hadn't hit any bestseller lists yet or been selling well enough for her to quit working. John was still looking for regular employment locally but had cut back his hours at the newspaper office and was devoting more time to writing and watching the babies.

"Thanks, boys," John said as Gilly's sons walked toward the back entrance of the library. It was the employee's entrance, but John knew the code and followed them. Alicia and Gilly walked behind talking.

"We really appreciate your coming," Alicia said.

"We wouldn't miss it for the world, honey. You look great, by the way. That's a new blouse, isn't it?"

"Yes. I got it at Chloe's last week during her sale. I asked you if you wanted to go with me to shop, remember?"

Gilly's smile shortened. "Yes, sorry. I've had a lot on my mind lately. I couldn't make it because things were crazy at the inn."

"I understand." Alicia knew that Gilly was having some trouble adjusting to the move to Cobble Cove and taking over the Cobble Inn from Dora and Charlie who had moved to a retirement home in Florida two months ago.

John had punched in the back door code and was holding it open for them as the three boys walked in carrying the boxes.

"Thanks," Alicia said as she took the door and beckoned her friend to enter.

Inside, Gilly changed the subject. "I want to be the first one to get an autographed copy of your new book signed by you and John."

Alicia laughed. "I can't have you cut the line, but I'll make sure you get one after we give our presentation."

"Presentation? I didn't know this was a talk."

"Well, we have to say a few words after Sheila and Mary Beth announce us."

"Your editor is here?" Gilly's grin widened again. "I bet John just loves that. I can't wait to meet this woman I've heard so much about."

Alicia nodded. "You won't be able to miss her, Gilly."

***

The party was taking place upstairs in the room next to the staff lounge that had been set aside for meetings and programs. It was on the opposite side of the hall from the lounge and the director's office. As they entered the main part of the library, Alicia suggested John take the boys up in the elevator because they were carrying boxes, and she and Gilly would meet them upstairs.

Rounding the corner by the staircase, Alicia noticed the sign with a red arrow pointing up that read, "Meet the Authors: Alicia and John McKinney of the Groucho Marks Mystery Series." It also featured a photo of her and John each holding a copy of one of the books. She remembered posing for it at Mary Beth's request. Nancy had taken the photo.

"Nice PR work," Gilly said also seeing it. "I'm sure you and John will pack the house."

"Nancy's doing a good job as our new public relations director. She also sent the press releases Mary Beth faxed us to other towns and newspapers in the area besides the *Cobble Cove Courier.*"

"I thought Mary Beth was just an editor, not an agent or publicist." Gilly seemed surprised.

Alicia was about to reply that Mary Beth did everything and expected no less back from her authors because after all, she was getting paid from the net sales of John and Alicia's books. Before she could address Gilly's comment, however, Donald came running from the front desk toward them.

"Alicia, Abigail." He was the only co-worker at the library, probably the only person in town, who called Gilly by her actual name Ramsay.

Alicia turned, her hand on the bannister, one step up the stairs. "Donald, what's wrong?"

In his late thirties and very thin despite a huge appetite and a high calorie diet, the librarian's red tie of scattered leaves was askew, his glasses slipping down his nose, his dark hair spiked up as if lightning had struck him, and his face was red as beets.

"That woman . . ." He pointed upstairs. "You better watch out, ladies. She's out for blood."

Alicia knew immediately to whom he was referring. "Calm down, Donald. Mary Beth is a bit controlling, but she's not going to harm anyone."

"I hope you're right, Alicia. She barged into the library a half hour ago ordering everyone around, including Sheila. She gave Gladys the third degree because she hadn't set up the room yet and then wasn't happy with how she arranged the chairs. Then she yelled at Nancy for not putting signs up on the front door or on Bookshelf Lane. She also somehow knew the flyers she sent to be distributed in the shops in Cobble Corner were not given to all the store owners. Even worse, she argued with Sheila about why the library didn't have a larger room for programs and one on the main floor that would be more accessible to everyone."

"That sounds typical of Mary Beth." Alicia wasn't surprised, but she took a deep breath hoping that Donald would mimic the action. "What did she call you out on, Donald?"

He sighed, and she was happy to see the flush of his face begin to lighten. "She wanted me to tell every patron that walked in the door about the event and urge them to attend. Now I don't mind spreading the word, but there are patrons who just come to the library to use the computers or take out videos. Some aren't interested in books at all, especially ones they have to buy."

"Don't worry, Donald. I'm sure you're doing your best. Remember, Sheila's your boss, not Mary Beth."

Donald sighed again, and his voice was much calmer as he replied, "Thanks Alicia, and good luck tonight. I wish I could attend, but someone has to be at the desk." Before turning and heading back to his post, he nodded to Gilly. "Nice seeing you again, Abigail."

Gilly smiled. "Likewise, Donald. Please say hi to Roger for me." Roger was Donald's partner who worked as a teacher in the elementary school next door. He had been especially accommodating to Gilly's three sons when they'd started classes at their new school at the beginning of September, as had Mrs. Stafford, the principal. Gilly's oldest boy, Danny, would be moving into the new high school that was scheduled to be completed next year on the site of what used to be Casey's diner. Alicia still felt sad about the town losing that landmark and about what happened to Casey last December. At least something good would come from the loss, as students graduating from the elementary school that went up to eighth grade would be able to attend classes in Cobble Cove instead of being bussed to a high school in another town.

***

When Alicia and Gilly arrived upstairs, the room was still closed off to guests. Most of the library workers were there. Sheila, Nancy, and Mary Beth were talking animatedly in a circle by the table over which hung a banner matching the one downstairs minus the arrow.

Alicia and John's books were on the table, but neither John nor Gilly's boys were in sight. Alicia assumed they might be attending to another task assigned by Mary Beth. The editor was raising her hands in exclamation, talking in the rapid-fire speech that Alicia recognized from their phone conversations. She was about Alicia's height and weight with shoulder-length auburn hair possibly a shade darker, but that's where the similarities ended. Alicia estimated Mary Beth to be in her mid to late fifties, ten to fifteen years older than she. Heavy makeup caked her face, and her hazel eyes were shaded by thick, false lashes. John liked to say that Alicia's eyes were pools of deep chocolate he could melt in and that he loved the fact the only cosmetic product she wore was light lipstick. Mary Beth was dressed in a tight-fitting gray suit with matching low-heeled shoes. At Alicia and Gilly's entrance, she dropped her hands, stopped talking a breath, and peered at them.

"Alicia, my dear. What a pleasure to meet you finally, and I love that blouse you're wearing." She extended her talon-like hands displaying long blood-red fingernails and an assortment of rings that would rival the ones that Sheila wore. Alicia was suddenly reminded that she had been instructed to have a manicure before the event so her hands would look attractive signing books. Shaking Mary Beth's hand, she was conscious of her unvarnished and uneven nails. She had completely forgotten to make the appointment at Wilma's salon and hadn't even gone there for a haircut. At least Mary Beth approved of her blouse.

"Nice to meet you, too, Mary Beth," she said, without much inflection.

"Your husband and those young men he arrived with are gathering more chairs to put out in the back row because your custodian refused and stormed out of here. She made some comment about fire laws and this room's capacity." She waved her arm, indicating she felt the statement ridiculous.

Alicia saw Sheila raise a red eyebrow. The director was obviously holding back an angry retort. She would be well aware that Gladys knew the regulations, and Alicia could not imagine how more chairs would fit in the already jammed space. She also knew that those chairs might end up not being filled, anyway. However, while most library events rarely saw more than twenty attendants, the extra publicity about her and John's appearance might bring more guests.

Mary Beth then focused on Gilly. "Excuse me, are you another cleaning person?"

Alicia watched her friend's face change and wondered if she would need to restrain her. Gilly wouldn't take such a demeaning remark lightly.

Alicia was proud when, instead of making a scene, Gilly simply replied, "No. I'm afraid you're mistaken, Ms. Simmons. I am Alicia's best friend, a part-time clerical employee here, and the new owner of the Cobble Inn."

Despite being corrected, Mary Beth just smiled, showing straight white, yet pointed teeth. They somehow struck Alicia as ones that might belong in the mouth of the Big Bad Wolf, who John imitated as he tried to blow down each of the little pigs' homes.

"Ah, the Cobble Inn. I checked that place out when I was planning to book my reservations in town. It's unfortunate there are no other places to stay. I opted for the 4-star Hilton Hotel in Carlsville."

Alicia could well imagine Mary Beth using the proceeds of what she earned from their mysteries for fancy lodging that she could also claim as a business expense. She was glad when Gilly didn't react to the insult. Her friend was probably relieved the editor hadn't booked a room at her inn.

Before any other words could be exchanged, John and the boys came back into the room each carrying a chair.

"Where did you say you wanted these?" John asked, looking over at Mary Beth.

"In the last row, please, John."

As the boys tried to fit in the chairs, John glanced toward Alicia and Gilly with a pained expression.

Sheila walked to the back of the room. "Just stack those chairs by the wall. If we need them, we can arrange them down the side, but I want the area clear before the program begins."

Nancy, quiet until now, joined Sheila by the back row, her small stature in contrast to Sheila's and Mary Beth's. "I agree. People have to walk down the aisles especially if John and Alicia are going to be autographing books."

Alicia was surprised that Mary Beth didn't argue. She busied herself straightening the books on the table into neat piles.

***

A few minutes later, when Sheila let in the public and the additional library workers who were attending the event, Laura hurried to Alicia's side at the front of the room. She held a small brown box in her hand. "Hi, Alicia. I wanted to give this to you before you began. I think you'll be able to use it during your signing."

Alicia was surprised. Laura was the Children's Librarian. She was also in charge of the library cat, Sneaky the Siamese, who had made the place his home after turning up there before Alicia came to town. The children especially loved it when Sneaky, and occasionally his guest Fido, her father-in-law's golden retriever, participated in the story times Laura conducted.

Taking the box Laura handed her, Alicia couldn't guess what was inside. The box was not shaped like a pen, so she couldn't imagine what else would be useful to her for autographing books.

"Sorry I didn't wrap it," Laura said. "It arrived just yesterday, and I didn't have time."

"Don't worry about that. You really shouldn't have gone through the trouble at all." Alicia glanced down at the box and noticed it was labelled "Custom Stamps."

"It wasn't any trouble at all except getting Sneaky to sit still while I made the print to send to the stamp company."

Alicia laughed, and it calmed her anxiety that had raised a notch upon meeting Mary Beth. The woman was still ordering Sheila and Nancy around on last-minute tasks. Alicia admired Nancy's quiet and controlled responses to the editor's commands but knew Sheila was only holding back her red-headed temper out of respect for her and John.

"Go ahead, open it, Ali. I think it's cute. I hope you like it."

Alicia lifted the box's lid and found a paw print stamp inside that said 'Sneaky' underneath.

"When you and John sign the books, you can use that paw print to pawtograph the books, too. I know you used Sneaky as one of the characters in your Groucho Marks books, and he always seems to point Marjorie Meyers and Detective Marks to the clues that solve the mysteries."

"What a great idea. Thank you, Laura. Is that actually the real Sneaky's paw print?"

"Sure is." Laura seemed proud of herself. "I saw an advertisement in one of the library's cat magazines for a personalized paw print stamp, and I followed the instructions on how to take one of Sneaky. I made sure to use non-toxic ink, of course, but it was still a mess."

"I'm sure it was. Thanks again, Laura." Alicia turned to John who had been cornered by Mary Beth after she'd finally finished with Sheila and Nancy. She knew he would be relieved to be interrupted. "Excuse me, John, look what Laura made for us to sign our books. Isn't it adorable? It's Sneaky's actual paw print."

Before John could reply, Mary Beth cut in. "Alicia, I'm surprised at you. Didn't you tell your friends that all promotional materials must be approved by me?"

Alicia was shocked. This was going too far. "The stamp is not a piece of promotional material, Mary Beth. It's a gift. If people don't want us to use it, we won't; but there are many cat lovers in town, and Sneaky is one of the main characters in our cozy mysteries."

Mary Beth sighed and threw up her hands. "Do what you want. I can't waste time arguing. The program is about to begin."

John grinned at Alicia as they walked to the side of the room to await their introductions and whispered in her ear, "Good going, honey. I think that stamp will work well for us, and MB should have no say in what presents we accept."

Laura had also smiled as she'd gone to sit in the front aisle that had been reserved for the library staff and John's father and his girlfriend Betty, who was also the President of the Library Board. Alicia was thankful Mac hadn't brought along Fido, even though Sheila would've probably permitted the dog to attend. Mac was keeping a close eye on his pet since the episode last December, but he probably figured there would be too many people in attendance and that Fido, despite being well trained, might get too excited. Gilly had also left Ruby, her Beagle, back at the inn.

***

After Sheila welcomed everyone to the book launch party and mentioned some upcoming library programs and events, she introduced Nancy as the new public relations director. Nancy joined her at the front of the room and said a few words of thanks and talked about some of the ideas she was planning. Although the ebony-skinned lady, close to Sheila's age in her early sixties, was petite, her perfect posture caused her to appear taller as she stood facing the audience. She announced that the first Cobble Cove Library newsletter would be published the following month and would include contributions from patrons as well as staff members. She also described the new writing club that would hold its first meeting in October. Alicia had volunteered to run that group, and several patrons had already expressed interest in joining. Alicia noticed how soft-spoken Nancy was as she addressed the group, although no one, not even those in the tight aisles in the back, had trouble hearing her. Alicia was reminded of how Gilly often told her that, when her boys misbehaved, whispering instead of yelling more effectively got their attention. She assumed that was a lesson Mary Beth with her booming cadence needed to learn.

When Nancy stepped down, Mary Beth took the stage. "Keep your fingers crossed people don't start walking out after her speech," John said next to Alicia as he leaned against the wall where they waited their turn to talk.

"My name is Mary Beth Simmons, and I'm honored to be here tonight," their editor began. "I've come all the way from New York City where I am editor of Prime Crime Books, a prestigious publisher."

John put his hand to his mouth, and Alicia heard him cough gently into it. She was sure he was thinking the same thing. Prime Crime Books was a small publisher compared to many of the others in the city.

Mary Beth continued in the same haughty tone but at a slower pace than her usual rapid-fire vocalizations. "I've taken time out of my busy schedule to attend this event to celebrate the publication of Alicia and John McKinney's second Groucho Marks mystery, *Written in Stone*. She glanced down at the books on the table and then toward the corner where John and Alicia were standing. "It is my pleasure to introduce Alicia and John who will read some excerpts from the book and then autograph any copies you purchase. If you missed the first book, there are still a few copies left that you may also buy at the end of the program. I will be happy to assist in the sales at that time."

Now it was Alicia's turn to suppress a laugh. "I bet she will," she whispered to John. "I guess that's our cue. I expected her to talk longer, but I think Sheila warned her that the library is only open until nine tonight."

John grinned. "Okay, sweetheart. Let's go break a leg."

***

The following hour passed in a blur. Alicia was barely aware of Andy, the young man who would officially take over the local paper that spring when he graduated college with his journalism degree, clicking photos as she and John spoke. Mary Beth was also using her iPhone to click shots, right on Andy's heels. She also noticed when Sheriff Ramsay arrived at the last minute and took the vacant seat next to Gilly that she suspected her friend had saved for him. Both divorced, it looked as though her initial observations about their mutual attraction were correct. Alicia recalled when Gilly and the new sheriff became reacquainted at the barbecue in July in honor of Dora and Charlie's retirement and Gilly and her son's taking over the Cobble Inn. Since then, the local grapevine was ripe with gossip about their developing relationship; but Gilly, not one to shy away from topics of sexual involvement, still had not confided in Alicia about whether she and the sheriff were more than friends. At least John's father and Betty had been more open about their affair. John had even told Alicia that the two eighty-year-olds might be planning a wedding soon. Alicia was happy for her father-in-law who had lost two women he'd loved; his wife, John's mother, and his first love with whom he'd fathered John's sister, Pamela.

After Alicia and John gave a brief introduction about themselves and their book and read a few passages from each of them, they invited people to come up to buy autographed copies of either or both of their mysteries. A left to right line was formed where those wishing signed books would take a book from the table and hand it to Alicia who would autograph it and add Sneaky's paw print if requested and then pass it to John who would give it his John Hancock as he joked. The purchaser's last stop would be by Mary Beth who would eagerly take their cash or check payments, and she even had a square card reader for her phone for accepting credit cards.

Alicia didn't expect the crowd that formed around the table. Although she wasn't surprised her friends and family would buy her and John's books, she hadn't expected so many of the patrons, used to borrowing books from the library, to do so. She also hadn't thought everyone would stay after the talk. Even though a few people in the back row left right afterwards and even one lady who walked out rudely after the first fifteen minutes, most people stayed to buy the books or converse with her and John.

Gilly was first in line, even though Alicia had promised her a complimentary copy of the book after the signing. She said she wanted to buy an autographed one for each of her sons. Alicia wanted to argue, but Mary Beth gave her a glare, so she signed all three books and passed them to John. Gilly paid Mary Beth, and each of the boys smiled as they took their own copy. Alicia wasn't sure if they were big readers or would enjoy the mysteries; but, since the books were cozies without explicit violence or sex, she assumed they were safe enough for the boys if they read them.

After the first two rows of people consisting of her friends, family, and co-workers had received their books, the back row of patrons came to the table. Claire, the blonde curly-headed, chubby baker who had supplied cupcakes for the book launch, was first to ask for a book. Wilma, the hairdresser, followed. She told Alicia she looked beautiful but still wanted to style her hair for her. Gary and Patty brought their daughter, Angelina, up for an autographed and pawtographed copy of the books for all of them. Alicia knew the family could not afford extra expenses even though John's wealthy sister, Pamela, had kindly gifted them money for Angelina's future bone marrow transplant. She considered returning the money afterwards, but she knew they wouldn't take it. It was only because of their love for their daughter that the Millburns had agreed to Pamela's gift.

Angelina was excited when Alicia added Sneaky's paw print. "Where is Sneaky? Why didn't he come to your talk, Mrs. McKinney?"

"You know cats don't like noise or too many people around them," Alicia explained. "He's probably hiding in his cat room."

"Can I go see him, please?"

Alicia didn't want to hold up the line, but Patty, Angelina's mom, gently guided the girl forward. "Not now, Angie. Sneaky is probably sleeping. We can come back tomorrow, and Miss Carson can bring him down to you in the Children's Room."

Angie's face lit up, and her freckles bounced. "Thank you, Mama."

The next group of people wanting autographed books were not familiar to Alicia except for Adele Wexler in her large-brimmed flowered hat who spoke in a hushed tone as she approached the table. As much as Adele enjoyed Alicia and John's books, she also loved the gorier, chop-em-up killer thrillers and was convinced Cobble Cove harbored murderers and psychopaths. After what had transpired there in the last two years, Alicia wasn't all that certain she was wrong. The remaining strangers who came to the table possibly saw the advertisement Mary Beth sent around to nearby towns. There was an obese, middle-aged man with a bald head who asked for his book to be autographed to Marvin; an Asian woman about Nancy's height with the American name Sue who reminded Alicia a bit like the receptionist at the Meow Parlour cat café she and John had visited in the city last December; and a black man named Kyle about the age and size of Detective Stryder who had been so helpful working with Ramsay on her and John's kidnapping case before Ramsay became sheriff.

When the last book was signed and the room was empty except for her, John, Mary Beth, Sheila, and Nancy, Alicia sighed. She felt exhausted as the nervous energy that had kept her going dissipated. She was thankful that Sheila and Nancy helped her and John pack up the remaining books and bookmarks that were a much smaller pile than the ones they brought. Gilly had told her the boys would wait downstairs to help them carry the boxes back to their car, but it seemed they could now fit everything into one box that John could easily handle. Gladys slipped in while they were putting things away, and John helped her fold up the chairs and stack them against the wall. Previously a part-time worker at the library, Gladys had accepted the full-time custodian position that replaced Walter. A retired school janitor and a college student occasionally assisted Gladys, but neither worked Thursday nights. Alicia noticed the look Gladys gave Mary Beth when she entered the room and realized no love had been lost between them.

"Alicia, you and John were marvelous tonight," Mary Beth said directing Alicia back to her. Sheila and Nancy had cleared off the refreshment table and gone next door to the staff lounge to put away the coffee urn, paper goods, and milk.

"Thank you, Mary Beth." Alicia was surprised at the compliment coming from one who found it easier to speak criticisms.

"You're welcome, my dear." Mary Beth handed Alicia the money collected from the book sales. "Now that you've done so well locally, I think we may consider taking you and John on tour."

"I can't speak for John, but I would have trouble with that. You remember, we have young children. It's one thing to leave them a night with a babysitter, but I don't like being far from them." Alicia recalled the horror of her experience when she and John spent time in the city last December.

She was surprised again that Mary Beth didn't argue the point. "I understand, but speaking of those babies of yours, when am I going to meet them?"

Alicia didn't like the change in Mary Beth's tone. She sensed something behind the friendly façade.

"We'd be glad to have you over our house when you're in the area again, Mary Beth."

Mary Beth's eyes lit up. "It just happens that I'm staying through the weekend, Alicia, and I'm free for dinner tomorrow night."

So that's was what the editor was up to. Before Alicia could reply, Mary Beth touched her arm lightly. "Of course, I know you need to ask John." She reached into her purse and withdrew a card. "I'm staying at the Carlsville Hilton, but my cell number is listed on my business card. Call me tomorrow whenever you can. No rush."

As Alicia took the card, Sheila called to them from the doorway. "The library will be closing soon, folks. Does anyone need a hand with anything?"

***

Alicia decided to save Mary Beth's invitation until she and John got home. When they arrived downstairs, Donald looked even more flustered than ever at the front desk. He barely acknowledged them as they walked by.

"Donald," Alicia said. "Is something wrong?"

The librarian pointed in the direction of the computer room. "Ever since your talk broke up, it's been a madhouse. I've been handing out computer passes like they were winning lottery tickets. A few people who attended your event also asked me reference questions or were looking for books to borrow."

Alicia glanced toward the PC's and recognized some of the out-of-town people whose books she'd signed as well as library regulars. "Sorry to hear it's been so busy, Donald, but the library will be closing very soon."

Donald let out a breath. "It can't be soon enough. These programs always draw patrons to the desk afterwards, and I'm always stuck working here alone."

Sheila, who was right behind Alicia, heard Donald's words. "Now Donald, that isn't true. We try to alternate coverage during events."

Donald lowered his head, looking chastised by his boss. "Sorry, Sheila. I'm just having a bad night."

Alicia knew he was referring to his run-in with Mary Beth. She found it strange that the editor was nowhere in sight and had possibly left without a goodbye. The only explanation she could think of was that Mary Beth was sure she'd be invited to her and John's house for dinner the next night. Alicia was not looking forward to that.

Chapter Four

By the time Alicia and John got home from the library, the twins were asleep, but Kim, even with her youthful energy, looked tired. They thanked her, and John paid her. As soon as she was out the door, however, Carol and Johnny woke up. It took another hour of Alicia and John reading them stories to put them back to sleep. Alicia was so exhausted that she decided to postpone telling John that Mary Beth had practically invited herself to their house for dinner the next night.

***

At the breakfast table in the morning, after they and the twins had eaten the eggs John had prepared, Alicia was about to broach the subject of dinner with Mary Beth, when she noticed John gazing at the laptop he'd brought to the table. It was his usual custom to check the news and emails in the morning while she saved that task for the library or after work on her desktop computer in her home office. The babies were babbling to themselves, interspersing the few real words they already spoke.

"Is something wrong, John?" Alicia had learned to recognize the signs of upset in her husband. His furrowed brow, deep concentration, and shallow breathing alerted her that there was a problem.

John looked up at her through blue eyes clouded with worry, but denied her concern. "It's nothing. Just a prank email. I'm surprised we haven't gotten more of them from crazy fans."

Alicia jerked and nearly spilled her coffee as she put down the cup. "What do you mean? Is it a threat?" She moved closer to his chair to peek at the screen, but he logged out before she could see what he'd read.

"John, tell me." Her voice was rising, and the babies began to fidget in response. Carol let out a cry.

John got up and took his daughter out of the high chair to comfort her. "Don't cry, sweetie. Nothing's the matter."

Alicia took a breath and let it out. Men could be so frustrating. "John, I know you saw something in your email you didn't like. Tell me what it said."

Carol quieted down. Johnny, in the other high chair, was just regarding his parents in his quiet, inquisitive way. Alicia considered he might grow up to be an author one day, taking in everything and filing it away to write about later.

"If you insist, dear." John placed Carol back in her chair. "It was rather silly actually. Some nut made up a yahoo email calling himself Mark Marks."

"The detective's name in our books? Why would someone do that?"

"Like I said, it must be some looney."

"What did he write? C'mon, John, Fill me in."

John grinned, but she could tell it was half-hearted. Looking away from her as he began to clear the breakfast dishes, he said, "Mark Marks wrote that Marjorie Meyers should be killed in the next book."

Marjorie Meyers was the amateur sleuth in their mysteries, often solving cases before Detective Marks, known as Groucho by the townspeople of Friendly Falls, loosely based on Cobble Cove. Besides being intuitive and often nosy, Marjorie was a librarian at the public library. When Alicia and John wrote the books, they alternated chapters but both wrote the female and male parts. Marjorie wasn't married, as John and Alicia were, but she was a young widow like Alicia and many of the men in town were trying to court her. Detective Marks was the only one who seemed immune to her charms. A divorced man in his fifties, obese and rather rude, he was based on Ron Ramsay before the Long Island detective retired, lost weight, and mellowed out after a health scare.

Alicia considered the email. "Is that a reader's feedback, John, or a death threat against me?"

John sighed. "That's why I didn't want to tell you, but you're not Marjorie, Ali, and the person who sent that isn't Mark Marks. I deleted it and that's that."

"You what? John, it might be evidence. Maybe we should show it to the sheriff."

"I can still take it out of trash, but I doubt it's worth it. Ramsay won't do anything unless something more significant happens."

"Like I'm killed. John, why aren't you taking this seriously?"

"I admit I was a little worried at first; but, like I said, it was just a matter of time before we started getting these crazy notes. All authors receive them."

"I haven't had any, John, and they're not always harmless. Retrieve the email, and I'm going to call Ramsay." She went to the phone.

"Wait, Ali. I'll get the email, but don't call Ramsay yet."

Observing her frown, he added, "Believe me, honey, if I believed you were in any danger, I'd go down to the sheriff's office myself, but I'm sure this is meaningless. Maybe it's even one of our friends joking with us. Hey, that's it!" John looked like he did when he came up with an idea for a plot twist or newspaper scoop. "What if it's Donald? He was pretty upset he had to work alone last night during our program, and he does like to pull practical jokes."

Alicia recalled how Donald gave Laura a scare one day when he told her Sneaky had caught a mouse in the staff lounge. With a straight face, he'd pointed to the creature under the table that turned out to be a very realistic-looking toy mouse. After composing herself and taking a good look at it, Laura realized it had just been a prank. The next day she retaliated by "accidentally" spilling tea on Donald's favorite Shakespeare tie he'd purchased at a library conference. The tea washed out, but Donald got the picture and never messed with Laura again.

"That's different, John. This is not something Donald would do, and the reason he was angry last night was the way that Mary Beth treated him. I know he wasn't the only enemy she made either. Speaking of Miss Personality, I just remembered that she's still in town and wants to come to dinner here tonight to meet the twins."

"Fine with me. I think she's a vegetarian, so I'll make something meatless. You always like my vegetable lasagna, and the zucchini, spinach, and carrots are great for the kids."

One advantage of having a work-at-home husband was that Alicia didn't have to cook. Since John's mother had taught him great recipes and Alicia was more of an out-of-the-box chef, it worked out well. "Okay, I'll call her on her cell and let her know. Do you think you can tidy up the house a bit while I'm at work, today, too?"

John glanced around at Carol and Johnny's toys littering the kitchen floor. Now that they walked, messy reminders of their presence were scattered throughout the house.

"No problem, Ali. Don't worry about a thing, not the house, the twins, or tonight's meal." He bent down and kissed her on the lips. "Most of all, don't worry about that stupid email."

***

Throughout the morning, Alicia tried to take John's advice, but she couldn't help think about the message he'd received. Her co-workers all complimented her on her and

John's presentation the night before, but Donald had called in sick complaining of stomach upset, and she imagined it was his encounter with Mary Beth that had rendered him literally sick to his stomach.

When people started taking morning breaks, and Gilly was alone at the desk with Alicia, she said, "You don't seem yourself today, Alicia. Are you still worn out from last night, or is something else bothering you?"

Alicia was creating computer passes. The librarians often made them ahead of time, so they wouldn't be swamped with requests to use the PC's while they were busy with other work. She looked away from her screen at her friend. Gilly was a very perceptive woman, and she knew she couldn't lie to her. "I am a little disturbed, Gilly. John got a strange email this morning. He didn't seem to think it was anything serious, but I'm not so sure."

Gilly's dark eyes widened. Alicia noted how round they were, a shape that could accurately describe the woman's entire face and body. In a whisper, although no one else was by the desk, she asked, "What did it say, Ali?"

Alicia waved her hand, "I can't recall the exact wording, but it mentioned something about killing off Marjorie Meyers, the main character in our book."

"Have you or John received anything else before this?"

Alicia shook her head. "No. What's even stranger is that the email came from someone calling himself Mark Marks, Detective Groucho's real name."

Gilly's eyes narrowed as she considered what she'd been told. "Is John talking to Ron about this?"

Alicia was surprised to hear her friend call the sheriff by his first name, but she knew they were friends and dating occasionally. If food was the way to a man's stomach, it was probable that her friend would have a new husband soon. Every morning, before work, Gilly brought a fresh batch of her famous brownies to the sheriff's office for him to start his day.

"I offered to call him, but John persuaded me to give the situation more time. He thinks it's just a prank."

Gilly looked doubtful. "It doesn't sound like one to me, Ali. Also, it's odd it came right after your talk. What time was the email sent?"

Alicia hadn't had a good enough look at it to tell. "I don't know. John didn't want to show it to me initially. When he did, I only got a peek."

"I'd like to see it, and I want to mention it to Ron, but I don't want to cause any problems between you and your husband. Do you know the password to John's email?"

Alicia laughed. "No, of course not. Even though we're married, we respect one another's privacy."

Gilly ignored that. "Do you think you can guess it? Most people use words that are familiar to them. John could be using his birth date, the names of one of the twins, or something else that's important in his life."

"I don't plan to hack into his account when he's away from home if that's what you're suggesting, Gilly."

"Then what if you ask him to see it again; and, this time, memorize it as well as the date and time stamp. Would you do that for me, Ali?"

Alicia tapped the pile of computer passes she'd finished. "Look, Gilly. I know you're concerned about this, and I'm sure John would show me the email again if I persisted, but maybe he's right and there's no point."

Gilly gave Alicia a direct and very intense stare. "But what if there is, honey? This could be a warning, like what happened last year when all those bad things were occurring in Cobble Cove, and you two ignored them and went away on the trip to New York."

"Gilly!" Alicia exclaimed as her friend's words hit a nerve. "Please don't bring that up. I went away reluctantly and my fears came true, but remember we got to see you first. The pen you gave John saved his life."

Gilly smiled. "That it did. Okay, I won't say another word for now. Just be careful, Ali. Stay alert and make sure John tells you if he receives any other emails. Also, keep an eye on yours."

"I intend to do that, Gilly. Thank you."

***

After Alicia and Gilly had spoken, the day went through its regular routine. It was Friday, and most of Alicia's co-workers, except those working the next day, like her and Gilly, were happy the week was almost over. Alicia had been off the day before, but her evening talk seemed like it had been a full shift in itself. She was tired, and her worries about the email were taking an additional toll on her. She brightened when she saw Patty and Angelina enter the library a little before noon.

Angelina ran to the desk. "Hi, Mrs. Mac. Mrs. Nostrand," she said. The young girl had trouble saying Alicia's full name and used the abbreviation that was also John's father's nickname. She added a "d" to the end of Gilly's last name.

"Hi, Angelina, Patty." Alicia smiled.

Gilly went around the desk and hugged the girl. "Hi, sweetie. I have a lollipop for you." Sheila always kept some candy around for the town's children, although she was careful about anything with nuts in case they had allergies. Gilly grabbed a red ring pop and handed it to Angelina.

"Thank you, Mrs. Nostran," Angelina's mother said as the girl ripped off the paper, threw it in the nearby wastebasket, and put the lollipop in her mouth. "Remember, you'll be having lunch soon, honey."

"What brings you to the library?" Alicia asked. "Laura's in the children's room if you're looking for something to read." Even though Angelina was only in pre-school, she was bright enough to read picture books with simple text.

"I'll go there later," the girl replied. "I want to see Sneaky first. Mama promised me last night when we were at your book talk that we could see him today even though there isn't a storytime."

Alicia recalled the girl being excited when she'd autographed her book with Sneaky's paw print and then asked to see the cat. She turned to Gilly. "Would you mind manning the desk while I bring Angelina up to Sneaky's cat room, Gilly? Laura's the only librarian in Children's, and I don't want to disturb her."

"No problem, hon. I know Sheila doesn't like patrons to go up there, but she'll make an exception for Angelina."

"I can stay here and chat with Mrs. Nostran," Patty told her daughter. "But don't take too long and don't wake Sneaky if he's sleeping."

The girl nodded. She grabbed Alicia's hand and started skipping toward the staircase. Alicia tried to keep pace, as she was dragged along. "Slow down, sweetie. Sneaky's not going anywhere."

***

Since it wasn't quite lunchtime and most of the staff had already had their coffee breaks in the lounge, the only person there was Sheila, finishing a late cup of tea and one of the last remaining brownies Gilly had brought in. The cupcakes from Claire's the night before were long gone.

Sheila wasn't surprised when Alicia entered with Angelina on her arm. "Hello, there. I suppose you're here to visit Sneaky," the director said.

Angelina's smile widened. "Yes, Mrs. Whitehead. Mama brought me to the library to see him, but I can't play with him if he's asleep. Is he up?"

Sheila took the last sip of tea, stood, and threw her napkin full of brownie crumbs in the trash. "Let's go see. I haven't heard a peep from him, but that doesn't mean he isn't up."

She glanced over at Alicia. "If your friend keeps bringing those brownies, the whole staff is going to become obese."

Alicia laughed. "You have nothing to worry about, Sheila."

The willowy redhead tossed back her hair, her gold headband shimmering in the lounge's light along with that of the sun from the room's open window. "I don't tempt fate. C'mon, let's go see that lazy pussycat. I'm surprised he didn't come out to gobble up those crumbs." She indicated the brownie pieces on the floor with the toe of her brown boots.

Sheila's rings glinted as she opened the door with Angelina on her heels. Alicia was behind them. As the three of them stepped into the room, Angelina began to call out to Sneaky. "Hey, kitty, kitty, where are you?"

"I don't see him," Alicia said. "Maybe he went downstairs. He still likes to hang out near the local history collection and the Children's Room. We could ask Laura."

Angelina pouted. "What if he left the library? He could get lost. Muffin ran out of the house one day, but he turned up in our neighbor's bushes."

"We were worried about that when Sneaky became our library cat," Sheila said, "because patrons come in and out of the front doors all day. Mac put a desensitizer strip in his collar like that we add to books, so if he does go out the entrance, an alarm will go off."

Angelina, an alert child, said, "What if he goes out a window?"

Alicia recalled the staff lounge window was open to let in some air. "I think it works on windows, too, Angelina."

"Not if he isn't wearing it," Sheila said bending down near Sneaky's cat tree to pick up the blue collar on the ground.

"Oh, no," Angelina exclaimed. "Did he break it off?"

"Looks that way." Sheila placed the collar on one of the shelves that Mac had built to store his cat supplies when the old man worked at the library.

"That doesn't mean he's missing," Alicia said trying to comfort the girl who'd begun to cry. "Lots of cats break off their collars. Let's go downstairs and check with Laura."

As they left the room, with Angelina in the lead, Sheila whispered to Alicia, "I didn't see him at all today. I hope he didn't get out last night when the library was crowded with people attending your talk."

Alicia said a silent prayer that they would find Sneaky in the bay window of the children's room, sleeping in the cat bed Laura had placed there.

Chapter Five

When they arrived downstairs, Angelina ran to her mother's side. "Mama, Mama. Sneaky is missing."

"Honey, I'm sure he's around. Cats like to hide in lots of odd places."

"But his collar is off. He could've run outside."

Before the girl started to cry again, Alicia said, "Let's go ask Laura if she's seen Sneaky." Patty and her daughter followed Alicia into the Children's room as Sheila and Gilly stood looking after them. Gilly wore a puzzled expression on her face.

Laura was helping a mother and her toddler son find some books in the low stacks at the back. Angelina ran over to her. "Have you seen Sneaky, Miss Carson? He's not upstairs, and his collar came off."

Laura handed the young boy some picture books about airplanes. "No, he hasn't been around here, Angelina, but don't worry. Sneaky wouldn't go far."

"But what if he got out through a window or door?" Angelina exclaimed in a tremulous voice. Alicia could tell the girl was again on the verge of tears.

Laura excused herself from the boy and mother, took Angelina's hand, and walked to where Alicia and Patty were standing. "If you want, I can help you look around the library, Angie. I'm sure Alicia wouldn't mind manning the Children's desk for a few minutes."

Alicia nodded, but Sheila had come into the room. "I'll do that, Laura. You and Alicia can help Angelina search for Sneaky."

"I'll come, too," Patty offered. "Maybe we should break up into different groups."

"Good idea." Laura glanced around. "I'll check this side of the library with Angie. Alicia can look on the other side, in the reading room and local history area; and Patty, if you want to look around upstairs again, it might not hurt. Remember, he could be curled up somewhere."

"Does he answer to his name?" Patty asked.

"Yes," Laura said. "Even though he came to the library when he was a few years old, he recognizes the name Sheila gave him."

"Should we shake a bag of cat food or open a can?" Angelina asked. "That's what me and Mom do when we can't find Muffin in the house. When she hears her food, she usually comes right out and runs to be fed."

"Sneaky's food is upstairs, but I don't think it's a good idea to open it in the public area of the library," Laura explained. "Let's just walk around and call him and see if we spot him hiding or sleeping somewhere."

When the search party had all their instructions, the three women and the young girl began scouting the building for Sneaky.

***

As Alicia was on her way back, empty-handed, Gilly called over to her from the Reference Desk. "I guess you didn't have any luck. Angelina will be so upset if Sneaky isn't found."

"I know. I feel terrible." Alicia looked at the clock above the desk. It was after twelve. Gilly only worked part-time in the mornings. "I know you have to get back to the inn, Gilly, and it looks like I'll be eating at one if we don't find Sneaky soon."

"Don't worry about me, hon. I have Edith and Rose working today, and the boys don't get out of school until three. I can stay as long as you and Sheila need me."

"Thanks. Without Donald today and Vera and Jean also out, we're pretty short-staffed in Reference." Jean was a part-time librarian who alternated her days at the library. She had a son about the age of Gilly's youngest boy, Joey. Vera was full-time but was still on vacation visiting her grandchildren in Connecticut.

Alicia's conversation with Gilly was interrupted by Angelina, Laura, and Patty who had returned with sad looks on their faces. "Miss Carson and I didn't see him anywhere. Did you or Mrs. Mac find him, Mama?" Angelina asked.

"I'm afraid I didn't, sweetheart," Patty said.

"Neither did I, Angelina, but he may still be in the library. If he's here, I'm sure he'll come out when Laura goes up to feed him before she leaves at five."

Tears formed in Angelina's blue eyes, already red from her previous crying bouts. "But what if he got out, Mama? He might be lost. Another dog or cat might fight with him and hurt him or . . ." She paused as fresh tears fell from her cheeks. "Mama, you always tell me to make sure I close the door behind me when I leave the house, so Muffin doesn't run out and get hit by a car."

Patty tried to console her daughter. "Try not to think those bad things, Angie. Sneaky is a smart cat. If he got out, and we're not sure he did, he would sniff his way back to the library. Cats have great senses of smell, and some have found their way home from many miles away."

The girl wasn't convinced. "Then how come he never found his way home when he came to the library the first time?"

Patty sighed, but Gilly tried to answer Angelina. "Sneaky was younger then, and it's possible the people who owned him dropped him at the library. They may have had too many cats or were planning to move or maybe one of them had allergies, so they couldn't keep him."

Angelina sniffled and seemed to accept the explanation. "Can I come back at five when Miss Carson feeds Sneaky and see if he comes for his food?" She asked turning to her mother.

"I don't know. I have to go to the school this afternoon. Even though the older grades have begun, Kindergarten is starting next week; and a few of us teachers have to meet with Principal Stafford to go over things, but Duncan said your dad could come home early today. Maybe he'll bring you back, Angie."

"I hope so. I'll be thinking of Sneaky all day."

Alicia's heart went out to the young girl who was currently in remission from leukemia and still on a bone marrow transplant list.

"Before you go," Gilly said, walking from behind the desk and signaling Angelina over to her. "I have a cherry lollipop for you." She took a red Dum Dum from her pocket and handed it to the girl.

Angelina's face lit up temporarily. "Thank you, Mrs. Nostrand."

Gilly didn't correct her name. Instead, she said, "Call me Gilly, honey. It's much easier to say."

The girl nodded, and her mother smiled. "That's very nice of you, but a bit too much candy for today. We'll save it for later." She took the lollipop and put it in her purse. "We'll be going then. Please call if Sneaky turns up. My husband may bring Angie back later this afternoon."

***

In all the excitement, Alicia almost forgot to call Mary Beth to confirm dinner that night. She dialed the editor's cell phone number on her lunch hour and left a voicemail when the woman didn't answer. She had gone home to see the babies and spend some time with John who had put together him and his Dad's famous PB&J sandwiches for her and the twins.

"You look a bit perturbed, Ali. Are you worried about Mary Beth coming over tonight? I've got it all in hand. The vegetable lasagna will be in the oven and the table set by the time you get home from the library. I'll also have the twins dressed in their best to meet our endearing editor."

Alicia laughed. John always had a way of easing her stress when she tended to look at the dark side of things. "Thanks, John, but I'm not concerned about Mary Beth. Sneaky is missing, and Angelina is very upset. She was there this morning wanting to see him. Sheila found his collar on the cat room floor, and the window in the staff lounge was open. It's also possible he sneaked out of the library door last night when people were coming and going during our talk."

John wiped Johnny's mouth after the boy ate the piece of sandwich he'd fed him. Although the twins could eat most things at this age, it helped to cut up their meals in small portions. "Sneaky is fine, Ali. Even if he did get out, he won't go far. He has the life being the town's library cat and getting all those food scraps the staff passes to him."

Alicia thought of the crumbs on the lounge floor and the way Donald always slipped Sneaky leftovers. "I hope you're right, John, not only for Alicia but the other children who have grown fond of him." She gave Carol a bite of her food, and the girl ate it up in one gulp. Neither of their children had poor appetites.

"I'll finish feeding the kids, Ali, if you want to get ready to go back to work. I'll bet Sneaky will have risen from his nap by now and made his catly appearance."

Alicia wiped Carol's face. "That would be great, John."

***

As she walked back to the library, taking advantage of the still pleasant weather and the short distance to Bookshelf Lane to help her burn up a few calories from Gilly's brownies, Alicia realized Sneaky's disappearance was helping keep her mind off the dinner with Mary Beth and the strange email John had received.

The rest of the afternoon passed uneventfully, but she found herself counting the minutes until 5 p.m. At a quarter to the hour, Laura came to the Reference Desk. "Sheila is in Children's. She said she didn't mind my leaving a little early to put out Sneaky's food. If Gary brings Angelina back, try to keep her downstairs until I know for sure that Sneaky is here."

Alicia nodded. "I'll do my best, but I can't stay too long after work, Laura. I have a dinner guest coming tonight."

"I know. I heard you're entertaining your editor. I can't believe how rude that woman acts. Can't you and John ask your publisher for someone else?"

"I suppose so, but she's good at her job. It's just her people skills that are lacking."

"I would think people skills are important in the editing field. Anyway, I'll serve Mr. Sneak something he can't resist. There'll be no doubt that he's missing if he ignores the bait."

Alicia crossed her fingers that Laura's temptations would bring the cat out of hiding as the young librarian headed upstairs.

***

Angelina and her father arrived a few minutes later.

"Hi, Alicia," Gary said as Angelina ran to the reference desk. She could hardly believe the dedicated father was a man she once believed took part in her children's kidnapping.

"Hi, Gary. Angelina."

"Has Sneaky turned up yet, Mrs. Mac?"

Alicia hadn't been given the all clear sign from Laura to send the Millburn's upstairs, so she had to think of a way to detain them but knew she should be honest.

"No, I'm afraid not, Angelina. Laura just went upstairs because the library is closing soon. She'll bring Sneaky down to see you if he comes out to eat."

"But I asked Daddy to bring me here, so I could feed him with Miss Carson." The girl's eyes were bright with held-back tears.

"I'm afraid you can't, honey. The library is closing soon." On Friday's the library closed at 5, although Laura usually stayed a little later to give Sneaky his meal for the night.

Before Angelina could protest, her father said, "Let's just wait down here for Miss Carson, Angie. Maybe you want to take out a book before the Children's Room closes."

"No, Daddy. I want to go up and see if Sneaky is eating."

Alicia was about to give in, when Laura joined them at the Reference Desk. Catching her breath, she looked like she was about to cry, too.

"He's not here. Sneaky's really gone."

Chapter Six

Alicia couldn't help but look for Sneaky on her way home. She checked the bushes and the low areas where a cat might hide along Bookshelf Lane and did the same on Stone Throw Road, but there was no sign of him. It had been hard calming Angelina down when Laura broke the news. Her father had dragged her from the library crying. He'd tried to comfort her with the false hope that Sneaky would be back soon.

Alicia noticed a strange car in her driveway when she walked up to her house. For a moment, she'd forgotten about her dinner guest but then realized the red Fiat had to belong to Mary Beth. Although she'd stayed a few minutes after work to help console Angie, the Prime Crime editor was nearly an hour early.

The door opened before she was at it. Mary Beth stood there smiling. "Hello, Alicia. Sorry I'm early, but I have some plans later. I called to let John know, but I guess he didn't want to bother you at work. Please come in. I've already met Carol and Johnny, and they are totally adorable."

Alicia stepped into the house, smelling the aroma of John's version of his mother's vegetable lasagna. While Mac grew his own herbs and was the mastermind behind the family's secret PB&J recipe, John's mother had been the true cook in the family, passing down many of her recipes to John.

She followed Mary Beth into the dining room. John had set the table for the three of them, and the babies were in their high chairs as usual. They normally ate in the kitchen when it was just the family.

"Please sit down, Mary Beth," Alicia said, trying to adjust to the role of hostess even though she felt Mary Beth was the one entertaining her.

Mary Beth complied taking her place by a glass Alicia noticed was full of white wine. A half-empty bottle stood next to it. While she and John occasionally had wine with dinner, they usually had only one glass. It looked like Mary Beth was on her way to emptying the bottle before dinner was even on the table.

After giving the twins each a kiss hello on their foreheads, Alicia joined John in the kitchen. He wore the apron and the matching oven mitts they shared and was checking the lasagna. When she entered, he checked the oven. "Not quite done yet, but you and Mary Beth can chat. I gave her some wine to quiet her up." He grinned. "Did Sneaky make it to dinner?"

"No." Alicia looked down. "He didn't."

"Sorry, Ali. I know you're as attached to Sneaky as Angelina. After all, when you first came to town and stayed upstairs in what used to be an apartment, Sneaky slept with you. That was before, I did." He winked.

She laughed at the memory. "At least he didn't take my covers. Oh, John. I really hope he turns up."

"You should place a sign at the reference desk, and I'll tell Andy to run an ad in the *Courier*."

"Thanks. I'm sure Sheila will agree to that, and Gary told Angelina he'd hang a sign in the supermarket and Patty would do the same at the school. Angelina offered to design it. It'll give her something to keep her mind off her worry."

"Does anyone have a photo of Sneaky? That would be useful to put on the signs and place in the ad."

"I'm sure Sheila has one. She took lots of them during the storytimes in which Sneaky was a guest. Now Nancy is in charge of photography."

"I like the new PR director," John said. "She's classy and, unlike tonight's guest, knows when to speak and when to keep her mouth shut." He walked away from the oven and approached Alicia. In a lower voice, he said, "You know, she even had the nerve to flirt with me. I didn't think that was in our contract."

"What?" Alicia was surprised. She was aware that Mary Beth treated men slightly better than women, although Donald had been one of her exceptions. Perhaps, she hadn't found him attractive or knew he wasn't interested in women. But coming on to a married man and one she worked with, was a new low for the editor. Alicia imagined that was why she'd arrived so early and not because of any appointment.

"Don't worry, honey," John assured her. "I think I put her in her place. I can put up with her editorial demands and non-stop chatter, but sexual harassment is where I draw the line, especially since I have such a beautiful wife to whom I am totally devoted."

Alicia smiled as he kissed her lightly on the lips, but she was looking forward to the rest of the evening even less.

***

The dinner with Mary Beth turned out better than Alicia expected. The wine definitely had slowed her speech, although she still talked nearly non-stop.

The twins seemed to find her funny, and Alicia wondered if Mary Beth had children of her own. As much as the editor wanted to know about her and John, she avoided revealing too much of her own personal life. Alicia only knew Mary Beth was divorced, which was no surprise.

Around 6:30, Mary Beth glanced at her watch. "This has been such a lovely evening, but I must make my appointment. Before I go, though, I have a question for you, Alicia."

"Yes?"

"Despite some of your co-workers' negligence and that rude Donald at the front desk, your talk at the library went well, and you looked absolutely stunning. I meant to ask you where you purchased that beautiful blue blouse. I'm looking for something like that to add to my wardrobe. Although I love the City stores, I know that you can sometimes find gems in small shops and pay a lot less for them." She smiled, and her foundation creased at the sides of her mouth. Even though John had added candles to the table to soften the lighting, Mary Beth's caked makeup was hard not to notice.

"I bought the blouse at Chloe's Closet in Cobble Corner," Alicia said. "It's a women's store that opened here last year. They sell business and casual clothing. There was a great sale there last week, and I picked up two blouses for the price of one – the blue, and a less dressy lilac top."

"How late are they open? I might make a quick stop there before I head to my appointment."

"They're open late on Fridays. I think until 8 or 9. The sale might actually still be going on."

"Wonderful!" Mary Beth stood up. "I'll be sure to mention that you referred me to Chloe. Maybe she'll give me a discount if the sale is over." She chuckled and, patting Carol and Johnny on their heads, she added, "I may drop by the library tomorrow morning and show you my purchases." Then she turned to John, "Thank you again for that delicious lasagna and the wine, John. When will you have the next manuscript to me?"

John gave Alicia a look that read, "I knew she'd mention the third book." Neither of them had started writing anything new yet. "We're working on it, Mary Beth," he said, helping her into her light jacket.

"Good. Your fans are waiting, and I expect at least several chapters of the first draft before I leave on Sunday.

You can drop it off at the main desk of the Carlsville Hilton before 11 a.m."

John swallowed. Alicia knew he'd probably want to finish what was left of the wine as soon as Mary Beth left. It would not be easy for them to write a few chapters in one day especially since Alicia would be at work tomorrow.

Without waiting for John's reply, Mary Beth headed for the door. "Goodnight, my dears."

John waited until the door closed behind the editor before he stuck out his tongue. Carol and Johnny broke out with gales of laughter at their dad's funny face, and Alicia had to laugh, too.

***

Alicia couldn't sleep well, worrying about Sneaky. Even though the night temperatures were still warm enough, he was still in danger of being attacked by other animals, let alone people who didn't like cats. Also, he would be growing hungry having possibly gone without food a whole day. She knew cats, especially ones that were a bit overweight like Sneaky, could survive a long time without eating as long as they found drinking water, but it was still a concern. She was also upset over the email John had received as well as Mary Beth's short deadline for three chapters of their next book.

***

The next morning, John commented on the circles under Alicia's eyes. "I felt you tossing and turning last night, Ali. I didn't sleep well myself. I have no idea how we can have something ready for Mary Beth by Sunday."

Alicia stifled a yawn as she cut up some of the scrambled eggs John had made and added them to Carol's plate. "That wasn't all that kept me awake, John. I was thinking about Sneaky and that strange email you received."

"Sneaky will be fine, honey. As far as the email, I haven't gotten anything further and nothing has happened. I'm still chalking it up to a prank."

Alicia watched as John served his son a portion of eggs. His laptop stood in front of him, and he had already checked his email. She had also checked hers last night and was tempted to check it again just in case the person pretending to be the detective in their series decided to write to her.

John read her mind. "If you want to read your email, I'll finish feeding the babies and clean up. I know you're working today and, even though Donald is notorious for surfing the web at the library and keeping up with his social media, I know you tend to just read email at home."

"Thanks John, but you're not entirely right about nothing bad happening after you received that note. Sneaky is missing, remember?"

Her husband gave her a curious look. "How would that be connected with the email?"

"I don't know, but it's strange he disappeared on the night of our talk and then you got the email the next morning." She decided to check the time stamp as Gilly suggested. "What time was it sent? Do you know?"

John frowned and tapped some keys on his laptop. "Looks like 8:35 p.m. Thursday night."

"We were still upstairs at that time putting things away, but most of the audience had already left."

John nodded. "Ali, please don't start building your famous mountains out of molehills."

She sighed. "I know I tend to overthink things, John, but I'm not convinced that email was a prank. I'll go check mine now. Thanks for finishing up with the twins and for dinner last night. Most of all, thanks for getting Mary Beth half-drunk to keep her mellow and not letting her have her way with you."

John smiled. "That was my pleasure, and I'm afraid I didn't get her mellow enough because she remembered to make her usual impossible demands on us."

"Gilly asked why we don't change editors."

"It's not that easy. As nasty and controlling as Mary Beth is, she's a workaholic and does more than most editors in helping us promote our books."

Alicia wasn't that convinced. "I still think we could find someone else who is nicer. I wonder if there's a backstory to her about why she's so demanding. You told me once that she's divorced. Do you know anything else about her?"

John wiped Johnny's mouth with his bib. "I don't, Ali, and I think it's a wonder she got married in the first place. Most men would not put up with her domineering ways. The only backstory I think she has is that she was spoiled and pampered as a child and grew up to be the word that rhymes with witch that we don't say in front of the twins."

***

After Alicia checked her email and found nothing suspicious, she began to consider that John was right and that the message he'd received had just been a bad joke. She changed into a pair of slacks and the lilac blouse from Chloe's that she'd mentioned to Mary Beth. The color went even better with her complexion, and John complimented her on it when she went back to the kitchen, gave him and the babies goodbye kisses, and left for work.

As she walked toward the library, she continued looking for Sneaky. Again, there was no sign of him, and she prayed he'd turn up today because the library was not open on Sundays until October.

Turning on to Bookshelf Lane, she suddenly had a feeling of being followed. Her pace and pulse quickened at the memory of her experience last December. But this time, it wasn't stealthy footsteps and breathing behind her but the sound of a car's motor slowly cruising by. She stepped onto the sidewalk, avoiding the car that brushed by her. Another old memory flooded back. Police officers coming to her door to tell her that her husband had been killed by a hit and run driver. She watched as the car pulled into the library parking lot and caught a glimpse of a blonde woman behind the wheel. Catching her breath, she walked to the back employee entrance. The occupant in the car just sat there staring at her waiting for the library to open. Alicia recognized her from somewhere but couldn't place the face. She'd seen her recently, but something about her was different.

Alicia jumped as she entered the library when a figure crossed her path.

"Good morning, Alicia. Oh, sorry I startled you." It was just Gerry, the new library guard who worked nights and weekends. Gerry's actual name was Gerald Fox. He was an ex-army man who'd served in Vietnam. With a sandy crew cut and standing taller than John, at six-foot three, he towered over Alicia. Retired from civilian work as a bodyguard, he now worked part-time for the security agency from which Sheila had hired him.

"That's okay, Gerry. I'm just a little on edge this morning."

"Too much coffee? That'll do it for me." He walked with Alicia into the main part of the library. Donald was back at the reference desk creating computer passes in advance of opening.

"Hi, Donald. Feeling better?" she asked.

"Not entirely, but I think I can make it through the day." Alicia noted the librarian's face was pale.

"Well, if you feel sick, please go home."

"Thanks, but I wouldn't want you to be left alone." Besides Donald and Gerry, the only other staff members working that Saturday were Gilly, who was in charge of the

Children's Room, and Bonnie, the young part-time clerk who had had the run-in with Walter last year. Gladys was also there, sweeping around the circulation desk before the doors opened.

"I appreciate that, Donald. Just don't throw up on me."

He grinned. "The nausea is gone, but I may need to make some bathroom stops for the diarrhea."

"As my babysitter Kim would say, tmi—too much information."

Donald laughed as Alicia took the seat next to him.

Chapter Seven

When Gladys opened the library doors, a few patrons were there waiting. Among them was the woman from the Mazda. Swinging back her blonde hair, she asked Donald for a computer pass. Alicia noted the way he appraised the woman as he handed it to her. As she walked toward the PC's, Donald whispered, "She's hot. If I wasn't gay, I think I'd like to jump her bones."

"Donald!" Alicia laughed, but she was still trying to place the woman. "There's something familiar about her. Have you seen her in the library before? I don't think she's from Cobble Cove."

"She was here the other night. It was a zoo here, but I recall her using the computers after your talk."

Alicia glanced at the woman again. "Yes. Now I remember. She sat in the back and left early. A kerchief covered her hair, and she wore sunglasses. She nearly ran me off the road this morning with her car while I was walking here."

"She seems friendly enough. You might've been mistaken."

Alicia didn't have time to consider that. Angelina ran in at that moment with her mother who was trying to catch up with her.

"Mrs. Mac. Is Sneaky back yet?"

The girl held a stack of flyers in her hands. Alicia saw a photo of Sneaky centered on them and the words, "Have you seen this Cat? $100 reward for anyone who finds him." The Millburns' phone number was listed on the bottom.

"Hi, Angelina. I'm sorry. He hasn't come back yet, and I haven't seen him in the neighborhood. It's nice of your family to offer a reward, but you really shouldn't have. I'm sure if anyone Sneaky knows finds him, they would be happy to bring him back without being paid."

The girl's face darkened and tears filled her eyes. "I helped my dad make the flyers. He said a reward might make people look harder. Can you put them out? Mom and I have placed some around town and near the shops already."

Alicia took the notices and promised to put them on the front door and in other areas of the library. She worried that Angelina's upset would cause a relapse before a bone marrow donor was found. She could also see concern on her mother's face as she put her arm on her daughter.

"Why don't we go to the Children's room and take some in there?" Patty suggested. "You could also pick up some books to read."

"Is Ms. Carson in today?"

"No, but Ms. Nostrand is in the Children's section today."

Angelina seemed happy to hear that as she skipped toward the Children's Room. Patty looked back at Alicia. "Thank you, Alicia. I hope Sneaky comes back soon."

***

Angelina and her mother spent about fifteen minutes in the Children's Room before leaving the library. The girl carried a couple of books along with some leftover flyers. She waved to Alicia as she walked out the door.

It was almost time for coffee breaks, and Alicia told Donald he could go up to the staff lounge first. Even though he said he didn't think he could stomach much coffee, he seemed thankful to get off the desk for a few minutes. Alicia had also arranged to cover the Children's Room for Gilly when she went upstairs after Alicia had her own break.

While she was watching the reference desk, Alicia couldn't keep her eyes off the blonde woman on the computer. When the woman suddenly logged off and came over to her, she turned away quickly. Then she remembered that she was a librarian and raised her eyes. "What can I help you with?"

The lady directed her blue-eyed gaze on Alicia. She noticed her features were nearly perfect with an aquiline nose, rose-bud lips, and large eyes set against ivory skin with just a natural blush of peach. "I'm sorry I didn't introduce myself earlier. I'm Lindsey Harrington."

Alicia searched her memory for that name, but came up blank. "Do I know you?"

Lindsey tossed back her spun gold mane of hair. "Maybe not. I thought maybe John might've mentioned me once. We're old school friends."

Alicia nearly choked. "No, he didn't. It's nice to meet you, though." She hesitated when Lindsey extended her hand.

"Likewise, Alicia. Do you mind my calling you that instead of Mrs. McKinney?"

Alicia was confused about how this woman would know her if they'd never met, but then she recalled Donald saying that Lindsey had been at her and John's book release party the night before.

Avoiding the question Lindsey had asked, Alicia said, "You were here last night. Why didn't you come up and talk with us?"

The woman waved her hand. It was unadorned, without a wedding ring or any other jewelry, and featured long, rose-polished fingernails that were neatly shaped and unbitten. "There were so many people, and I didn't want to disturb you. I figured, while I was in town, I'd drop by the library and meet you. I still have to contact John. Would you mind if I called him later?"

A wave of anxiety punched Alicia in the stomach. "You have our number?"

Lindsey laughed. "Of course not, although your emails are all over the bookmarks you put out last night. I think calling is much more personal. I'd also like to surprise John. Can you give me his number? I'll be heading back to my hotel soon. Maybe the three of us can get together for dinner or something before I go back to New York. I noticed a nice Italian place near those quaint shops. Cobble Cove is enchanting, a lot less expensive than the City, too."

Alicia found it hard to talk around the lump that had formed in her throat. When she and John first started their relationship, he told her about his wife and how he had not had any meaningful girlfriends after her death. He'd never mentioned Lindsey; but, hopefully, that was because she'd just been a friend. Looking at the woman, Alicia had doubts. Against her better judgment, she took one of the sticky pads from the desk and jotted down her home number. Passing it to Lindsey, she said with a false smile, "I'd be happy to go to dinner with you and John at La Bella if he's interested. We would just have to find a babysitter for our twins."

Lindsey shook her thick hair again. "Why not bring them? I'd love to meet them, too." She put the phone number slip in her purse. "I have to do a little research before I leave, but thanks again for the chat. By the way, I'm sorry about this morning. I wasn't watching the road as well as I should've been, and the sun was in my eyes. I didn't see you until you stepped on the sidewalk."

"No harm done," Alicia said, even though she knew the skies had been cloudy when she'd walked to work and were still overcast.

"I hope to see you later then," Lindsey said. As she strode off to the back of the library, Alicia noted her heels and skirt were both too high. She took a deep breath as Donald returned to the desk.

"What's wrong, Alicia? You look pale. I hope you're not catching my stomach bug."

Alicia still felt tongue-tied. "No, Donald, but I do need a break now. When I get back, I'll relieve Gilly, so she can take hers."

***

As she entered the staff lounge, Alicia saw Gerry and Gladys eating donuts at the table. She was reminded of Faraday and Ramsay when she and John were interrogated by them on Long Island after her house fire. While Ramsay no longer ate fattening desserts because of his health concerns, she knew he still craved them. She wondered if Gilly had said anything to him about the email John received, but she knew her friend was good at keeping secrets, so it was likely she hadn't.

"Hi, Alicia," Gladys said, biting off a piece of a Boston crème donut. She slid the open pink and white box toward her. "You better take one before they're all gone. Gerry brought them in, and they sure hit the spot when you have to work a Saturday."

Alicia's stomach rumbled as she glanced inside the box. Only one Boston crème remained. She couldn't resist, and grabbed it. "Thanks for ruining my diet, Gerry," she told the guard.

Gerry grinned. "You only live once, Alicia. Enjoy the small things in life." Tossing his crumb-filled napkin in the trash, he walked to the coffee maker and took one of the mugs on the counter. "Want something to wash that down with? I'm grabbing another cup myself."

"Thanks, Gerry." Alicia watched as he brewed two coffees and brought them to the table. There was a small pitcher of milk and some sweetener packets already there.

Alicia added a drop of milk to her cup and stirred the brown liquid before taking a sip.

"Anything out of place down there?" Gerry asked taking the seat next to Gladys again.

"Only some books that patrons pull from the stacks and put back in the wrong area without leaving them on the reshelving trucks." Alicia mentioned her pet peeve. She still had her mind on Lindsey, but was trying not to dwell on the encounter.

Gladys laughed. "If that's all that's mixed up, it should be an easy day and probably a boring one."

"I don't mind working Saturdays," Alicia said. "The afternoons generally get busier, but Sheila isn't around to complain about anything, although she's a great boss."

Gerry grinned. "You know what they say. 'When the cat's away, the mouse will play.'"

Gladys gave him a gentle tap on the arm. "You aren't even employed by the library, Gerry."

"Sheila's still my boss. I like the lady. By the way, did that cat ever turn up?" He glanced at the door with the cat flap.

"No." Alicia took another sip of coffee. She hadn't yet eaten her donut. "Angelina came by this morning with some flyers to put around the library offering a reward. It's sad. I hope he comes back or someone finds him."

"I have cats," Gladys said. "They are smarter than people give them credit for. He's probably nearby. He'll come back when he's good and ready. Cats are like that. Do you think he left because he was mad over something?"

"What could've gotten him mad?" Alicia was stumped. Although she loved animals, she didn't quite attribute human feelings to them the way Laura and Gladys did.

"Maybe it was that shrew of a woman, Mary Beth, and all the commotion she made last night. If I were a cat, I would've gone into hiding myself."

Gerry laughed. "I wasn't lucky enough to meet her, but I heard the rumors. I'd suggest you check with that Dr. Donna, the vet lady in town. She might have an idea of where you could look for Sneaky."

Alicia considered that idea. "I might do that if he's not back by Monday."

***

Before Alicia went to the Children's Room so Gilly could take her break, she stopped back at the Reference Desk to see Donald.

"I just wanted to remind you I'm going to Children's now for fifteen minutes. Was everything okay while I was on break?"

Donald looked up from his computer where he was reading his Facebook news feed, a habit Sheila was aware of but allowed as long as it didn't interfere with his work. "It got a little busy when you went upstairs, Alicia, but I think it's simmering down now. We had an influx of patrons as if the bus let off." He grinned. "A few of them were from your talk last night. I guess some out-of-towners are staying at Gilly's Inn for the weekend and decided to visit the library again."

Alicia knew that Cobble Cove allowed residents of nearby areas to check out books, but she noticed the computer room was full again and there were also a bunch of people reading newspapers and magazines by the Periodicals section. Most of them were library regulars including Adele Wexler, her high-brimmed hat tipped over her head, gazing into a mystery book with a bloody cover.

"Has Mary Beth been here?" Alicia asked recalling that the editor had mentioned stopping by the library that morning.

Donald grimaced. "I can't say I've had the pleasure of seeing her again." He emphasized the word "pleasure" to indicate the sarcasm.

"Maybe you'll luck out, and she'll stay away. She was talking about shopping at Cobble Corner last night, but maybe she went today and decided not to bless us with her presence."

Donald brought his eyes back to his computer screen. "That would be peachy. See you in fifteen, Ali."

***

Gilly was waiting at the Children's Room desk when Alicia got there. The room was pretty empty except for a few kids playing on the iPads in the corner, their parents standing nearby.

"Hi, Alicia. Thanks for coming to cover my break. There are no storytimes or other programs here today, so it should be quiet."

"You'll only be gone a few minutes, Gilly, but make sure you grab a donut. Gerry brought them in, but I nabbed the last Boston Crèam."

"What nerve you have!" Gilly made a face. Alicia knew Boston Creams were her favorites, too.

"Don't worry. There are plenty of powdered jelly ones and crullers, too."

"Then we're still friends." Gilly smiled; but as she headed to the stairway, she paused. "Oh, I almost forgot. Ron asked me to pick up a book for him today. I'll go look for it before I get my donut."

"You could get it on the way back. There may not be many left now, Gilly. If Donald didn't have an upset stomach today, they would've all been gone already." Donald's legendary appetite despite his trim frame was known around the library.

"I think I'll risk that. As much as I love donuts, I should be watching my weight."

Alicia wondered if her friend's comment had anything to do with her budding relationship with the new Cobble Cove sheriff. She'd noticed Gilly was wearing nicer clothes lately and even a bit of makeup, which was not typical of her. She watched Gilly walk toward the true crime aisle and disappear into the stacks.

**

The scream echoed through the library. Patrons looked up from their books and computer screens. Those near the 360 section made their way toward the sound. Questioning exclamations and puzzled whispers mingled with footsteps. "What was that?"

Alicia, Gerry, Donald, Bonnie, and Gladys rushed to Gilly. She stood with her trembling hand pointing down at a woman lying face forward on the carpet, a gaping hole in the back of her skull.

Mary Beth. Alicia took this in, even as she went numb with shock. She was further chilled by the fact that they wore the exact same blouses. Had this been meant for her?

As Gerry called 911, people converged around them. Donald suggested they call Ramsay, as the victim was clearly beyond help.

Gerry nodded, and made that his next call.

Donald said, "I don't think we should let anyone leave just yet. I'll put up the "Closed" sign and lock the doors.

Patrons were unhappy about that. "Please, be calm," Alicia said. "We need to wait for the police."

There was some mumbling, but everyone settled down.

"We need to contact Sheila immediately," Alicia said, turning back to her co-workers.

"You're the librarian in charge," Donald reminded her.

"What if the killer's still in the library?" Gilly asked softly, her voice shaky.

"We stay together and follow orders." His phone buzzed. "Yes? All right. Will do. Thanks." He lowered his phone. "Ramsay wants us to wait by the back exit. The police will meet us there."

"Crime books," Gilly said.

"What?" Alicia asked.

"A murder by the murder books. Isn't that ironic?"

***

The next few minutes were chaotic. Alicia felt as if she was asleep, having a nightmare. She couldn't believe there'd been a murder in the library. Even more unreal was that the victim had been her and John's editor dressed in literally the same clothes Alicia had worn to work.

Ramsay was first on the scene, with backup officers behind him and a crime scene investigator. They all wore vests she imagined were bulletproof and had their guns drawn. Alicia recognized Stryder, the Carlsville detective who had helped on her kidnapping case last year. It seemed the tall black officer had been called to assist Ramsay along with other Carlsville cops. The policemen didn't storm in the back door but approached the group quietly and in an orderly fashion. Alicia saw Gilly, standing beside her, send Ramsay an admiring look as he took command. He glanced in her direction and nodded. The sheriff then issued orders to the officers and told the group to go outside and wait together behind the library.

As soon as Alicia stepped through the door, John and Andy came running up to her. "Oh, thank God you're okay, Ali," John said with relief. "As soon as I heard what happened, I notified Kim, and she came right over to watch the babies."

"How did you find out?"

"I told him," Andy said, "but I can't reveal my source."

Alicia knew the young man who had taken over John's paper took his job as a reporter seriously. She assumed, since the *Courier* was only a few doors down from the sheriff's office, that he was tipped off by Ramsay on the way to the scene.

"I understand, and I'm thankful," Alicia said. She was looking around at the people who were gathered by the wall, some standing and a few crouched down on the pavement covering their eyes with their hands. Mrs. Wexler was one of those standing. Her eyes still gleamed with excitement, but she had toned down her voice in response to the sheriff's directive. She was talking with a few other patrons who were also library regulars. However, Alicia didn't notice any of the people who had attended her and John's release party. Lindsey Harrington was not among the bystanders, and her car was gone from the parking lot. An ambulance sat in its place, its flashing lights on, ready to transport.

Chapter Eight

Sheila arrived a short time later. The police were still inside the library. Stryder had come back out a few minutes after what Alicia assumed was the first sweep of the building. He refused to answer questions the crowd began tossing at him. But when Sheila rushed over to him, her boots pounding the sidewalk, he took her aside and spoke to her. Alicia noticed the director's hair was astray. It seemed she hadn't had time to brush or contain it with her usual headband. The red strands were flung around her face by the strong winds on this early September afternoon. She struggled to brush them back with one hand as she gesticulated comments to Stryder. After their brief talk, she walked over to Gerry and had some words with him. Then she approached Alicia. "Thank you for calling me. I came as quickly as I could. Detective Stryder tells me Sheriff Ramsay is still inside with some officers making sure the library is empty. They have someone checking the body." Her voice sounded shaky, even though Alicia knew Sheila was adept at handling emergencies. After losing her husband to a brain aneurysm early in their marriage, she had raised her daughter alone.

"It's Mary Beth Simmons," Alicia said. "The Prime Crime editor. John and I had dinner with her at our house last night."

John put his arm around his wife as Alicia choked on the last words. She turned to him. "I didn't even see her come into the library, John. I was on a break, and when I came back, I had just relieved Gilly. She was looking for a book for the sheriff in the true crime section and found Mary Beth. We all heard her scream and rushed over."

John drew his brows together, his blue eyes darkening with worry. "I know this is such a shock for you Ali, and you too, Gilly." He looked over at the woman who had found the body. Gilly seemed more concerned that Ramsay hadn't come out of the building yet. "What's taking them so long? They must've been able to check everywhere by now. The library is not that big."

"They have to be thorough," Stryder said. "You'd be surprised how many small areas there are where someone can hide."

"Do they really think the killer is still in there?" Andy asked. Although he wasn't taking any notes, Alicia figured he was already memorizing facts for a story.

"Most likely not, but we have to be sure." Stryder moved away from them toward the front of the group and addressed the crowd. "I know you're all impatient to get home, folks, but we need to keep everyone together a little while longer. Once the building is clear, we're going to ask you all to go back inside for a few minutes, so we can ask you a few questions."

A murmur spread throughout those gathered, and Mrs. Wexler spoke up. "Excuse me, Officer, but are you going to be interrogating us?" From the light in her eyes, Alicia could tell the woman wasn't asking the question in the hope of a negative reply. It was obvious the avid mystery reader wanted to be in on the murder investigation.

"It won't really be an official interrogation, Ma'am. We just want to see what each of you remembers about what occurred."

"Why are you taking people back into the library?" Sheila asked. "Shouldn't you take everyone to the sheriff's office or the police station?"

"We need to keep people together," Stryder replied. "No one is under suspicion yet. It's possible the person who committed this crime is already gone. The library's been open since 9 a.m. We need to figure out exactly when Ms.

Simmons arrived, how long she was in the library, and when she was shot."

"Who was at the desk when this happened?" Sheila asked.

Donald, standing by Bonnie, said, "I was at Reference, and Bonnie was at the Circ desk." Alicia noted he looked even more pale than he had earlier and knew the sight of Mary Beth's body had done nothing to calm his sick stomach.

Alicia saw Bonnie's eyes widen behind the round lenses of her glasses. The young clerk looked like she was about to faint.

Before Sheila could ask anything else, Ramsay walked out of the library with a few officers behind him. "The coast is clear, Steve. You can bring them inside."

***

As they entered the library, Alicia gasped at the sight of men carrying out the body bag that contained Mary Beth. John hugged her. "It's okay, honey. They'll catch who did this." She had to look away, but several people couldn't keep their eyes off the grisly scene. Alicia wasn't surprised that Mrs. Wexler watched in fascination, but she couldn't understand how Gilly could look without screaming again. Donald was taking deep breaths and telling Bonnie he felt nauseous. "I hope your co-worker doesn't toss his cookies," Stryder commented. Alicia sympathized with Donald. Her stomach didn't feel all too settled either.

Sheila suggested they go upstairs, and she offered to make coffee for everyone. Ramsay quickly took her up on the offer. Alicia excused herself from John who seemed to be keeping a watchful eye on her and went to assist her boss. She considered John was guilty that the email he'd ignored had almost cost Alicia her life. Gilly had told him, while they were waiting outside, that she had thought it was Alicia lying in the aisle when she first saw the body. Her horror had only been assuaged knowing that she'd just left her friend at the Children's desk; and, when Alicia came running in response to her scream, Gilly realized it was someone else's dead body she'd found.

When Alicia and Sheila brought coffee and what was left of the donuts Gerry had brought into the room where Alicia and John had celebrated the release of their second mystery the night before, Gladys and Donald were placing chairs around for people to sit. Most chose to remain standing. In front of the room, where Alicia noticed they'd forgotten to remove the banner, Ramsay and Stryder stood with officers on both sides of them.

The group settled down a bit as a few people helped themselves to coffee from the urn Sheila had set up on last night's refreshment table. Ramsay, breaking his diet most likely due to the stress of the situation, had been the only one to partake of a donut. When people were back in place, Stryder called them to attention.

"Excuse me, everyone. But I know you all want to get this over as quickly as possible. For those who don't know me, I'm Detective Stryder from Carlsville. I came to aid Sheriff Ramsay and brought some of my men." He nodded left and right to the policemen and then turned to the sheriff who was wiping his mouth.

"Thank you, Detective Stryder," Ramsay said, tossing his napkin into a nearby wastebasket. "We asked you all back inside just for some brief questions. As far as we can tell, whoever killed Ms. Simmons has escaped. We apologize for the body and bag checks outside, but they were necessary to rule out any weapons any of you might've been carrying."

A few murmurs were heard around the room and then Mrs. Wexler stood up from her seat in the front row. "Sheriff, may I interrupt for a moment?" Before he could give her permission, the lady, moving the brim of her hat to reveal curious gray eyes, said, "Do you have any suspects yet?"

Stryder was the one who replied. "It is way too early in our investigation to make any assumptions. Ms. Simmons attended the McKinneys' book release party at the library Thursday night. She was staying at a hotel in my town, so I will be making some inquiries there."

"But the murder happened here," Mrs. Wexler pointed out.

"We're well aware of that," Ramsay said. "I'll be checking things out in Cobble Cove, as well."

"What about Alicia?" Gilly asked. She was also seated in front next to Alicia and John. "Ms. Simmons was dressed like her. Do you think . . .?" She let her words trail off, but everyone knew what she was insinuating. Alicia wanted to warn Gilly not to mention the email John had received. She felt that would best be shared privately with Ramsay, and since she knew how close her friend had become with the sheriff, the opportunity to do that wouldn't be difficult to find.

"We are considering that, Abigail, I mean, Ms. Nostran," Ramsay said. "But as Detective Stryder explained, we are not jumping to any conclusions right now without the proper evidence."

John took Alicia's hand and whispered in her ear, so low she could hardly hear and knew no one else could. "I wish Gilly hadn't brought that up. I'm going to speak with Ramsay privately about the email."

She nodded. Andy, on John's other side, was now openly taking notes on a pad. She hoped he wouldn't mention in the newspaper story that the dead woman had been wearing an identical blouse to the one she had on. She assumed John would make sure the young reporter kept that off the record.

Ramsay spoke again. John's warm hand in hers helped calm her.

"We're going to let you all go home to your families. I've already spoken to Sheila, who has agreed to close the library for the next week. All library employees will still be paid. There may be a few people who need to come in for brief periods to allow us access to the building to continue our investigation." He looked toward Sheila and Gladys.

When people started standing and getting their belongings together, Stryder added, "Hold on one minute. We still have a few questions. Does anyone here remember seeing Ms. Simmons enter the library?"

The room became quiet. Some people shook their heads in a negative response. Stryder was about to ask another question when Bonnie stood up. Her voice quivering, she said, "I remember."

Ramsay fixed her with the beady eyes Alicia once recalled as being cold but were now warm with concern. Gently, he asked, "When was that, Miss?"

Bonnie flipped back the cocoa curls from too-long bangs and pushed her round glasses up her nose. "Donald needed to use the rest room, so I kept an eye on the reference desk while he left. A few patrons came in. I wasn't really paying attention to them because they didn't stop at the desk, but I think I saw a woman in purple blouse headed toward the crime section." She gulped as the words spilled out in a high pitch of fear. "I may be wrong about seeing her because I was answering the phones, but I thought I should mention it."

"What time was that?" Stryder's voice was not as gentle as Ramsay's.

"I'm not sure about that either. It must've been when Alicia had just gone up on her break. Donald was there alone but had to leave to go to the restroom."

Ramsay addressed Donald who was looking even whiter after hearing Bonnie's words. "How long were you away from the desk, Mr. Davis?"

Alicia wondered if the sheriff was actually considering Donald as a suspect in the murder. She also didn't understand why he hadn't asked her to wait before she took her break so he could use the bathroom. She knew stomach pains could hit quite suddenly, but she still found it odd, and she realized Ramsay might find it incriminating.

"I have a stomach virus," Donald said in his defense. "I was out yesterday and shouldn't have even come in today. I was off the desk until maybe five minutes before Alicia came back."

And yet, Alicia thought, *he seemed like he'd been there the whole time when Alicia returned.*

Chapter Nine

When the group was finally released, Ramsay and Stryder assured them the killer would soon be caught and brought to justice. They urged everyone to contact them with any information they might recall later. Ramsay's final message was not to panic. Although it was very early in the investigation and the sheriff and detective were hesitant to make any assumptions, the theory they were hypothesizing so far was that this was a targeted murder. Someone had followed Ms. Simmons to the library with the intent to kill her. Stryder believed the person wasn't from Cobble Cove but someone who was following Mary Beth. No money or credit cards were taken from her, so the killer wasn't after money. The victim was shot from behind with a small caliber bullet, the gun very likely concealed upon the perpetrator who fired it at close range. Alicia imagined it would fit nicely in a purse. She shuddered as she recalled Lindsey Harrington, the beautiful woman who claimed she knew John. The black purse she carried was bulky. Alicia had not paid much attention to it at the time because her own pocketbook was overstuffed. But even as her thoughts turned in that direction, she remembered Lindsey opening the bag to put in the slip of paper on which Alicia had written her and John's phone number. If the woman had meant to kill her, why hadn't she done it then? The obvious answer was that Lindsey was in full view of the library entrance, and Bonnie was at the circulation desk right across from Alicia. She tried to take her mind away from placing her in the role of a murderer. Lindsey likely just came to town to visit an old friend and not kill off his wife. But was friendship all that had been between her and John?

Alicia knew she had to mention Lindsey's appearance, but it would be better to wait until they were home alone.

***

Ramsay asked that the library employees stay upstairs a few minutes longer and dismissed everyone else. Stryder and his men accompanied the patrons downstairs while the sheriff addressed the remaining people in the room. Andy had stayed behind to continue taking notes, but Donald had asked to leave owing to illness and been refused. Ramsay spoke to the remaining members of the group.

"Although Stryder is focusing his investigation on Ms. Simmons' background and the Carlsville Hilton where she was staying, nothing has been ruled out. This is a safe town, and I'm honored that you chose me to protect you. However, unlike the Detective, I'm not convinced the killer has left Cobble Cove. I've asked for a couple of Stryder's men to remain in town to help me check things out locally. As we mentioned, the library will be closed until further notice." He glanced at Sheila who was standing by the door. "I will keep Ms. Whitehead informed of our progress in solving this case. I advise you all to remain vigilant and keep your windows and doors locked until we determine the motive that leads us to the murderer."

"Aren't you considering that Mary Beth wasn't the intended victim?" Gilly asked. "She and Alicia were wearing the same clothes."

Ramsay waved away the question. "We haven't ruled anything out yet. We need to first contact Ms. Simmons' family to inform them of her death. The body has been moved to the Carlsville coroner's office where the ME will examine it further. We then need to trace Ms. Simmons' steps since she came to Cobble Cove. We also need to dispatch some officers to Prime Crime publishing in New York."

Alicia suddenly realized they'd lost their editor. Would that jeopardize her and John's contract?

"Mary Beth was divorced," John said, directing the information to Ramsay. "She still used her maiden name. She told me she never changed it when she married. She's been divorced at least five years. No children, though."

"Do you know anything else about her family? Are her parents still alive?"

John shook his head. "I have no idea. She was a very private person."

Ramsay nodded. "We'll find her relatives. For the time being, if you remember anything else, please call me."

"She was at our house last night," Alicia offered. "She asked where I purchased the blouse I was wearing. I told her about the sale at Chloe's Closet. She must've gone there and bought the one I have on today." Alicia's voice caught, and John squeezed her hand.

"We'll need to speak with Chloe," Ramsay said. "Do you know if Mary Beth had plans to go anywhere else last night?"

"She mentioned a meeting," John said. "An appointment of some kind."

Ramsay's beady dark eyes seemed to double in size. "What did she say about this meeting? Do you know where it was taking place?"

John shook his head again. "No. Sorry."

"Are we free to leave yet?" Donald asked. "I'm still feeling queasy and would like to go home and lie down."

"You can all go," Ramsay said, "but if any of you recall anything else we should know about Ms. Simmons or anything unusual that happened at the library this morning, call me immediately."

Alicia thought of Lindsey Harrington but kept her mouth shut. Gilly joined Ramsay as people began to leave. Donald was first out the door, followed by Bonnie who had sat throughout the whole time with her eyes wide, staring straight ahead in fearful silence. As John guided Alicia to the staircase, he whispered, "Betty will have to be told about what happened."

Alicia knew her father-in-law's girlfriend, if that was the term for an eighty-year old woman, would be informed by Sheila along with the other members of the Library Board. Gilly would likely break the news to Edith and Rose when she got back to the inn.

Since Alicia had walked to work that day, she headed with John toward his car. The ambulance was no longer in the parking lot, and only the sheriff's car and those of the library staff members remained.

John opened the door of his pickup and then went around to the driver's seat to let Alicia in. Andy, who was behind them, came over and spoke to him. "I've never covered a murder before, so I'm going to need some help with the story, Mr. McKinney."

John smiled at the young man. "I had a feeling you would. It will need to be handled delicately. There are still a lot of questions, and we can't rile people up more than they already are with the thought that a murderer is still on the loose."

"I understand. I'll do my best and email you the draft for you to read before I publish the piece. We should get something out as soon as possible."

"Right. I'll look it over, Andy. Don't worry." John rolled up his window as the young man walked to his own car. Alicia watched as Gilly and Ramsay, last out of the building before Sheila, headed to the sheriff's car. It seemed Gilly was driving with Ramsay and picking up her car later to take to the inn. They were deep in conversation, and Alicia noted the way they walked close together. Gilly waved toward them as Ramsay opened the cruiser's door for her to enter. "I'll call you later," she yelled across to Alicia.

As the sheriff's car pulled away, Sheila came to the passenger side of the pickup.

"Alicia, I'll be in touch with you. I heard what Gilly said, but I think she's wrong. Even if you were dressed similarly, Mary Beth wasn't a pleasant woman. I don't like to speak ill of the dead, but I have a feeling she had a lot of enemies."

Alicia wanted to believe her boss's words, but there was one thing Sheila didn't know. It wasn't just the clothing. The strange email John received may have indeed been a warning that Alicia's life was in danger. Could the killer really have mistaken Mary Beth for her?

***

When Alicia and John arrived home, Kim was playing with Carol and Johnny. Alicia admired the energy the young woman had running after the toddlers who were now into everything. She felt a pang of guilt at the fact that she still worked full-time at the library, leaving John to watch them as he worked on his half of their books from home. It was no wonder progress was going so slow on the third mystery. The twins were sleeping less now, and it wouldn't be much longer before they stopped their afternoon naps altogether.

"Is everything okay?" Kim asked as Alicia and John walked in the door. Carol and Johnny were running around the room, but they stopped when they saw their parents. John went to the kids and scooped them both up while Alicia went to talk with Kim. She noticed a few strands of the girl's brown ponytail were loose and that, despite her youth, she was catching her breath from chasing the twins.

"The sheriff is handling things. We should know more soon, but the library is closed for the time being," Alicia filled Kim in as John brought the kids upstairs. Although they wouldn't be two until the spring and would probably not understand the conversation about what happened to Mary Beth, she knew John would not want them to be frightened of anything they might hear. Their grandfather would say, "Little pitchers have big ears," or, knowing Mac, he would modify the phrase.

"Is it true that your editor is dead?" The girl's blue eyes opened wide from under bangs that could use some trimming.

Even though Carol and Johnny were not nearby, Alicia lowered her voice as she replied. "Yes, Kim. They don't have much information right now, but they're investigating. I'm sure they'll catch whoever did it soon." Alicia wasn't confident of that at all, but she didn't want to alarm Kim. From last years' experience, she knew how distressed the babysitter could become.

Kim wasn't satisfied with that answer. "Oh, my God! A murder in the library. Do they have any suspects at all?"

Alicia shook her head, thinking of Donald and Lindsey. "No. Detective Stryder's helping Ramsay by questioning people at the hotel where she was staying in Carlsville. Ramsay will be contacting Mary Beth's relatives, although neither John nor I know much about her background."

"That's awful," Kim said. "I remember Detective Stryder. He was that black cop that worked with the sheriff during the kidnapping." Her voice broke as she mentioned the crime in which her boyfriend had been suspected but who John knew was innocent.

"Yes, some of his men are staying in Cobble Cove to continue checking things in town and at the library." Alicia had taken a seat on the couch. She felt like taking a stiff drink, but maybe she and John could just have some wine after Kim left.

Kim seemed to take her cue to go. "I hope they solve the case quickly. I'm sure Andy will be busy for the next week keeping up with the news."

Alicia saw from Kim's saddened expression that she wasn't too happy with being second place to her boyfriend's job. When Andy worked only as John's assistant at the *Cobble Cove Courier*, things were different. But between taking his last journalism classes at college and being responsible for publishing the paper each week, it didn't leave him much time for dating Kim.

"I'm sure Andy will do a great job. John has also agreed to assist him in covering the story."

"That's nice of him." Kim began to walk toward the door, and Alicia got up to lead her out.

"Thanks for coming to watch the twins on such short notice."

Kim smiled and pushed back her bangs. The light was back in her eyes. "It was my pleasure, Mrs. McKinney. They are so much fun. We played hide and seek, and I have to tell you that Carol is a real sneaky one."

Alicia laughed. She knew her daughter was the more extroverted of her two children. Johnny, like his father, was a deep thinker but still mischievous in his own quiet way.

"You can call me at any time," Kim added as Alicia opened the door for her.

"I appreciate that." As the girl waved goodbye and stepped outside, Alicia couldn't help adding, "Take care."

***

Alicia closed the front door and locked it behind her, something she'd started doing after last year's kidnapping. Even though the culprit was behind bars and his accomplice, someone who was once her friend, had moved away from town after serving a brief sentence, she was still uneasy. She then went to join John upstairs and found him slipping out of the nursery, switching off the room light and then placing his finger to his lips.

"Shhh, they're asleep."

She was shocked. "How did they go from fifty miles an hour to out like a light?"

"I think that's the norm at their age. Kim must've exhausted them." He grinned.

"You know I hate it when they fall asleep in the middle of the afternoon and are then up all night."

"It's okay, Ali. I think we need some time to ourselves now."

She agreed. She wanted to ask him about Lindsey. "Yes, John. I need to talk to you about something. Can we go downstairs? I'll pour us a glass of wine, and we can sit by the fire."

"I like the sound of that." He followed her to the living room where he took a seat in the rocker by the unlit fireplace. It was not yet cold enough to light it, although the nights were starting to grow cool.

Alicia went to the wine cabinet and brought back an unopened bottle of sherry and two glasses. "Can you help me with this, John?" She always had trouble opening cans and bottle caps. She once teased John that that's what husbands were for, but if she was out with Gilly or Sheila, they would pop the tops off and tell her she needed to exercise her hand muscles. Then they would add that the only thing men were good for were in between the sheets, and then only a few of the talented ones. Alicia knew John would qualify, but she wondered what Gilly thought of Ron Ramsay's performance in that area. As far as Sheila, the widowed director didn't seem to have any interest in male company, but she was attractive enough to have secret lovers that no one in town knew about.

John opened the wine and poured them both a glass. "Would you like me to light the fire, Alicia? It's a little chilly in here."

"I'm cold, too, John, but it's not from the temperature. I can't believe Mary Beth was murdered."

John stood and turned on the fireplace. It was an electric one, unlike the one he'd had at home with Mac who insisted on a "real" fireplace.

When he sat back down, he faced his wife. "I don't like that Gilly is implying that Mary Beth was mistaken for you because you both were wearing the same blouse."

"Isn't it a possibility, John? I mean, you got that email yesterday and ..." She let her words trail off.

"I'm still convinced that was a prank. Gilly has Ramsay's ear now, so he'll be hounding me about the email. He'll probably confiscate my laptop, and I'm in the middle of the second chapter of our next book."

Alicia recalled the unreasonable deadline Mary Beth had given John. She must've done the same to her other authors. Maybe one of them preferred her dead to meeting her deadlines.

"I think you can do without your laptop if you have to, John. We still have the desktop in my office, and since we network them, it's easy to share the files. But I'm not sure Gilly will say anything to the sheriff. She's my friend. She won't do that without my permission."

John took another sip of wine and then placed the glass on the table by his side. "I guess it doesn't matter, Ali. If you're actually in danger, which I don't believe, I want to make sure you're safe."

She took a breath and decided to ask the question that she'd been postponing. Her heart began to race as she formed the words. "John, who is Lindsey Harrington?"

Her husband almost choked. When he'd cleared his throat, he turned away from her and looked toward the fake flames. "How did you hear about her?" His voice was too controlled.

Alicia felt the pit of her stomach drop. She replied in a flat tone, "She was in the library today."

John's expression remained neutral as he turned back to her. "I assume she introduced herself. Did she say why she was in Cobble Cove?"

Alicia realized he hadn't answered her question. "She was at our book release party. She must've seen one of the flyers Mary Beth had Nancy send to other areas."

Even though Alicia thought she was adept at reading her husband, she couldn't figure out what he was thinking as he looked at her through cool blue eyes. "I wonder why she didn't introduce herself. I didn't notice her in the audience."

"I thought the same thing, but you haven't answered my question. She said she was a college friend. Is that true?"

She was relieved when John answered honestly. "More than a friend, Ali. We were lovers."

"Before you married your first wife, I guess."

"Yes, and also after she died."

Alicia was surprised. "When we began our relationship, John, you told me there hadn't been anyone else after Jenny."

John lowered his eyes, and Alicia noted the long lashes that so many women in town envied. "I'm sorry I gave you the wrong impression. I said there was no one serious in my life after Jenny. Lindsey had been a friend of hers. The three of us were friends. Lindsey understood when I broke up with her and married Jenny. But after I lost Jenny and the baby, Lindsey consoled me. It wasn't enough. I was still in love with Jenny and her memory. I told Lindsey I needed some space away. I moved here with Dad, and you know the rest."

"Do you think Lindsey expected you to come back to her again?"

John stood. "Is that what this is for, Ali? Don't tell me you're jealous of a woman I left twenty years ago?" His voice had started to rise and his face redden.

Alicia remained seated. "It's not that, John. It just seems strange she would attend our release party and not come up and talk with you. She asked for our number and said she would be in town for a while and would like to go to dinner with us."

"She hasn't called, Ali. I would tell you about that. She probably felt uncomfortable approaching us with so many people around last night."

"That's what she said." Ali looked up at her husband standing by the fireplace. She put her full glass down.

"And you don't believe that? You think she had another reason? Maybe you even think she was plotting to do away with you and win me back and then mistook Mary Beth for you?"

Hearing it put that way, Alicia realized the craziness of her reasoning.

It was then that the doorbell rang.

Chapter Ten

Alicia half expected Lindsey to be standing on the doorstep. Instead it was her father-in-law with Fido, his golden retriever, beside him.

"Mac, c'mon in," she said, calling him by his nickname. He'd given up some time ago her addressing him as "Dad." Alicia's parents had died in a car accident while she was in college.

Mac ambled in on his cane, tugging gently on Fido's leash. Fido was more than middle-aged, but it wasn't true you couldn't teach old dogs new tricks. The golden retriever had recently taken some police dog training lessons after being drugged during Alicia's children's kidnapping. Prior to that, Fido had helped locate his owner during a snowstorm.

"What brings you here, Dad?" John asked from behind Alicia.

"I was out walking Fido, John, when I passed the library. I saw a sign outside saying it was closed and police cars were in the parking lot. I was wondering what was going on."

"Have a seat with us in the living room. We can all talk in there."

After Mac sat on the couch and Fido settled on the floor next to him, Alicia offered to make tea or coffee. Mac told her not to go to any trouble, but she put hot water on and served a few of the leftover chocolate chip muffins from the second batch of baking Gilly had done before the book release party.

As Mac bit into one, he exclaimed, "Now I know why Sheila hired your friend and had her and her boys move to town. These almost match my delicious PB&J sandwiches. They must be a secret recipe, too."

Alicia laughed as she sat down in the chair across from the men. John was also eating a muffin. Since Fido had looked up at her with his big brown eyes when she'd brought them out, she'd slipped him a dog bone she kept on hand when he visited. She didn't want her father-in-law tossing him some scraps as he usually did because chocolate can be poisonous to dogs.

As Fido lay there munching his bone, Alicia was reminded of Sneaky. She wondered if the dog could sniff out Sneaky's whereabouts and considered asking Mac after they filled him in on Mary Beth's murder.

John broke the news to his dad first. Never one to mince words, he simply said, "The reason the library is closed, Dad, and probably will be for a while, is that our editor, Mary Beth, was found murdered there this morning."

Mac's blue eyes, so like John's, glanced toward Alicia with concern. "How awful. Did you find her, Alicia? Betty will be so upset when I tell her the news. As you know, neither of us knew Mary Beth personally, and, to tell the truth, we didn't particularly enjoy meeting her last night." He grimaced. "I don't condone murder, but I can see how she could flare someone's temper."

"We're not sure that's why she was murdered," John said, bringing his father's attention back to him. "She was wearing a blouse she'd bought in town at Chloe's Closet where Alicia shops. They both wore the same one to the library today. I still think that's only a coincidence, but Alicia is worried that the killer mistook Mary Beth for her."

Mac considered John's words as Fido, done with his bone, took a nap by his owner's feet. "Well, I can understand that, but I agree with you, John. What possible motive would anyone have to kill Alicia?" He looked back toward his daughter-in-law. "Betty shops in Chloe's Closet often. It's a nice place. She buys lingerie there."

Alicia smiled at the thought of an eighty-plus woman buying negligees like the one Gilly gave her when Alicia went on her second honeymoon.

"I imagine the police will be speaking with Chloe," John said ignoring his father's statement about his girlfriend's nightwear. John, despite being quite imaginative in bed, did not like hearing about his father's intimacy with Betty. Alicia thought they made a rather cute couple. Recalling how Betty was once an angry recluse, shutting out the world after her own family was killed in a mugging in New York City, she was glad Mac could bring the old lady some peace and contentment. It worked both ways. Mac mourned two women, John's mother and Pamela's. While their relationship was still new, it seemed Betty had done a good job of consoling the widower.

"I'm sure Ramsay will catch the killer," Mac said, bringing Alicia's attention back to the murder. "I must admit I didn't have much faith when he was elected sheriff, but he did a good job during Carol and Little Mac's kidnapping." Mac liked to call his grandson by his middle name. Mac's real name was also John, but Betty liked to call him by his full name, Jonathan. Everyone else in town referred to him as Mac.

"Ramsay was helpful," John acknowledged, "but Alicia and I were the ones who found the kidnapper, literally by accident."

Mac frowned at the memory of seeing his two children in the same hospital room in Carlsville. "Lucky for you Gilly gave you that Christmas gift that saved your life, Son."

Not wanting to dwell on that awful memory, Alicia changed the subject. "You know, Mac, Sneaky is missing. He's been gone since our book release party. We found his collar and think he broke it off and then went through the staff room window."

"Oh, no!" Mac exclaimed. Alicia watched Fido's ears perk up at the mention of the cat.

"We've been looking for him. Angelina is very upset. Haven't you seen the signs she put up around town? Her family is even offering a reward for anyone who finds him."

Mac shook his head. "My vision isn't what it used to be, so I may have seen the signs but not been able to read them. I did notice a sign with a photo of a Siamese. I hope he comes back soon. We had cats when John was young, and they always came home as long as they were fixed. They have a strong sense of smell that leads them back to their territory."

"I hope you're right." Alicia got up and cleared away the empty tea cups and the remains of the brownies. When she came back, Mac was saying to John, "If you'd like, I could have Fido do some sniffing around. I don't think we can get back into the library to get any of the cat's toys so Fido could smell them, but I know you've kept Sneaky here during long weekends when the library was closed and Laura wasn't able to take him. Do you still have anything here with his scent?"

"I keep a cat bed for him in my office, Mac, but the last time Sneaky was here was over Labor Day weekend. Laura and her family were away then."

"That should work fine, Alicia. Did he sleep in it when he was here? Have you washed it since then?"

"Yes. Sneaky loves cat beds, but he did end up in our bed a few times that weekend."

John rolled his eyes. "I remember. I rolled over one night and thought Alicia had grown fur on her arm."

Alicia ignored that comment. "I didn't clean it, Mac. I know how cats like to use things with their own scents on them, and it wasn't dirty. I'll show you. Come with me." She got up and waited while Mac took his cane and followed her down the hall with Fido. John also came along.

Before they even got to the room, Fido had rushed in and headed over to the round, Sherpa-lined pet bed where he dug his nose into the cushion.

"There you go," Mac said. "I'll take that with me if you don't mind, and I'll give Fido a few more laps around town. If we find Sneaky, I'll let you know."

"Are you sure you can carry that, Dad?" John asked. "Why don't I drop it off at your place later? Fido's already had his whiff of Sneaky. That might be enough to get him started."

Mac agreed, although Alicia knew the man hated to admit his inability to do things on his own. "Sounds like a good plan, John. I also want to get back home to talk to Betty and let her know what's going on at the library."

"Sure, Dad. I'll give you two some time to talk and bring it over later."

Alicia and John walked Mac and Fido to the door. Alicia hoped the golden retriever would locate the Siamese and, even more important, that Ramsay and Stryder's men would find Mary Beth's killer.

***

When Mac left, John went up to check on the babies. Like Alicia, he didn't want them to sleep too long for fear they might stay up at night.

Alicia was about to start some housework, wondering how she would keep herself occupied and her mind off the murder investigation while the library was closed. Being a mother of toddlers, a co-author of a mystery series, and a full-time librarian, there never seemed to be enough time in the day to accomplish everything she wanted. Yet, when faced with the possibility of days and probably weeks off from work, Alicia realized she would not be as productive despite the additional hours. She recalled the saying, "If you want something done, ask a busy person." She knew retired people such as Mac and Betty who filled their days with activity. Betty volunteered as President of the Library Board, and Mac still repaired damaged books and maintained his part-time real estate business. John also had grown used to organizing his twenty-four hours around caring for the twins, writing their books, and assisting Andy at the newspaper. While he still talked about finding a full-time job locally, it seemed they were managing financially as their royalties were beginning to grow as their book sales increased. However, without Alicia's income, they would not be able to afford even the low cost of their home in Cobble Cove. Although John was no longer accepting his sister's monetary gifts, he had agreed to keep the money she'd given them for the babies at their baptisms in a tax-free, high interest earning account that would eventually be used for their college funds.

Alicia jumped out of her reverie at the sound of the ringing phone. Again, her thoughts turned to Lindsey, but the voice on the other end belonged to Gilly.

"Hi, Alicia. I'm just calling to check on you. Is all okay?"

"We're fine, Gilly. You sound anxious. What's wrong?" Alicia recognized her friend's high-pitched tone as nervousness.

"I'm back at the inn. Ron is questioning some of the guests here. I told him that wouldn't be good for business, but he insisted."

Alicia wondered why the sheriff was talking to Gilly's guests. Then she remembered that most of the out-of-towners who attended the book release party were staying in Cobble Cove. As far as she knew, only Mary Beth, with her fancy tastes, was staying in Carlsville.

"Are people from our book release party still at the inn?"

"A few, but some left this morning. Ron checked my register. He also spoke with Edith and Rose. I hope he hasn't frightened them. You know how sensitive they are, especially Rose."

Alicia knew the two women who helped Gilly at the inn and were known as the town's "cousins" because they had lived there so long and worked on all the village committees, could get easily excited. Rose was the shy sister deferring to her older sister, Edith, but both ladies preferred the quiet life in Cobble Cove.

"Ron even talked to the boys," Gilly went on. "They know about murders from watching TV, of course, but I made sure he was careful about what he told them. I don't want them having nightmares. Danny would probably offer to investigate with him, but that could be dangerous."

Thinking of Lindsey and the possibility that John's old flame had chosen the Cobble Inn while she was in town, Alicia asked hesitantly, "Gilly, you didn't happen to notice a pretty blonde woman among your guests, did you? She's in her mid-forties but looks younger. She would've checked in a day or so ago."

"I know who you're thinking of, Miss Harrington. Yes, she checked in on Wednesday and is still here. Ron spoke to her a little while ago, and I have to admit I had a touch of jealousy. Why do you ask? Do you know her?"

Alicia didn't want to go into the story yet. "Not exactly, but she was at the library this morning and came to the talk last night, although she left early. I wondered if she was staying at the inn."

Gilly may have found Alicia's answer suspicious, but she hid any curiosity she had from her voice as she replied, "Yes, she's one of the few who are still staying with us. I think Ron spooked some of the guests because I had a lot of checkouts after he left."

"Didn't he ask people to stay in town?"

"No. He seemed satisfied they all had alibis except Miss Harrington."

Alicia felt her stomach begin to knot. "Did he ask her to stay?"

Gilly chuckled, but it wasn't a happy sound. "Unfortunately, I think he only asked her because she's so pretty. I bet he'd like to get her in handcuffs."

"Gilly!" Alicia knew her divorced friend tended to come out with crazy and sometimes lurid expressions. "I hope no one is listening in on this conversation. I'm sure the sheriff only has eyes for you."

Gilly gave another chuckle. "He's a man, Ali. Men have eyes for all women. Except those who are like Donald, of course."

The mention of her co-worker had Alicia recalling his run in with Mary Beth and his agitation afterwards. She assumed Donald would be one of the library employees Ramsay would be talking with again. She also surmised that Gilly's fears rose out of her experience of finding her ex in bed with his secretary. But wouldn't she feel the same if Lindsey made good on her promise to call John, and his attraction for her was re-ignited?

"I have to go, Ali. There's more people at the desk, and Edith needs a break. Rose is cleaning the vacated rooms."

"Would you like me to come over there?" Alicia volunteered. "Maybe I could help Edith, and you could get some rest or go shopping or something."

Gilly sighed. "Thanks, Alicia, but I need to hang around here. Ron will probably want to talk to you and some of the other library people again soon."

"What about Stryder? Have you heard what he's doing?"

"Ron told me he's been questioning the guests at the Carlsville Hilton. He's also trying to find any relatives of Mary Beth to contact with the news of her death. Her body is still being examined for evidence, but it's clear she was shot from behind. The weapon hasn't turned up, so it's likely it's still in the possession of the killer."

The thought of that frightened Alicia. The only thing that comforted her was the knowledge that the murderer had targeted his or her victim. Unless, of course, they'd shot the wrong person.

Alicia heard the twins stirring as John woke them, and she said a quick goodbye to Gilly, thanking her for checking in on her and promising her she'd keep her doors locked. She was thankful Gilly hadn't brought up the possibility of Mary Beth being mistaken for her, but she wondered if it was because Ramsay had talked her out of the idea or if she was trying not to unduly scare Alicia.

***

Alicia's fears were wiped away momentarily as the twins came bounding down the stairs, stumbling in spots as their chubby legs buckled. John followed behind them, trying to help them down. The site of her husband with their kids always made her feel better.

"Hey, Ali, I have an idea. Since it's a beautiful day out and we have some time together, how about we take the twins to the park?"

"Mommy, park," Carol screamed excitedly as she ran into her mother's arms. Alicia patted the girl's blonde locks. John was probably right that they should take advantage of her day off. "I think that would be nice," she said looking at her husband as he took Johnny's hand and walked him over to Alicia and his sister.

John smiled. "Great! We can go to the Bookshelf Lane Park. It's less crowded than the one by Cobble Point."

Bookshelf Lane Park was located next to the elementary school on the other side of the library. She considered it might not be wise to be in that area so soon after the murder. "I don't know, John. Some of the kids hang out there after school, but I think they must've had an emergency closing today. Gilly just called and mentioned that Ramsay was talking to the inn guests and also to her kids about what happened at the library."

John's brows furrowed as Carol and Johnny both cried out in unison, "Park, Park, Park."

"It'll be fine, Ali. The kids need some exercise and fresh air. I'll get their jackets. We won't stay there long, an hour tops."

Feeling outvoted by her family, Alicia nodded. "Okay. Just for an hour."

Carol jumped up and down squealing with delight as Johnny grinned from ear to ear, showing his father's dimple.

***

As they walked to the park, Alicia took deep breaths of the sweet September air. It was warm, but not hot, and there was no humidity. The days were still long, but the leaves on a few trees were already starting to turn. While most kids hated to see summer end, Alicia had always felt September's special magic. It was a time of new beginnings. She believed that although change wasn't always easy, embracing it was the only way to allow positive things to enter your life. Like her awakening two years ago when she learned the truth about Peter. If she'd continued to let her fear of losing the love she thought lay between them, she and John would never have met.

They had to pass the library and school to get to the park. Johnny, walking next to John in his faulty steps, pointed toward the front of the library and said, "Liberry." Alicia was relieved to see the police cars were gone, although a yellow tape surrounded the area and a large sign notified people that "Cobble Cove Library is Closed Until Further Notice."

"Yes, that's where Mommy works," his father told him, "She's going to be home with us for a little while, so we can all spend more time together. Isn't it fun to go to the park with her today?"

Alicia knew John took the twins to the park often. She sometimes went with them on weekends. As a mother who worked full-time, she could relate to the divorced dads she often saw there on Sundays. It was tough being a part-time parent, and she envied John the time he had to share with Johnny and Carol even if it meant changing diapers, doing the wash, and cooking.

The school had the same sign as the library, although it stated that the building would reopen on Monday. There was one police car on the street, and Alicia saw Ramsay head toward it as he left the building. Bridgette Stafford, the school principal, stood on the school's steps, seeing him out.

Ramsay tipped his head as he spotted the McKinneys passing by. "Good afternoon. Where are you folks headed?"

"Hello, Sheriff," John said. "We're going to the park. It's a nice day, and the kids were getting antsy." The children were tugging at his and Alicia's hands, urging them to hurry up.

Alicia worried the sheriff might advise them to go back home. From what she could see from where they stood, the park was completely empty. Instead, Ramsay smiled and glanced up at the sun. "Nice day for it." But as they began to walk away from him, he said, "Before you go, I'd like to speak with Alicia a moment."

Alicia looked at John. "Would you mind taking the kids while I talk with the sheriff?"

"Not at all." John took Carol's hand as Alicia released it. "Isn't Mommy coming?" the little girl asked.

"I'll be there in a minute, honey. You go with Daddy now."

Alicia watched as John with Johnny and Carol on either side of him walked into the park. Then she turned to Ramsay. "What can I help you with, Sheriff?"

"You know you can call me Ron, Alicia. In private, of course." Ramsay leaned against his cruiser. "I just wanted to update you on the case. Gilly said you would want to know. She's worried about you, but nothing I've turned up points to the victim being mistaken as you except for what she was wearing."

Alicia considered telling him about the email, but decided to listen to whatever information he wanted to relate first.

"Do you have a motive or suspect yet?"

He shook his head, and she noticed his dark hair, touched with gray strands, also seemed thicker. Hair treatments? It was possible. The sheriff, having lost weight and adopted a new attitude, seemed like a younger man. He was taking care of himself and his appearance. When she'd first met him on Long Island, his rudeness made him look ugly. Now his demeanor highlighted his attractiveness. No wonder her friend had an interest in him.

"We are still investigating, but we've managed to locate Ms. Simmons' ex and her relatives. They're planning a memorial service on Long Island on Monday."

Alicia was surprised. She knew Mary Beth was divorced, but John said she'd never talked about other relatives.

"Mary Beth came from Long Island?"

"Yes. Her mother and sister live in Hewlett."

Alicia and Peter's home had been in Syosset, but she was familiar with the South Shore town of Hewlett-Woodmere. "What about her husband? Is he also from the Island?"

"No. He's a stockbroker in the City. Works on Wall Street. He remarried, you know. Although we tend to pin these types of murders on the husband, even the ex-ones, I don't see him as the killer. I only spoke with him on the phone. Stryder spoke with Mrs. Simmons. It seems Mary Beth never took her husband's name. He also talked with the sister. She's single but doesn't live with her mother. She has an apartment in New York, like her sister did but on the opposite side of town. I was a bit curious as to why they didn't share. Rents in the city aren't cheap."

Alicia tried to assimilate the details of what she was being told. It wasn't difficult to figure out why someone wouldn't want to live with Mary Beth, but Alicia was surprised to learn she had a sibling. John had conjectured that Mary Beth had been a spoiled only child. "Is Mary Beth's sister younger or older than she?" she inquired, interested in knowing more.

A strange look passed over the sheriff's face. "That's the odd thing, Alicia. Mary Beth was Mary Lou Simmons' twin."

Chapter Eleven

Alicia spent a few more minutes talking to the sheriff before joining John and the kids in the park. She tried not to let her mind run away with her envisioning Mary Beth's twin as the woman who had been killed in the library. The scenario didn't work because she was sure Mary Lou Simmons was in the city at the time of the murder and that she surely wouldn't have purchased a blouse from Chloe's Closet. Besides, if that were so, where was Mary Beth? She also believed Ramsay and Stryder had already ruled out the sister being involved whether as the victim or the perpetrator.

John was pushing Carol and Johnny who were seated on the baby swings when she arrived. He smiled at her. "Wanna help, Mom?"

She walked over to them and stood behind Carol. "Mommy, push," her daughter requested as the swing slowed.

She took over as John continued pushing Johnny. "So, what did Ramsay say?"

"He and Stryder have made some calls. They found Mary Beth's mom on Long Island and, get this, John. She also has a sister who lives in the city named Mary Lou who is her twin." Alicia waited for his reaction as she gave her daughter another tap on the back to send her forward in tandem with her brother.

"Hmmm. That's interesting." John didn't seem all that shocked. "She never spoke about her family. I think they were estranged. I wouldn't be surprised if they aren't too broken up about her death."

Alicia thought of Peter and Pamela. "I don't know. Ramsay said he found it strange Mary Lou lives in a different part of the city. She isn't married. I wonder what she does for a living and if she has the same personality as Mary Beth."

John grinned as he pushed Johnny. "I don't think twins share personalities like they do looks, but I do understand them staying as far away from each other as they could get."

Before the conversation could be continued, they saw Mac ambling down Bookshelf Lane with Fido at his side. He waved to them. "Nice day for the park. Mind if we join you?"

Johnny said, "Grampa. Down."

John stopped pushing and slowed the swing to let his son off, who ran to his grandfather. Carol also wanted to stop swinging, but she was more interested in Fido. She began putting her hands out to him as soon as Mac walked through the park gate.

"He's been walking a while, Carol, but I thought I'd let him loose for a run around the park. It's his favorite place," Mac told his granddaughter.

Mac went over to a nearby bench. Alicia wondered if it was he and not Fido who was tired. Her father-in-law was in his eighties and, although he kept active, he didn't have as much energy as a younger man.

John and Alicia joined Mac on the bench as he unhooked Fido's leash. "Now you kids watch that he doesn't go by the gate," he instructed. Fido bounded away with Johnny and Carol at his heels.

"Any luck with Sneaky?" Alicia asked, remembering that Fido had sniffed Sneaky's cat bed before he and Mac left their house.

Mac shook his head. "Sorry, Alicia. No sign of him. John can still bring over the cat bed, but I have a feeling we won't be able to track him."

Alicia's heart sank. "Angelina will be heartbroken, and I'll have to tell Laura, too. She knows a lot about cats.

Maybe she has some ideas on how to find him." Alicia also recalled that Laura and other library workers who hadn't been working that Saturday did not know about Mary Beth's murder. She was sure Sheila would contact them before the news hit the paper the next day.

"I hope he turns up." Mac watched as Carol tried to mount and ride Fido, something her father had taught her. "No, honey." He called from the bench. "You don't want to hurt Fido, and he might get mad at you." Fido was a gentle dog, but it wasn't good to tease him.

"I'll go watch them," John offered, slipping off the bench. "You and Dad can chat."

When he walked away, Mac turned to Alicia. "I'm heading to the inn before going home. That's the only place I haven't brought Fido to check on Sneaky."

"Gilly would've known if he was there," Alicia said. "but it's on your way, and we can walk with you. How is Betty holding up? How did she take the news?"

Mac's blue eyes clouded. "She's upset, of course, but you know, Betty. She's a lot stronger now after having finally put her family's death behind her."

"Yes, but this would certainly bring that experience back." Alicia knew Mac was a big part of the reason Betty had overcome her paranoia and agoraphobia.

"She'll be okay." Mac looked toward his son romping with his grandchildren and dog. Then he turned back to Alicia. "What about you? It must've been a shock finding Mary Beth dead in the library and dressed in your clothes. I also heard you received a death threat shortly before that."

Alicia couldn't believe John had told his father about the message when he'd denied the email was anything but a prank. "John didn't seem to think it was serious."

"What about now?" Mac probed. "I think your friend Gilly believes someone was after you and not Mary Beth."

Before Alicia could reply, John came back with Carol seated across his shoulders and Johnny holding his hand walking next to Fido. "I think we should head back. I think Fido has worn the kids out and vice versa."

Mac grinned. "Looks that way, but I think you're more worn out than they, John."

"Mac is headed toward the inn, so I thought we would walk him there before going home," Alicia said.

"Sure." John pushed back a strand of dark hair tipped with gray that had fallen over his right eye as he'd run after the twins and the dog. "Hopefully, Gilly has baked a batch of her delicious brownies."

Alicia doubted that. On the phone, Gilly had seemed harried, keeping up with all the people who were checking out after learning about the murder.

Things seemed to have settled down at the inn by the time they arrived. Alicia felt a bit of nostalgia at the sight of the white clapboard building where she first met John and where they'd spent some happy hours touching up the paint on the porch. She was still in contact with Dora through email, but she missed the kind woman even though it was great to have her best friend in charge of the Cobble Inn.

Gilly was sitting out on the porch when they arrived, having a cup of tea. Sure enough, as Mac had hoped, a plate of brownies lay in front of her. Ruby sat at her feet, her ears perking up as Fido walked up the steps next to Mac.

"Hi, there," Gilly said starting to stand. "You're all just in time for afternoon tea."

"Don't get up, Gilly," Alicia said. "We were at the park and just dropped by to walk Mac and Fido home."

Mac grinned as he ambled over to the table. "I'm in no rush, and those brownies certainly look good."

Carol and Johnny ran up to the table. "Bwownies," they both exclaimed.

Alicia shook her head. "Just one, kids." She didn't like them getting into a habit of eating sweets.

John joined his father, taking a seat and grabbing a brownie himself as Alicia sat down next to Gilly.

"Go ahead, honey. Take one, too. There's plenty."

"What about the other guests and Edith and Rose?"

Gilly's eyes darkened. "Most of the guests are gone. Edith is upstairs keeping the boys company, so I could have a little rest, and Rose is shopping for dinner. I don't know what I'd do without them."

Alicia realized her friend was concerned that the murder might impact the inn's business. Fido had joined Ruby on the floor next to Gilly as Mac took the chair next to her. Both dogs were starting to beg. "Sorry, pups, but you know you can't have chocolate."

"Hold on, Mac. I have something for them." Gilly got up and went inside. A few minutes later, she returned with bones. "I keep these as treats for Ruby, but I'm sure she won't mind sharing with Fido. I have some cat treats, too, for when Sneaky comes by. Laura takes him here sometimes with her."

Gilly paused. "Has Sneaky turned up yet?"

Alicia shook her head. "No. We're very worried. Mac let Fido sniff Sneaky's scent from a cat bed, but he's had no luck locating him on his walk."

"Angelina must be sad. I saw her putting up signs with her father around town. I have one by the front desk."

Just then, the sheriff pulled up in his cruiser. Alicia assumed he wasn't there on business because Gilly had said all the guests had been questioned and most of them had checked out.

"Hello, Abigail. Long time no see, John, Alicia," he said, mounting the steps.

"You'd better hurry, Ron. The brownies are almost gone." Gilly moved the plate containing the last two toward the sheriff.

"I'm still dieting, but I can't turn down your brownies, Abby. I'll just take the smaller one." He grinned as he took a brownie less than an inch smaller than the other.

"In that case," Mac said, "I'll finish off the plate. I already walked off the calories."

"Sure you did, Dad," John said as his father took the other piece and bit into it.

Gilly smiled. "I'm glad you all enjoy my baking. Rose is a pretty good baker herself. We take turns making treats for our guests."

"I hear most of them left after I questioned them," Ramsay said, taking a seat next to Gilly. Alicia had to admit they made a nice-looking couple. Who would've thought?

"You frightened them off," she teased, but Alicia could tell her friend was worried about the drop-off in business. She'd put all her savings into the inn because her ex-husband's alimony could barely pay for the boys' expenses and the college fund Gilly had set up for the three of them. Alicia wondered if she and Ramsay would marry, but she knew Gilly might not be ready for it. Ramsay was also a divorcee, but he had no children.

"I couldn't detain them, Abby. I don't think any of them were involved." He took a bite of his brownie and wiped his mouth with the napkin Gilly had put in front of him. "I have located Mary Beth's relatives. Did Alicia tell you about that?"

"No. We were talking about Sneaky."

"Sorry he's gone missing. I had cats as a kid, but after Mr. Clyde died, I told my mother I didn't want another one."

"Mr. Clyde? I didn't know you had cats, Ron."

Ramsay looked wistful. "Mr. Clyde was my buddy. I didn't have any siblings and not a lot of friends, so he kept me company from the time we found him hanging outside our house as a stray kitten until he passed away the year I left for college. I'd had him twelve wonderful years."

"They say cats are good for your blood pressure," Gilly said. "I know your diet and the exercise plan the doctor put you on is helping, but maybe if you got another cat you might be able to get off medicine completely."

Alicia was accustomed to her friend trying to be everyone's mother, but she saw Ramsay, like most men, was stubborn in his beliefs. "I don't think I could take another one. I'd be afraid of getting close to a pet again, and I work such odd hours that it wouldn't be good for the animal either."

"I've been thinking of getting a kitten at the inn, but I'm not sure how Ruby would react to that," Gilly said looking down at Fido and Ruby chewing bones under the table. The two dogs got along well and were not trying to steal away the other's treat.

"A cat would be good to have here at the inn," Mac said. "It'll keep the mice away. Sneaky does a great job being the library's mouser." As soon as he said Sneaky's name, he looked down as he remembered the cat was missing.

Gilly said, "My kids have had pets from fish to birds to hamsters, and I was always the one left to care for them, even Ruby. We might get another pet one day, but we're still breaking in here." She looked at Ramsay. "What did you find out about Mary Beth's relatives? How did they take the news?"

Ramsay reiterated the story he'd told Alicia including the fact that Mary Beth had an identical twin, but he also added the further detail that Mary Lou Simmons was a literary agent.

"Maybe that's why Mary Beth took on so much more than being an editor entailed," John suggested. "Perhaps she was in competition with her sister."

"Mary Lou told me they hadn't spoken in five years," Ramsay said. "The mother told Stryder the same thing. It seems Mrs. Simmons favored Mary Lou. It'll be interesting meeting them both at the memorial service on Monday."

"Memorial service?" Alicia hadn't thought of that. "Where is that taking place?"

"At a church on Long Island that her mother attends. The ME hasn't released the body yet, but the family wants to have a service in Mary Beth's honor." He glanced across at John. "You two might want to go since she was your editor."

Alicia had no idea why Mary Beth's relatives would want to hold a service for her if they weren't on good terms, but she agreed she and John should attend even if they weren't exactly friends.

"I guess we could get Kim to watch the kids," John said looking over at Carol and Johnny who were still munching into their brownies and giggling together as they petted Fido, "or I could go myself."

"Don't worry about the twins," Mac said. "Betty and I would love to spend some time with them. Kim will probably be in school."

"Are you sure, Mac?" Alicia asked.

"Of course. You two should even stay overnight. It's a long drive."

Alicia had been back to the Island to take care of all the details of selling her house after it was repaired from the fire. She hadn't yet met the buyers, but wasn't sure she'd be interested in doing so or visiting the place where she lived through lies with her first husband.

"Sounds like a plan," John said.

"I'd like to go, too," Gilly said as she started cleaning off the table. "Now that most of the guests are gone, I think Edith and Rose can handle the place. The school should be open Monday, so the boys will be occupied most of the time in classes."

"That's a great idea," Ramsay said. "We can all drive down together."

Alicia wondered if Ramsay was attending the service to observe Mary Beth's relatives. She assumed Stryder would be there, too. She couldn't help but feel curious about what Mary Lou and her mother were like. She also had to admit that another reason she wanted to go with John was because she'd feel a little safer away from Cobble Cove.

Chapter Twelve

When they arrived home after dropping off Mac and Fido, John took the twins upstairs to give them their baths. There were two voicemail messages on their house phone. Alicia played them back. The first was from Laura, her voice strained with agitation. "Alicia, it's Laura. Sheila called me about what happened at the library. It's awful. I also heard from Patty. She says Angelina is so worried about Sneaky that she isn't eating. I'm going to visit her, but you can call me on my cell. I want to talk to you." She left her cell number, even though Alicia already had it. She dialed the number quickly, fear about Angelina taking hold as she waited for the line to be picked up.

"Hello," Laura's voice still sounded shaky.

"Laura, it's Alicia returning your call. Sorry, but we were at the park and then stopped at the inn to talk with Gilly. Are you home or with Angelina?"

"I'm at Angelina's house. I managed to get her to eat some food, but not much. At this rate, she's going to make herself sick. Are there any leads at all on Sneaky?"

Alicia was as concerned as Laura about Angelina's condition. She was worried that the upset over the cat's disappearance might cause the girl to have a relapse of her leukemia. "No news, Laura. Mac even had Fido try to sniff him out. It's like he's not even in Cobble Cove."

"Cats can travel far, but he's never gone any distance from the library before, even the few times he got out the door."

"There's nothing much we can do, Laura. I'm glad you went over to see Angelina. Maybe Muffin can comfort her a little." Muffin was Angelina's cat.

"I don't think Muffin will help. Seeing her makes Angelina even more worried about Sneaky."

"Laura, I have to tell you something. John and I are going to Long Island on Monday with Gilly and Ramsay. They're having Mary Beth's memorial service there. We'll be back Wednesday next week. Hopefully, Sneaky will return by then, if not by tomorrow."

Laura sighed. "Fingers crossed, Alicia. I'll stay with Angelina as long as I can. She's starting kindergarten on Monday, but I don't know if she'll be up to it if she's not sleeping or eating properly."

"I'll check on her before we leave," Alicia promised, "and I'll be sure to let both of you know if I hear anything further about Sneaky."

After Alicia hung up, she listened to the second voice mail message. The water was running upstairs, and she heard John singing, "Rub a dub dub. Two kids in a tub," changing the tune of the famous nursery song. If she wasn't so concerned about Angelina, she would've laughed at his off-key serenade. Instead, she focused on the second caller and felt her heart start to race as she realized the throaty voice on the recording was Lindsey Harrington.

"Hello, John. Alicia's probably told you by now that I'm in town. I couldn't resist going when I saw your book release party advertised in the paper. I'm sorry I didn't come up for an autographed book, but I thought it would be nicer if we got together privately." Her sexy voice paused and then continued. "How is tonight? I've been meaning to try that Italian place I noticed in the shopping area. I know how much you like Italian food. Oh, and, of course, I'm looking forward to meeting your children … and Alicia again." Leaving her number, she clicked off.

Alicia just stood there holding the phone. How much worse could this day get?

***

Alicia considered erasing Lindsey's message, but she knew the woman would call again or, worse, show up at their door if she'd figured out where they lived. She took a deep breath and went upstairs to tell John. He was in the nursery changing the twins. The room smelled of a strange mix of baby powder and dirty diapers, but it also smelled of love. As Alicia watched John with their children, tickling their tummies and telling them jokes that made them giggle, she realized she couldn't make the same mistake she'd nearly made before they were born. She had to have faith in her husband. Their marriage was built on trust, and she would not threaten its foundation.

"John," she said in a low voice as she entered the room. "I can change Carol while you finish Johnny."

"Sure, thing, Mom. Thanks." He often referred to her as "mom" or "mother" in front of the kids.

As John let her slide by to get to her daughter's bed where the girl was rolling around in a towel, he looked up at her. "Should I put on Johnny's pajamas? I know it's still early, and we haven't eaten yet."

"You might as well put on a new set of clothes." She reached for a diaper along with one of her daughter's dresses and a pair of tights. "We actually may be going out to dinner."

"Really? I was planning to cook tonight, but that's fine with me. Where do you want to go?" John had finished changing Johnny and picked him off the changing table, slinging him over his shoulder and allowing Alicia to have her turn with Carol.

"We won't be dining alone with the kids, John." Alicia started to undo Carol's diaper. "Lindsey Harrington left a message while we were out. She wants to go to La Bella with us."

John was silent as he took one of his son's shirts from the nearby bureau and unfolded it. "Are you sure you're okay with that, Ali?"

She wanted to assure him she was, but she couldn't lie. "I wasn't happy about it when I played the message, but this is probably Lindsey's last night here." Then she added, "And I'll be looking over your shoulder all night."

John laughed. "I love you, Ali. I'll call Lindsey back and let her know I and my family"—he emphasized the word "family"— will meet her at La Bella at 6."

***

Ever since Casey's diner closed, whenever they ate out, the McKinneys usually dined at La Bella, the family-owned restaurant in Cobble Corner.

It was a few minutes before six when they entered the dimly-lit building with the lovely murals featuring famous landmarks in Italy that John liked to identify to the twins and which they could hardly pronounce. Carol called the Leaning Tower of Pisa the Leaning Tower of Pizza and wanted to know if she could have a slice. Johnny termed the Venetian gondolas, "very good boats."

Teresa Romano and her daughter, Lucia, welcomed them at the check-in counter where delicious cheesecakes and cannolis were displayed. If it were up to the twins, they'd have their desserts first. Both pointed to the glass window.

"Later, guys," John told them. "Good evening Terry, Lucia. How are you, ladies tonight? We need a table for three adults and two babies."

"Good evening, folks. It's nice to see you again." Teresa turned to her daughter. "Can you please show the McKinneys to a table, and I'll bring over two high chairs for Carol and Johnny."

Lucia nodded. Her dark hair was long like her mother's but tied back in a ponytail tonight like Kim usually wore hers. The two young women were about the same age. "Right this way," she directed, walking toward the main part of the restaurant and leading them to a table with a flickering candle. Alicia sometimes went on date nights there with John and found the lighting and atmosphere quite romantic. Tonight, she was hoping it would be otherwise.

As they took a seat and the menu Lucia handed them, Teresa arrived with the high chairs and placed them on opposite sides of the table, one next to Alicia and the other by John. This was the type of arrangement they also used at home.

"If you need anything else, let us know. We'll be back to take your orders once the other member of your party joins you."

"Thank you," John told Teresa. "How are Sal and Vinnie?" He inquired about her husband and Lucia's younger brother.

"They're fine. Sal is cooking in the back, and Vinnie will wait on your table. It's early yet, and we aren't too busy." Teresa glanced around the room. Only a few tables were occupied.

After the ladies went back upfront, John fashioned two of the white table napkins into a bib and tied them around the twins' necks. Then he sat back down and looked over at Alicia. "Lindsey tends to run late. I'm sure she's on her way. Would you like a glass of wine? I can signal Teresa to bring a bottle of red to our table."

Alicia was tempted to take John's offer, but she wanted to be clear headed when she faced his old girlfriend. "Not yet. Let's see what Lindsey wants. I'll probably just have my usual order." Alicia and John often shared the house special, Romano Carbonara, a linguini in red sauce. The twins liked the traditional spaghetti and meatballs and shared one child's serving.

A few minutes later, as Alicia put down her menu, she saw a blonde woman enter La Bella. It was Lindsey. Lucia directed her to their table.

John stood up, a smile on his face. "My gosh. You look the same, Lynn. Nice to see you after all this time."

Lindsey smiled catlike, her blue eyes sizing up John and ignoring the rest of the table. "I could say the same of you, John, but I'd be lying because you've aged even better." She gave him a quick kiss on the cheek. Alicia noticed the slight reddening that was left from her lipstick and what appeared to be a bit of a blush on her husband's face.

"Have a seat," John said, pulling out the chair next to him. Then, as if remembering his family, he introduced Alicia, Carol, and Johnny.

"What beautiful children," Lindsey exclaimed, claiming the chair John indicated. Alicia watched as he helped her off with her jacket wondering if this meal together had been a good idea.

After they'd all ordered, Vinnie, in his white waiter's uniform which Alicia noticed was slightly too big and too long, brought them their food. The boy had just started high school in Carlsville. Next year, he would attend the new high school that was being built on the site of Casey's restaurant. Vinnie carefully placed the hot plates down and warned them to be careful, making sure John and Alicia got the baby's plates. "*Mangia,*" he said, using the familiar Italian phrase for "eat up," but Alicia lost her appetite when Lindsey offered to cut up the babies' pasta and meatballs.

"Thank you, but I can handle Carol's dish," she said, taking the plate. John had already handed Johnny's over to Lindsey who was chopping up the meatball.

"I saw some notices around town about a missing cat," Lindsey said. "Even though I'm deathly allergic to felines, I'll keep an eye out for him. His owners must really love him to offer such a large reward for finding him."

"He doesn't belong to the Millburns," John corrected. "He's the library cat. There's a little girl in town with leukemia who's really fond of him. She met him during the kids' storytimes at the library in which he sometimes makes a guest appearance. Even my dad's dog, Fido, goes to a few of them."

Lindsey chuckled. "I'd love to meet your dad while I'm still here." She paused and then continued, "I also saw a sign on the library when I passed it earlier. Did something happen there? Everything was fine when I left, but I see it's closed now. Did someone get hurt?"

Alicia did not feel like reliving the experience so was glad when John explained the situation. Lindsey's blue eyes widened. "A murder? Oh, my God! I remember that woman from your book release party. She wasn't very friendly, but I'm sure that's no excuse for someone killing her." She looked over at Alicia. "I'm so sorry it occurred in your library. You must've been so afraid."

Alicia looked down at her full plate. While she and John had split the family portion of linguini, she was just moving it around on her plate as she tended to do when she wasn't hungry. However, her rumbling stomach betrayed her.

"Looks like you're upset. You're hardly touching your food," Lindsey pointed out.

"Eat something, Ali," John added. "The sheriff and Detective Stryder are investigating. It's only a matter of time before they find the killer."

Alicia took a sip of water instead. "I know that, John, but let's not talk about it at dinner. Okay?"

"That's a good idea," Lindsey said before John could reply. "Let's talk about old times instead." She turned to John. "What have you been up to the last, oh gosh, twenty years?"

Alicia spent the next half hour listening to Lindsey and John recount events she'd been absent from. She focused on the twins instead, feeding them and wiping their mouths.

When everyone except Alicia had finished eating, Vinnie returned to clear away their plates. "Would you like a bag to take this home?" he asked Alicia.

"That would be nice. Thanks, Vinnie," she said, glad he didn't question her leaving so much on her plate. The leftovers would make a nice lunch for the twins the next day and maybe she could manage some herself after this night was over and Lindsey was on her way home.

As John helped Lindsey back into her jacket, she said, "This has been delightful, John. Maybe we can all do something else before I leave. I've decided to spend the rest of my weeks' vacation in Cobble Cove. It's such a charming town despite what happened at the library, but I'm sure that was an isolated incident. Murders are practically daily occurrences in the City. I don't look forward to returning there." She shuddered theatrically to allow her long hair to flip over her shoulders, so John could feel its silkiness as she slipped her arms through her jacket.

Alicia's already upset stomach took a turn, but then she remembered she and John would be going to Long Island for a few days. "We're actually attending Mary Beth's memorial service on Long Island next week," Alicia said. "Tomorrow, we'll be busy packing."

Lindsey raised a light eyebrow. "Are the babies going with you? They're quite young to attend a memorial service."

Alicia suddenly recalled the last time she'd left the twins and the horror of learning they'd been kidnapped. It wouldn't be easy leaving them with a murderer possibly still in town, but now she had even more reason to go. "No. My father-in-law and his, uh, girlfriend will be watching them."

"I see." Lindsey stepped away from the table as John freed the twins from their high chairs. Teresa came back to them and helped him fold up the chairs. "I hope you enjoyed your dinner," she said, her eyes on Alicia's takeaway bag.

"It was wonderful," Lindsey said. "I'll be sure to come back before I leave."

Teresa's dark eyes lit up. "That's great. I'm glad you enjoyed everything. We always enjoy serving Cobble Cove visitors."

As John allowed Lindsey to pass in front of him, Alicia could've screamed when he said, "We'll only be away two days. Maybe we can catch up with you before you head back to the City, and maybe you can visit Dad and Betty then, too."

Chapter Thirteen

Alicia was accustomed to clear, sunny days in mid-September on Long Island – not the downpour that greeted them when they arrived in Hewlett for Mary Beth's memorial service. Luckily, she had checked weather.com and knew to pack a rain jacket and umbrella. Gilly, with her own umbrella, was well prepared, too, but Ramsay and Stryder's street clothes were getting soaked as the five of them climbed the stairs of Trinity-St. John's Church. The rain had only been a light drizzle when they'd gotten into town that morning, but as they drove to the church, the skies had let loose.

Diving into the vestibule as she shut her umbrella, Alicia stood next to John and waited with the others before entering the nave. They were early, but a few other people joined them rushing out of the rain. Alicia pegged the two women who entered behind Gilly, the detective, and sheriff as Mary Beth's mother and sister Mary Lou, both dressed in black. Her hair was styled differently, cut short and highlighted with red streaks. She also used a lot less makeup on her face. Her mother also wore her gray hair short. It was curly and thick. It reminded Alicia of a steel wool pad. Neither woman smiled or greeted them when they entered, and despite matching neutral expressions, Mrs. Simmons and Mary Lou did not look like they were grieving.

Stryder took over and made the introductions, and everyone offered the women their condolences which were met with curt nods. Then the group took their seats inside. As a private service, there weren't many other attendants. Alicia, John and the others took up the front row of one pew, while the Simmons' sat on the opposite side with a few people that entered after them. Ramsay and Stryder sat together on the end of the aisle. Gilly sat next to Ramsay with Alicia on her right next to John.

The bald-headed minister came around and shook hands and then took his place at the front of the room. After saying a short prayer that hardly anyone joined in for except John, he raised his eyes toward the small gathering. "Before we lay Mary Beth's memory to rest, I just want to say that whoever committed this grievous sin will pay for their crime." He glanced in the direction of Ramsay and Stryder. "This woman brought joy to many people by her lifelong work of editing mystery novels. It is with a sad heart that we release her into God's hands." He paused and then, glancing again at the group, asked, "Would anyone like to step forward and say a few words about Mary Beth?"

The room took on a deep silence as people looked around at one another. Alicia expected Mary Beth or her mother to take up the minister's offer and speak about Mary Beth, but the tall, sandy-haired man who walked up to the altar was someone she didn't recognize and doubted was a family member. His head was down, and he looked sadder than anyone else present. Alicia thought he might be hiding his tears as he took a few gulps and prepared to talk. She wondered if he was Mary Beth's ex.

Gilly whispered to Alicia, "Wasn't that guy at your book release party?"

"I don't recognize him, Gilly. I think he might be the ex."

"He isn't," John said even though Alicia didn't realize he had heard them. "I'll fill you in later."

Alicia considered that might not be necessary because the man at the podium, after taking some deep breaths, introduced himself. In a tremulous voice, he said, "I'm Cooper Halliday, and I was one of Mary Beth's authors. She was a professional and a friend. I will miss her dearly."

As Halliday went back to his seat next to Mary Lou, John asked Alicia, "Should I go up, too?"

"If you want, John. It doesn't look like too many people here intend to add anything else." She had been surprised at Halliday terming Mary Beth a friend. She knew John had never seen the editor that way.

Like Halliday, John kept his words brief. "I'm John McKinney, and Mary Beth was also my editor as well as my wife's," he said looking toward Alicia. "Some people may have found her a bit overbearing, but she expected no less from herself than what she demanded of others." He paused, and a slight grin turned up at the corner of his mouth. "I'm sure she's giving St. Peter a hard time admitting her." His attempt at a joke did not elicit any smiles or laughs.

After John rejoined Alicia, the minister said some parting words and spent a few minutes afterwards talking in the pew with Mary Beth's sister and mother. Cooper Halliday was the first person to leave without saying anything to anyone.

Alicia and her group waited in the vestibule for an opportunity to add more words of sympathy.

While they stood together gathering their umbrellas because the downpour outside was still heavy, Alicia asked John, "How did you know Cooper Halliday?"

"He said a few words to me when I was setting up the chairs with Gilly's sons the night of our book release party. I was surprised he attended but not that he didn't come up for an autograph."

Alicia was still in the dark. "Have I met him before?"

"Probably not, although Sheila might carry his books in the library."

"He said he was an author."

"Yes. You could say he's one of our rivals and as he mentioned, one of Mary Beth's clients."

Gilly's eyes widened, and Alicia knew the way her friend's thoughts were turning. Sure enough, she verbalized what was on her mind. "He could've been her lover. His mysteries are a lot racier than you and John's."

"I thought you only read romances, Gilly."

"I prefer them, but I've read your books and Cooper Halliday's. I like them both, of course, but you should really consider putting some sizzle into Detective Marks' life. Maybe have him hook up with Marjorie Meyers."

Hearing the name of her two main characters who were both included on the strange email John received, made Alicia recall the unsettled events she'd left behind in Cobble Cove. A sudden feeling of *deja vu* struck her as lightning crashed outside. Was it raining back in Cobble Cove? Had Sneaky returned? Even if he had, the library was closed. What about Lindsey? Why was she staying a whole week in town, and why had she wanted to reconnect with John after all this time? Most importantly, was the email John received an actual threat on Alicia's life that had resulted in the wrong woman being murdered?

***

"Mary Beth and her mother certainly don't look like they're grieving," Alicia whispered to John as the two women came through the vestibule doors. Neither woman had shed a tear, and if Alicia had imagined any love had been lost between them, the thought had been erased when Mary Lou told Ramsay as he reiterated his condolences that the world was a better place without her sister, and Maureen Simmons said her daughter's murder was no surprise to her because so many people hated her.

John, after the Simmons' left, said, "People show their sorrow in different ways." She knew he'd bottled up a lot of his grief after his wife died, but finding out he'd allowed Lindsey to comfort him afterwards, didn't make Alicia feel all that sympathetic. "I still can't see them crying on the inside, John. They actually said they couldn't care less that Mary Beth is dead."

***

Hewlett was one of the five towns on Long Island that consisted of Woodmere, Cedarhurst, Lawrence, and Inwood. For their overnight stay, the group had booked rooms at the Five Towns Inn in Lawrence. It was pricier than John wanted to spend, but Ramsay told him he and Stryder would offset the cost as business related expenses. The sheriff and detective would share a room, while Gilly would have her own next to John and Alicia's.

Before heading back to their hotel, the rain had let up, and they had all repeated a few words of sympathy to Mary Beth's ungrieving relatives. There had been no gathering planned afterwards, as most families did following funerals. Instead, Mary Lou said she'd be spending a few days with her mother until she returned to work. Alicia found it somewhat surprising and a bit uncouth, when the agent took John aside in the church parking lot and asked him what his plans were with Prime Crime now that her sister was gone.

"I'm really not sure," John hedged. "I did notify them about Mary Beth's death. I assume they're going to assign us another editor." Alicia was glad he included her in the conversation.

Mary Lou turned eyes as shrewd as her sister's at him as she took a card out of a pocket in her black slacks. "I'll be back in the City on Wednesday. Call me, and we can talk about setting up some representation for you. I realize you most likely have a contract with Prime Crime, but contracts can be broken. You and your wife could do a lot better. I've made deals with top publishers, and I think I can even sell your series to a movie producer." There was a glint in her eye, not unlike the look Mary Beth often exhibited when she was promoting their mysteries.

Alicia almost laughed at John's dumbfounded expression. "Uh, okay." He took the card hesitantly. "I'll be in touch with you, Ms. Simmons."

The agent got in the car next to her mother. "I'll be looking forward to it, Mr. McKinney. Before she closed the door, she added, "And please say hello to my good friend Chloe Gibbons. I know she has a store in your town. I must come visit some time."

Alicia recalled Mary Beth buying the blouse at Chloe's Closet the night before her murder. Chloe was new to Cobble Cove, and Alicia did not yet know much about her. But if she was as good a friend to Mary Lou as she said, why wasn't she at her sister's memorial service?

As the Simmons' car pulled away, Gilly said, "I think she killed her or maybe she was in cahoots with Chloe."

Ramsay drew a breath. "I already spoke with Ms. Gibbons, and her alibi for yesterday morning was corroborated, Abigail. However, regarding Ms. Simmons, I agree it's usually a family member who commits the crime. Did you notice that Mary Beth's ex did not make the memorial service?"

Stryder nodded. "I certainly did. I questioned him, but it might be worth paying him another visit. Maybe on our way back through the City tomorrow, we can do that, Ron."

"Can I come, too?" Gilly asked. Alicia knew her friend had the makings of a Miss Marple, the homebody type with the curious personality of the fictional amateur sleuth who liked to solve puzzles.

"You're driving back with us," Ramsay said.

Alicia almost wished she could also go, but John was giving her a warning eye, and she was reminded he had mentioned visiting his sister on the way home. He'd also asked if she wanted to pass her old house, but she told him she wasn't interested. She'd left it behind when she started her new life with him in Cobble Cove. Like the fictional Phoenix, the house that was once her home had been reborn from its ashes but was no longer the same place; or perhaps, she had undergone an even deeper change.

"Don't worry. I'll fill you in," Gilly whispered to her as they walked to their cars. Ramsay had not brought his cruiser but an undercover car which he'd used to pick up Stryder on the way to Long Island. John had driven Alicia's car because he felt the pickup was not an appropriate vehicle for a memorial service.

***

Back at the hotel, Alicia said to John as he was helping her unpack the small bag they shared, "You know, I was kind of hoping Mary Lou would be nicer than her sister. Maybe my original thought that twins shared personality traits is true."

John grinned as she handed him a pair of socks, underwear, and pajamas. At home, he usually just wore the bottoms in case the twins woke them up at night. The remainder of the bag belonged to Alicia, and he'd already teased her about how much more women packed than men even for a simple overnight trip.

"You might be right, Ali. I wonder how much of a good friend Mary Lou is with Chloe. From what I know of the woman, she doesn't look like she would hit it off with her."

"I thought the same thing, John. Isn't it odd that she knows Chloe, and Mary Beth bought a blouse at her shop before she was killed?"

John placed his clothes in a bureau drawer. "From what she said at dinner, Mary Beth didn't know Chloe."

"Maybe I can talk to Chloe when we get back to Cobble Cove."

"I'm sure Ramsay already did and, if he suspected anything, he'd have filled in Stryder. They seem to be focusing on the ex-husband."

Alicia put her own things away and then sat on the bed. "I think Gilly wants to help Ramsay solve this case. She's a bit like Mrs. Wexler in her crime fascination."

"That's because she's a lonely divorcee with nothing else to do in her spare time."

"Not anymore, John. Besides the inn, taking care of her three boys, and working part-time at the library, Gilly's new pastime is Ron Ramsay."

John quirked an eyebrow, and gave his wife a sultry look. "Let's not gossip about other people right now. We have a night alone. We should take advantage of it." Joining her on the bed, he removed his shirt.

Alicia's heart began to race. "It's early. We haven't even had dinner yet, John. What if Gilly, Ramsay, or Stryder come by? They're right next door." They were in a middle room situated between Gilly and the two officers.

"Okay, hon. I'll wait until everyone is tucked in before I jump your lovely bones."

It was then that John's cell phone beeped, indicating an incoming message. Alicia panicked fearing it might be her father-in-law or Betty contacting them about a problem with the twins, but why were they texting and not calling?

"John, what is it?"

John had pulled his cell phone out of his pocket. "That's strange," he said looking down at it.

"What does it say?" Alicia had her hand out, reaching for it, her heart rate had accelerated again, not from anticipation of their lovemaking but from the awful thoughts that raced through her mind about her babies. It couldn't be happening again.

John pulled the phone away from her. "It's nothing, Ali. The kids are fine." He knew what was on her mind. "Just a prank text."

"John, let me see. What do you mean it's a prank?" She recalled the email John had received right before Mary Beth was killed.

"I guess we should show this to Ramsay in light of what's happened, but I don't want you to freak. Whoever's doing this is just trying to frighten us."

Alicia gave John the look that she knew he recognized from past experience as one that demanded he pay attention to her. He tapped the phone and handed it to her.

The text, like many spam ones she'd received on her own phone, was from an unknown source. The message was brief: "Marks missed Marjorie."

"This must be the same person who sent you the email, John. "You should have reported it."

"I know." John took back his phone and then grabbed his shirt. "Come with me, Ali. I'm going to Ramsay's room and show this to him now. It doesn't make sense. I can't believe the killer would bother contacting us. It's got to be to throw us off the trail."

Alicia wasn't sure. "Either that, John, or what he wrote is true. Maybe Mary Beth really wasn't the intended victim. Maybe this person who calls himself by our detective's name really means to kill our main character—who obviously is me."

Chapter Fourteen

Ramsay and Stryder were divided on their views of the text. Ramsay sided with John that it might be an attempt to throw them off track of the investigation. Stryder, however, wasn't convinced it should be treated lightly. He asked for John's phone and cell company information and his email address. He said that he wanted to run checks to see where the messages were originating from. He could start the process immediately by calling some contacts back in Carlsville, but he also needed to question Mary Beth's ex-husband with Ramsay before they headed back upstate. "Nothing should be overlooked. I also suggest, when you get home, that some men are placed outside your house and someone follows Alicia if she goes out," he told John. "Ramsay doesn't have the staff, so I'll arrange that with some of my officers."

"Do you really think Ali is in danger? It's strange the killer would keep sending these messages if that's his intent. Even if he's bluffing, I wonder why he's not just keeping himself hidden."

"It could be a game to this sicko," Stryder explained. "I've seen it before on cases, and I'm not ruling out the possibility Alicia is his target. We can't take any chances."

Gilly was listening in on the conversation. "Mary Beth had plenty of enemies, but everyone likes Alicia. I can't imagine who would want to harm her."

Alicia could think of one person, the woman who had extended her visit in town. Lindsey Harrington still seemed to have eyes for John.

***

The silent shadows of the September setting sun splayed across Pamela Morgan's face as she opened the door to her Brookville home to John and Alicia. The tall, willowy blonde was dressed casually in jeans and a gray sweater with a Harvard college logo that she must've borrowed from one of her daughters. In her right hand, she held a gold pen. Alicia recalled the last two times she'd been to Pamela's house and how she had greeted her with a riding crop the first time and a paintbrush the second. But in those instances she hadn't expected their arrival. This time, John had called her as they were checking out of the Hewlett hotel to let her know they would be dropping by. He hadn't wanted to contact her earlier until he knew they could make the stop.

"Hello, John, Alicia, please come in," Pamela said, opening the door wider to allow them entry. "I was just working on my memoir."

"Memoir?" John raised his eyebrows. "I see you holding a pen, but I would expect you to be using a computer."

Pamela, despite her wealth and the amenities of her large home, preferred to do some things the old-fashioned way like her dad, Mac. She didn't have any household help except for a cleaner who came in a few times a week and two stable hands that took care of her horses.

As Alicia and John followed Pamela into the sunken living room that was twice the size of theirs in Cobble Cove, Pamela said, "I find that it's easier for me to compose my thoughts on paper than on a screen. I've always kept diaries, and I've been going through them lately. I'm using some of those experiences in the book." She glanced at John. "Writing talent seems to run in our family, but I don't have the patience or imagination to write fiction. A memoir will be a legacy for my daughters as well as for you, your children, and Dad, of course."

Alicia saw the open notebook on the couch with a half full glass of wine on a table next to it. Pamela gestured for them to sit and offered them something to drink, but they both declined.

"This is just a quick stop, Pam. We have to get home to the twins. I just wanted to see you since we were on the Island." John had filled Pamela in about the murder.

"I'm glad you did. I'm moving into Caroline and Cynthia's apartment in the City soon. There's plenty of room for me, and they are hardly there. This place is much too large for me, although I'd like to keep it as a summer home."

"Are the girls still studying in Europe?" Alicia asked, sitting in a chair next to John opposite the sofa.

Pamela, closing her notebook with the gold pen to mark the page, laughed. She tilted her head back, and a few strands of her short, ash-blonde hair fell across her forehead. Alicia noticed her face looked thinner. Her high cheekbones were more pronounced, and her neck showed her age more than it had last year during that horrible time when she was injured during Carol and Johnny's kidnapping. *Maybe the experience had taken its toll on her, or could it be something else?* Alicia wondered.

"Caroline has gone to Egypt to follow her professor boyfriend, and Cynthia is still in France. I wish those girls would settle down and make me a grandmother already. How are your little ones doing?"

"Growing up fast," Alicia said. She noticed John observing his sister, too.

"Pam, is everything okay? You look a bit tired."

She smiled, but it seemed to be half-hearted. "I'm well, John. I just need to go in for some surgery in Manhattan next month. I have an excellent doctor, so I'm not worried."

That's what she meant by a legacy. Even though her words sounded positive, Pamela was afraid she might die.

"Do you mind if I ask what type of surgery?" John directed his gaze on his sister's face.

She reached over and took a sip of wine from the glass, swallowed before she replied. "I had a mammo a few weeks ago. There's a lump in my left breast. I need to have it removed."

"Oh, Pamela. I'm so sorry," Alicia said.

She waved her hand. "It's not a big deal, Alicia. They caught it relatively early. They assure me my chances are good."

"Are your daughters coming home when you have the operation?" John asked. Alicia could tell he wasn't convinced by his sister's words.

Pamela finished the rest of the wine and put the empty glass back on the table. "I haven't told them, John. I can handle this on my own."

"Dad's right. You're as stubborn as I am. But I won't let you go this alone. Let me know when you're being admitted, and I'll be there. I won't tell Mac if you don't want me to, but I'm coming to hold your hand. I'm your brother, and even though I've only known you a few years, I want to be there for you."

Alicia imagined Pamela had tears in her eyes, but she blinked them away. "I'll be at Sloan Kettering on October 15th. The surgery is at 9 a.m. You may want to come the night before. After the operation, I'll be staying at Caroline and Cynthia's place uptown. I'll email you that address. I don't expect you to stay during my recovery, but thank you for offering to be there when I go under." She smiled ruefully. "It'll be like old times with us in the hospital together as we were last year."

John grinned. "I may even bring you one of Dad's PB&J sandwiches."

"That would make my recovery even faster." Pam looked over at Alicia as she changed the subject. "Now, tell me more about what's going on in Cobble Cove? Do they have any idea yet who could've killed your editor? It's hard to believe they murdered her in the library."

John shook his head. "The memorial service was strange. The mother and sister were not very friendly. Ramsay and Stryder and Alicia's friend Gilly who moved to town last month are talking with the ex-husband before they head back to town."

"I don't think Mary Beth's ex would've done it. Mark and I are not on amicable terms, but he would never consider harming me. What motive would he have? I was the one with the money, thanks to Peter."

Alicia flinched at the mention of her first husband. John saw it and put his arm around her. "Mary Beth wasn't rich. Her husband worked on Wall Street, so he must've made a good salary. They didn't have children, so I doubt she was getting any alimony from him."

"What about the sister?" Pamela asked. "I know I could've murdered Peter, but someone beat me to it." As she said the words, she realized the effect it had on Alicia. "Sorry, Alicia."

"That's okay, Pamela. I know what you're saying. You would've never killed anyone, but my first husband was not the man I thought he was." She looked at John. "I was in love with an image, but now I'm in love with a real man."

Pamela smiled.

"Mary Lou is not any nicer than her sister," John said. "She's shrewd. She even wants to represent me with another publisher."

"Would you be interested? How long are you under contract with Prime Crime?"

John sighed. "It's not the contract that would stop me, Pam. I'm not interested in getting involved with a Simmons again. I hate to say it, but I'm relieved not to be working with Mary Beth anymore."

Alicia didn't think John had shared the messages he'd received with Pam or the fact that Mary Beth had been wearing the same blouse Alicia had worn to work the day the editor had been found dead in the stacks. She didn't see a point of mentioning it now and was glad when John said, "I think we should leave the investigating up to the detectives. Alicia and I need to head home now, Pam. You can get back to your memoir. I'll be here in October as I promised, and we'll be in touch by phone." He got up, and Alicia and Pamela joined him.

As they walked to the door, Pamela gave Alicia and John kisses on the cheek. Not a demonstrative woman, she allowed them both to hug her. As John released his sister, he said in a soft voice, "Don't worry, Pam. You'll be fine. I'll make sure of that, and mum's the word to Dad."

"Thank you." Her eyes looked misty again. "Give Carol and Johnny big kisses from their aunt. Maybe I'll visit them again for Christmas." She paused. "I hope everything is settled by then. Cobble Cove is such a lovely town. I hate to think of it becoming overridden with crime."

"So would we," John said, putting his arm around Alicia again as they walked to the car.

***

When they were back in Cobble Cove, a police car was stationed across the street as it had been when the twins were kidnapped. Sheila called to report that the library would be closed until the following week, and Laura informed Alicia that Sneaky was still missing. Angelina's mother was distraught by her daughter's lethargy and weight loss and was keeping her home from school. Patty also reported that a donor match had been found for Angelina and the doctors were hoping to schedule the operation in October. However, unless Angelina was stronger, they might have to postpone the procedure which might mean losing the donated marrow and starting again from scratch to seek another donor. Alicia felt awful about the news. She was still praying Sneaky would come home, but he'd already been gone nearly a week, and even the reward the Millburns had offered for his return had not turned up any leads.

Gilly came over that night to fill Alicia in on the interview with Mary Beth's ex. "He seems like a nice man," she said, "and Ron says his alibi checked out for the morning of the murder. He was at work." She gave Alicia one of her looks of motherly concern. "Ron also told me Stryder checked John's cell phone records and email account. The email was sent from the Cobble Cove Library the night of your talk from a fake yahoo account. They're still checking to see if they can find out where the cell phone message came from, but they think it was sent from a burner phone. I'm so sorry, sweetie. You must be a wreck, but at least you have protection. One of the officers outside—" she gestured toward the window "—is kind of cute. I wanted him to frisk me, but he only asked what my business was visiting you."

That made Alicia laugh. "It's nice to have someone watching out for me, but I think it's going to make me restless after a while. I can't even go to work, and my mind just isn't on writing."

"At least you have the babies to keep you occupied. It's a good opportunity to spend more time with them."

"That's true, Gilly. They're growing up fast. Before I know it, they'll be in school."

"Tell me about it. My eldest will be in high school next year." Gilly glanced at Carol and Johnny who were playing tag with their father. Mac and Betty had left as soon as John and Alicia arrived home, both looking a little exhausted from their babysitting.

"I'm going to pay Chloe a visit tomorrow. It gives me an excuse to do some shopping, too."

Alicia knew what her friend was up to. "Are you thinking of playing Miss Marple, Gilly?"

"I just want to give Ron a hand. I think Chloe will be more likely to open up to me. Would you like to come along?"

"I don't know, Gilly. The police will be following me around."

"You said yourself you might go stir crazy here. I'll speak to the hunky cop and assure him I'll keep an eye on you." As she watched Alicia's face consider the request, she added her final plea. "Besides, aren't you curious as to how Chloe knows Mary Beth's sister?"

Alicia couldn't argue with that. She secretly hoped the messages John had received were indeed red herrings to confuse the detectives. She doubted Chloe was the killer, though. As far as she knew, the shop owner hadn't even attended the book release party because she was working that night. She also hadn't been aware of her coming to the library Saturday morning.

"Okay, Gilly. John may not like it, but I'm sure he'll understand how cooped up and restless I'll be if I'm stuck in the house for a whole week. I can't even help him write our next book because things are so up in the air with our publisher."

"I'll pick you up at noon tomorrow. Maybe we can do lunch at La Bella."

Alicia walked Gilly to the door. "Thanks for your help, Gilly. I have faith in Ramsay and Stryder, too, but I know people often aren't comfortable talking to the police. I can't live my life in fear hiding out because of some messages that might or might not be from someone who botched up killing me and still means to go through with it."

"Don't worry, Ali. If someone is planning to murder you, Ron and Steve will get to the bottom of it, or I will first." She smiled, a glint coming into her eye. "Besides, it might give me a chance to spend more time with the hunky cop across the street."

"I thought you and Ramsey were . . ."

"We are, but that doesn't mean I can't look. If you notice, sweetie, there's no ring on my finger."

That made Alicia wonder if Gilly envisioned marrying the sheriff. Before she could ask, John met them at the door, the twins at his side. They all looked sweaty and tired from their play.

"Not saying goodbye to me or your nephew and niece?" he teased. Alicia considered Gilly the twins' aunt if not by blood, then by the strong friendship they shared.

Gilly looked a bit guilty. "Sorry. I didn't mean to rush off." She opened her arms and ran to hug Carol and then Johnny, planting a kiss on both their cheeks. Then she turned to John. "I still think you're the handsomest hunk in Cobble Cove, but Alicia beat me to it."

John hugged her. "I overheard that you're taking Ali out tomorrow to question Chloe. I'm not thrilled with the idea, but I know she'll be anxious sitting in the house all day asking me to check my messages every fifteen minutes. A little shopping therapy won't hurt to take her mind off things."

Gilly smiled. "Shopping therapy has always done the trick for me. That and a batch of my brownies."

Chapter Fifteen

Chloe was in the back of her shop arranging some outfits as Alicia and Gilly entered, the tinkling windchime over the door announcing their arrival. Alicia noticed the blouses in the window had been replaced by Chloe's new men's line of fall shirts and sweaters. She made a note to mention that to John when she went home.

Chloe came up to greet them, her bracelets jangling softly. Her fingers were adorned with rings. Alicia imagined Chloe had a larger ring collection than Sheila, and though she kept her long brown hair pulled back, it was tied with a bandana instead of a headband. She was dressed in her usual multi-colored ankle-length gypsy skirt topped by a yellow peasant blouse. Alicia thought the Boho style was reminiscent of how women dressed in the seventies; but Chloe, like her, appeared to be in her forties, so was too young to have adapted the fashion from memory.

"Hello, ladies," the shop owner said. "What brings the two of you here today?"

Alicia was about to say they were shopping in Cobble Corner and stopped by to browse, but Gilly was her direct self.

"We want to talk to you about your friend Mary Lou Simmons."

Chloe's kind expression changed. "The police have already questioned me." She looked at Gilly. "You should know that since you and the sheriff are so close."

Gilly didn't back down or deny her implications. "He doesn't share all his information with me. I don't believe that when he spoke to you he knew Mary Beth had a twin sister and that the two of you were BFF's."

Alicia almost laughed at the term for best friends forever, but it was apparent Chloe didn't find it funny. "We weren't friends. She was just a good customer. I used to have a store in the City. Mary Lou liked my merchandise. When I moved here after the rents got too high, she kept in touch with me. She asked me to email her photos of my new stock. Then she placed orders, and I would send them to her. I had no idea she had a sister."

"But didn't you know that Mary Beth was attending John and Alicia's book release party at the library on Thursday night?" Alicia found Gilly's follow-up questions well-worded and wondered if she had learned the skill from Ramsay.

"No," Chloe replied. "I'm sorry I couldn't be there, but I was working that night."

"And Mary Lou never mentioned she had a sister?"

Chloe's expression had lightened, and she smiled. "I don't ask my customers about their families."

"So what did you think when Mary Beth came to your store on Friday?" Alicia was silent as Gilly continued her unofficial interrogation.

"I thought she was Mary Lou finally deciding to pay me a visit in person."

"And when you found out she was her sister …?" Gilly let the question trail off.

"You have to understand I hadn't seen Mary Lou in over a year. The last order I'd received from her was in the spring, and I thought our mail order business was over. I figured she'd found another store near home where she could get similar clothes. That's why, when her twin came into the shop, I was surprised. I said I was glad she'd made the trip but asked why she hadn't called me first."

"What did she say?" Alicia asked. She had been afraid of interrupting Gilly, but her friend gave her the go ahead with a nod.

"She said I must've mistaken her for her sister and then she introduced herself and told me that she was looking for the blouse I sold you last week, and was it still on sale."

"Did you tell the sheriff this?" Gilly asked. Alicia wondered if they should be playing good cop/bad cop the way Ramsay and Faraday had during her case nearly three years ago.

"Of course. Why would I lie?" She touched the long amber stone at her throat that matched the ones in her bracelet. "I'm sorry the woman was murdered, but that was the extent of our contact. I sold her the blouse, and she left my store."

"What about Mary Lou?" Alicia asked. "Did you hear from her after that?"

"No. The next thing I knew I saw Mary Beth's photo on the front page of the *Courier* and read about her murder at the library. I wanted to call you and see how you were holding up, but then the Sheriff came to the shop and started asking me the same questions you two just did."

Gilly glanced over at Alicia. "We're sorry we took up your time. But, while we're here, do you mind if we do some shopping?"

***

As they exited Chloe's Closet, both carrying a logo bag with a large CC on it, Gilly said, "I think we can rule her out. I found it odd that anyone could be a friend of either of those sisters."

"Well, at least we got some deals," Alicia said. She'd purchased a sky-blue sweater for John that would complement his eyes and was part of the new men's line's discount special. Gilly had picked up another sweatshirt similar to the one Alicia got her for Christmas last year off the final sale rack. This one featured a woman holding a book with the words, "I love the classics, especially the classic heroes."

As they walked toward the Cobble Corner exit, Alicia's cell phone buzzed. She thought it was John, but the display showed otherwise.

"It's Stryder," she told Gilly, coming to a stop as she answered the ring. Her friend looked on curiously as Alicia spoke to the detective.

"Hello."

"Mrs. McKinney, I'm sorry to call you on your cell, but I tried you at home. Your husband gave me this number. I'm at the Carlsville Hilton right now. I went back to interview some people here, and I found something you might be interested in."

"Put him on speaker," Gilly asked straining to hear the conversation.

Alicia tapped the phone's speaker button and replied, "Is it about the murder?" She wondered why the detective was calling her about that when surely he'd be speaking to Ramsay first.

"No. It's about that missing cat. The Siamese."

"Sneaky?"

"Yeah. It seems he's been making himself comfy at the hotel. I thought you might want to come down and bring him home."

Alicia was shocked. How had Sneaky gotten all the way to Carlsville? It had to be a few miles' walk. "Are you sure it's the library cat?"

"I've seen the posters all over town, but there's another way I identified him."

Since Sneaky's collar had broken off and they'd never microchipped him, Alicia had no idea how else Stryder would know the cat at the hotel was Sneaky. "How?" she asked.

Stryder's voice came through the speaker. "Ramsay called me a few minutes ago. They had inspected Mary

Beth's car and found some strange hairs in the back seat. They were actually fur, not hair. Beige-colored. I think your cat hitchhiked a ride with her Thursday night when she drove back to the hotel after she attended your party at the library."

"I'll be right there," Alicia said, relieved and thinking how happy Angelina would be at the news, but she wouldn't tell anyone until she got Sneaky back to Cobble Cove. "Thank you for calling."

When she turned off the phone, Gilly said, "I'll drive you there. We can pick up my car at the inn. It's closer than your house."

Alicia knew her friend's offer was not only to keep her company and continue to protect her but because she wanted to question Stryder and the people at the hotel about Mary Beth.

***

When they got to the inn, Alicia said to Gilly, "I'm going to call John and let him know where I'm going. Stryder called him first to get my number, so he's probably wondering."

"Good idea, but I hope you don't worry him. Let him know I'll be with you."

"There are a couple of problems, Gilly. First, how do we get Sneaky if we don't have a cat carrier? Second, when we do get him, where will he go? The library is closed the rest of the week."

Gilly unlocked the passenger side of her car to let Alicia in. "Maybe you need to call Laura. Doesn't she keep Sneaky when the library isn't open for an extended time?"

Alicia nodded. "Yes, and she has cats, so should have an extra carrier. She also lives in Carlsville, not too far from the hotel."

"Perfect. You make the call while I run inside for a minute and let Edith and Rose know where I'll be. They're watching the boys and the inn while I'm out."

When Gilly came back to the car, Alicia had spoken to John and explained about Sneaky and then arranged everything with Laura who was excited to hear that he had been found. She promised she wouldn't tell Angelina anything until the cat was at her house.

***

As Gilly drove toward Carlsville, Alicia wondered how Sneaky had ended up in Mary Beth's car. Had the editor tried to catnap him? Or did he, after jumping out the open staff lounge window, board her car as she was leaving the library Thursday night? The latter scenario seemed more realistic as she doubted Mary Beth liked animals.

They stopped at Laura's house briefly to pick up a cat carrier. Laura had apologized about not being able to come along and assist, but she was on her way to a dental appointment. She said she didn't expect to be long but, if she wasn't home, her sister Lily would be there and would help settle Sneaky in when they brought him back.

***

The Carlsville Hilton could hardly compare with the Park Lane Hotel in New York where Alicia had stayed with John last December for their second honeymoon that had been cut short with the horrible news of their twins' kidnapping. However, it was larger, with more amenities than the Cobble Inn or the motels that had sprung up as the town expanded over the last three years.

"You'd think Stryder would've waited for us," Gilly remarked as they entered the lobby where they expected to find the detective. However, Alicia noticed her friend didn't seem too upset. She probably was anticipating talking to people without the police looking over her shoulder.

They walked up to the desk where a man in his fifties stood checking people in. When it was Alicia and Gilly's turn to be helped, the man whose name tag read, "Gordon Devlyn," observed the cat carrier in Alicia's hand and said, "You must be the ladies picking up the cat. I'm the hotel manager. I don't normally man the desk, but there are a few employees out today."

"Yes, we're here for Sneaky," Alicia said. "I'm Alicia McKinney and this is my friend, Abigail Nostran." She watched Gilly eyeing the man over but also noticed he wore a gold band on his left ring finger.

He smiled. "Nice to meet you. Detective Stryder had to get back to the station, but he told me you'd be coming. We don't normally allow cats in the hotel, but my son was persistent. He found him wandering around outside and thought he was a stray because he wasn't wearing a collar."

"His collar broke off," Alicia explained. "That was nice of your son to take him in."

"Matthew is a big animal lover. We don't have any pets because my wife is allergic, but Matt will probably have a house full of them when he gets married or an apartment of his own, which I hope will be soon. He's nearly thirty and still lives with us."

"So where is Sneaky?" Gilly asked.

"Sorry I know you two must be in a rush to get your cat and head back to Cobble Cove. Matt brought the Siamese to one of our vacant rooms upstairs. He's been popping in and feeding him, changing a litter box he made out of a paper carton, and playing with him. Matt's between jobs right now, so he helps sometimes at the hotel. I had hoped he would work here full-time because he has a degree in hotel management, but he declined my offer of a position. He said he wouldn't want to work for his father."

Alicia realized that Gilly was enjoying the fact this man was talkative, so she took advantage of his openness by asking, "I understand Ms. Simmons stayed here before her, uh, death. I'm sure Detective Stryder questioned you about that."

"Ah, yes." The manager pushed back the wire-rimmed glasses that covered his hazel eyes. "It was very unfortunate. I was afraid the guests would be upset by seeing the police here, but the detective was very discreet. I checked Mary Beth in Thursday morning. She insisted on our suite instead of a standard room." He paused and, as if he remembered something, he added, "One thing Matt didn't tell the police was that, when he brought your cat inside on Friday, he headed straight for the room Mary Beth had occupied. I was surprised because there were officers all over the place. I would think the cat would've been scared off by all the commotion."

"Would you mind showing us that room?" Gilly asked. "And taking us to where Sneaky is now, of course."

"I'll be happy to. Just let me get Amanda to watch the desk while I bring you up upstairs." The manager went through a door labeled "Staff" and came back a few minutes later with a young red-headed woman who took his place behind the desk.

"Right this way." He motioned Alicia and Gilly toward the elevators. As they got in and he tapped the button for the highest floor, which was the third, he said, "The cat didn't board the elevator. We have a set of stairs around the corner. He just jumped out of my son's arms and padded his way up to Ms. Simmons' room. We decided to keep him on the same floor, but not in the same room."

Alicia nodded. She could almost see the wheels turning in Gilly's head. Her friend knew that Sneaky had once before led Alicia to a clue. What if he had headed for Mary Beth's room because there was something there that would help solve her murder?

***

It turned out that Sneaky was being kept in the room next to where Mary Beth had stayed. Mr. Devlyn explained that the police had asked that they keep the room unoccupied in case they needed to check it again. Alicia noted the yellow tape across the door. "Not that anyone would want to stay in there," the hotel manager grinned wryly. "That's why Matt thought the room next door would be a good choice in which to keep the cat. These rooms are suites and not cheap, so they usually don't fill up on the off season during midweek."

Gilly glanced down the corridor. "Looks like there are only four other rooms on this floor. Are they occupied?"

"No. A few people stayed up here after the police came by, but they checked out shortly after."

Alicia thought of the mass exodus at Gilly's inn.

"Matt is with your cat now. I'll just knock on the door." As he tapped the room to the left of what had been Mary Beth's, Alicia didn't correct him that Sneaky wasn't her cat but the Cobble Cove library's. She was eager to see him again and if he was being well treated.

Her concerns evaporated as a younger version of Mr. Devlyn answered the door. Sneaky stood perched on his shoulder, somewhat fatter than she remembered and looking like the proverbial cat who ate the mouse.

"Matt, these are the Cobble Cove ladies who have come to take Sneaky home."

The man with hazel eyes like his father's, smiled. Alicia noticed he had a dimple like John in his left cheek. "Come in. I was just playing with Sneaker."

Sneaker? How had the manager's son known Sneaky's name? Laura often referred to the cat as Sneaks, another nickname for the moniker Sheila had given him when he'd arrived at the library.

Letting them in, the young man explained the name. "I was trying to figure out his name and then he started playing with the laces on my sneakers." He looked down at his white Addidas. "When I asked if he liked my sneakers, his ears perked up. That made me wonder if that was his name."

"That's very observant," Alicia said. "His name is actually Sneaky."

As they entered the room, Mr. Devlyn remained in the hall. "I have to get back to the desk. You help them with the cat, Matt."

The room was huge, and Alicia couldn't help but notice that it had been turned into a cat's playground. There was a cat tree facing the window, a makeshift cardboard litter box tucked in the corner, a multitude of cat toys on the floor, and a feeding station in the kitchenette that featured a tray on which lay bowls of water and cat food. Cans were stacked on the kitchen counter along with a bag of dry Friskies.

"Looks like you've taken good care of Sneaky," Gilly said, her eyes scanning the suite.

"It was my pleasure. I volunteer at an animal shelter, so I was able to get some supplies for him. I'm just glad Detective Stryder recognized him and contacted you when he did because Dad was only giving me until tomorrow before I had to bring Sneaker, I mean Sneaky, to the shelter." He lowered Sneaky, and the Siamese jumped down and ran toward Alicia, sniffing around her ankles.

She scooped him up. "Oh, Sneaky, you remember me. Angelina will be so happy when she finds out we've found you."

"Why were you keeping Sneaky here in the first place?" Gilly asked.

"I didn't want to put him in the shelter. He's a Siamese. You don't see many good breeds there, and I knew he had to belong to someone. I tried asking around and even put a photo of him in the lobby if you noticed. I thought he might belong to a guest, even though the hotel doesn't allow pets. I wasn't sure if I should list him in the lost and found. I was just hoping someone would claim him. Honestly, I would've taken him myself if my mother wasn't allergic."

"You found him Friday morning?" Gilly asked.

"Yeah. He was walking around outside. As soon as I brought him in, against my father's wishes," he looked slightly embarrassed, "he made a beeline up to this floor."

That was the story Gordon Devlyn had told. "What about the woman who was in the room next door? Your dad said he checked her in Thursday morning. Is that correct?" Gilly continued her questioning as Alicia stroked Sneaky, who was purring by her feet.

"Yes. He told me she was pretty full of herself. I felt bad when I heard she was murdered, though. Dad was just relieved it didn't happen here."

"Was there anyone staying in this room?" Alicia asked, and Gilly gave her a smile as if to say it was the question she was about to ask.

"Yes, a man. He checked out Friday morning before I found Sneaky. That's how I knew the room was vacant."

"What time was this? Did Detective Stryder ask you about him?" Gilly took back the questioning.

"I spoke to the detective. He wasn't too concerned about who had been staying in this room. His focus was on the victim's room, of course. I was glad he didn't ask to check in here. Luckily, Sneaky knew enough to keep quiet when the police were searching the room next door." Matt grinned again, showing his attractive dimple.

"Well, thank you for taking such good care of Sneaky," Alicia said bending down and undoing the latches of the cat carrier. "We're going to be bringing him to one of my co-workers who just happens to live in Carlsville."

"Wait a minute," Gilly said as Alicia gently slid Sneaky into the box. He went without a struggle, as if he was eager to go home.

Gilly had been walking around the room, and now she was crouched down on her knees, looking under the bed. First, she pulled out a catnip mouse that Sneaky must've swatted under there, then a book. Standing up and holding it out to Alicia, she said, "If this belonged to the man who had this room last, we might want to mention it to Ramsay and Stryder."

Alicia glanced at the cover of the novel. It was her and John's new release, *Written in Stone*, the second book of their mystery series. Her heart began to race. "Would you happen to remember the name of the man who stayed here and what he looked like?" She asked turning back to the manager's son.

Matt pushed back a strand of his sandy hair and then his wire-framed glasses. "I can't remember his face well. I think he had a moustache. I couldn't tell his age. He wore dark glasses, so I couldn't see his eyes. Sorry I can't recall too much else about him, but I couldn't forget his name because it was short and simple. He also paid for his room in cash. We are so used to people paying with credit cards that I found that odd."

"So, what was his name?" Gilly asked, dropping the book on the bed.

"His last name was Marks, but all he used for a first name was an initial, M."

Alicia felt faint as she processed the information the hotel manager's son was relating. "M. Marks. Mark Marks," the name of the detective in their series. The same name the man pretending to be their character had used.

Chapter Sixteen

After Alicia thanked Matt again for taking such good care of Sneaky and Gilly was already texting Ramsay about the information they'd discovered, they were about to leave when Matt called them back.

"Wait. I can help you bring the cat to your friend. I'm not working for Dad here today. I only came to check on Sneaker. Whoops, I mean Sneaky. Sorry, it's a habit now." He picked up the cat carrier. Sneaky had begun to cry for release. "It's okay, Sneaks." He soothed him, unknowingly using one of his actual nicknames.

Matt sat in the back of Alicia's car as she drove with Gilly next to her. He'd placed the cat carrier next to him and had calmed Sneaky down with a toy he removed from his pocket.

"You're really good with cats," Gilly told him.

"Thank you, Ms. Nostran. This has catnip and was one of Sneaky's favorite toys when he was at the hotel. I figured it would come in handy to settle him down during the drive. It wasn't from the shelter. I bought it in a pet store. You can keep it."

"That was nice of you. Please call me Gilly. That's short for Abigail, and Ali is Alicia."

"Thanks. You can both call me Matt."

Alicia was not concentrating on the conversation. She was thinking about the man who'd stayed in the room next to Mary Beth. She was eager to get home and talk to John about what they'd discovered at the Carlsville Hilton besides the missing cat.

***

Alicia had only been to Laura's home once before when she attended her sister Lily's college graduation party last May, but she remembered the address, and her GPS did the rest. But when she found the place, it seemed smaller than she recalled, definitely too small for five children and their parents. The yellow ranch had a basement where Laura told Alicia her brothers slept. Henry was the youngest and there was a brother who was one year older than Laura who was the second eldest in the family. Lily came next and then there were two daughters in high school.

Alicia hoped Laura would be home because she had mentioned her dental appointment and said they could leave Sneaky with Lily. Although Lily suffered from asthma, it was controlled; and, luckily, she didn't have any difficulty being around cats.

Matt followed Alicia up to the front door. Gilly didn't want to wait in the car, so she joined them. At the sound of the bell, Mrs. Carson answered. She was as fair as Laura, with some streaks of gray in her shoulder-length blonde hair. "Hello, Alicia," she said. "Laura told me you were bringing Sneaky to stay with us until the library reopens. I was so upset when Mrs. Whitehead called to tell us what happened. Come on in."

"This is my friend, Gilly," Alicia said, introducing them as they entered the house. "And Matt Devlyn was the one who found Sneaky and put him up at the hotel that his father manages."

"Nice to meet you both," Mrs. Carson said. "Laura should be home soon. Why don't you have a seat in the living room? I'll go get Lily. I know Laura asked her to settle Sneaky in if you got here before she returned."

Alicia was eager to get back to John and the twins, but she did as Laura's mother requested. Gilly sat next to her on the couch which they had to share with a calico cat who was snuggled next to a pillow and didn't move when they approached. Another cat, a black one with a speck of white on its chest, entered the room and headed for Sneaky's carrier that was on the floor next to Matt's chair Alicia's mind was temporarily taken away from her worries as she saw the two cats touch noses through the carrier's grilled front. Matt laughed. "Looks like these two like each other. Otherwise, they'd be hissing."

"I still would keep him in that carrier," Gilly said. "There seems to be a bunch of cats in this house." Alicia followed her gaze toward the alcove that led to the kitchen where three other tabby cats of varying shades and patterns were standing.

"Well, Sneaky will be in good company," Alicia remarked. She wondered what was taking Lily and her mother so long to come down; but, just as she was considering that, she heard a car pull up outside and Laura rushed in, her blonde hair tossed behind her. "Hi, Alicia, Gilly. Sorry I wasn't here when you came."

"We just got here," Alicia told her. "Your mom went upstairs to get Lily, but they haven't come down yet."

Suddenly, Matt from across the room, stood up. "Laura," he said. Alicia watched the young man's face change. He smiled widely.

"Matt," Laura replied, nearly running to his chair. She gave him a quick kiss on the cheek. "You're the one who found the cat? How lucky for Sneaky." She looked down at the carrier. The black cat had scooted away, but Sneaky was starting to make himself known with short cries that seemed to be a greeting for Laura.

"Do you two know one another?" Gilly asked.

"We sure do," Matt said. "Laura is a frequent visitor to the shelter where I volunteer. She's found homes for many of the strays there as well as the ones she rescues."

Alicia should've known when Matt mentioned helping out at the town's animal shelter that it was the same place that Laura spoke of often.

***

Mrs. Carson and Lily came down a few minutes later and invited everyone to stay for some refreshments. Alicia and Gilly made excuses about needing to get back to Cobble Cove. Alicia had to speak with John, and she knew Gilly wanted to see how Ramsay was handling the new information she'd supplied.

They left Matt, Laura, and Sneaky at the house. Laura had taken Sneaky out of the carrier and started to introduce him to her cats. Alicia noted how easily the children's librarian handled the Siamese in her home as expertly as she did at the library.

"You know," Gilly said as Alicia drove back, "I think those two would make an excellent pair."

Alicia was considering the way she would present her story about the anonymous Mark Marks to John. "Sorry, Gilly. I wasn't paying attention. Who would make a good pair?"

"Laura and Matt. They both love animals and they're about the same age. Is Laura dating anyone, do you know?"

"I'm not sure, Gilly. I don't think so. She doesn't talk about any boyfriends."

"Hmm. I should invite them both over to the inn one day."

"Are you thinking of matchmaking them, Gilly?"

Her friend smiled her Cheshire cat smile. "You know me better than that, Ali."

"Yes, I do, and that's why I know what you're planning." She laughed. "I want to get home as soon as possible, do you mind if I just drop you at the inn?"

"Sure. I asked Ron to meet me there. I want to fill him in on what we found at the hotel."

"Along with matchmaker, you're also playing detective, Gilly. You need to be careful about both roles."

Gilly just nodded, making no promises about her intentions.

Alicia dropped Gilly off at the inn. Ramsay was waiting for her, playing a game of catch with Danny on the front lawn.

Gilly waved to Alicia as she got out of the car. Danny, grinning, tossed her the ball as Ramsay motioned her to join the game. Alicia watched the three of them play, wondering if one day they might become a family.

***

As she pulled up to her house, her happy thoughts of seeing her friend having fun with her son and boyfriend dissipated as Alicia noticed the car parked in the driveway in her spot. It was Lindsey Harrington's car.

Taking a deep breath to try to calm herself from the awful thoughts that began to fill her mind, she opened the door.

Although the reality of what she saw was not quite as frightening as what she'd imagined, she was far from relieved at what met her eyes. John and Lindsey were seated on the couch in the living room. Lindsey had Carol on her lap and Johnny was between them. Both babies were giggling as Lindsey and John played with them.

Alicia just stood there, mouth agape as if she'd found her husband and his old lover wrapped around each other.

Chapter Seventeen

What bothered Alicia the most was how nonchalant John acted after having invited his old girlfriend to his house while his wife was away. Even worse, the woman was playing with her children!

It took every ounce of control for Alicia to adopt the happy hostess persona until Lindsey left, giving all of them a kiss, even her. She brushed Alicia's cheek, but the one she gave John came very close to his lips.

When she was gone, Alicia's temper let loose. "John, how could you have her here while I was away? What were you thinking?"

The smile that was still pasted on his face disappeared. "I didn't invite her, Ali. She showed up at the door. What was I supposed to do? Slam it in her face?"

Alicia lowered her voice as she saw the babies cower toward John. Even they were taking his side. "I don't want to argue in front of the twins, John, but I would appreciate it if you bid that woman goodbye."

"I don't believe this." John's voice had also lowered as he picked up the babies, one in each arm. "I'm taking them upstairs and putting on some cartoons for them to watch. I'll be down in a minute to discuss the rest of this with you." The expression he gave her was as cold as a February morning in Cobble Cove.

***

Allicia was pacing around the room when he returned. She was still mad, but she was less close to murdering both John and Lindsey than she was earlier.

John was as calm as Cove Point with sailboats drifting lazily on a summer day. But, like an iceberg, danger lie behind his steely blue eyes. "Please explain to me, Ali, why you're so jealous."

She couldn't look at him, so she turned toward the door. "I can give you several reasons, John. She's beautiful. She and you were once lovers. She's appeared after all these years and is spending way too much time in this town."

"I thought you trusted me more than that, Ali. We've been through this before, and it almost tore us apart." His voice had dropped to a whisper. She felt him move closer, but she remained with her back to him. "I love you and the kids. I would never do anything to hurt any of you. These aren't false words. Believe me, she was nothing to me then and even less to me now. You're the one I married. You're the one who gave me my life back." The last words came out almost on a sob. Alicia turned to see him with his arms open, and she fell into them.

"I'm sorry, John. I was just so surprised when I came home and found her with you and the twins."

"I know." He patted her back. "I can see how that would look to you, but there was no way I would have let her into this house if I had any inkling of feeling for her left. We're old friends and that's it."

Alicia took a deep breath as he held her at arm's length. Then he placed a light kiss on her lips. She put her arms around him and kissed him deeper. When they'd spent a few minutes making up, Alicia said, "When does she leave? Has she seen your father and Betty yet?"

"Tomorrow is her last day here. She had planned to spend the whole week, but something came up at her office. I sort of promised her we'd have dinner with Dad tomorrow night. He already knows she's here, and he offered. I couldn't turn down his herbed meat loaf. He makes it as good as my mom did." He grinned at the thought, but then became serious. "If you're not comfortable with that, I could cancel."

"No. It's okay, John. I can't deny you your dad's cooking." She smiled. "And the twins and I will love it, too."

"Thank you. Now would you like to tell me what happened in Carlsville?"

Alicia beckoned John to the couch where she related her and Gilly's visit to the hotel, Sneaky's posh digs there, and the man Matt Devlyn described who was using their character's name as an alias.

John's face darkened again, but it wasn't directed at Alicia. "Does Ramsay know all this?"

"Yes. Gilly texted him, and she met him at the inn when I dropped her off."

"It's strange. Why would this guy book a room next to Mary Beth and disguise himself? It's too much of a coincidence that he left the morning she was killed."

"I've thought about that, John. The detectives should've checked that room, but at that point they probably had no reason to. I'm just wondering if this mystery man calling himself Mark Marks came to town for our book release party and knew that Mary Beth was coming, too."

"Hmmm." John had adapted his Thinker's pose, with his chin rested on his hands. "That's very likely, Ali, but I'm also considering that if he was the person who sent those messages to me, his intended victim may not have been Mary Beth."

"You're thinking it was me?"

John's eyes clouded. "I don't know. He checked out of the hotel, so he must be gone."

"He might return if he hasn't finished the job."

John shook his head as he let his arms slip to his side. "Maybe not. If he knows they're looking for him, he might just give up and hide far away."

"Let's hope. But then why would he send you the message you got at the memorial service?"

"Ali, I think we have to leave the detecting up to Ramsay and Stryder. I know you're worried and Gilly is her curious self, but neither of you are trained professionals." Before she could argue that it was easy for him to say because his life wasn't in danger, he added, "At least you got Sneaky back. When are you letting Angelina know?"

"Laura's calling Patty today. Did you hear that they have a donor for Angelina? If she learns Sneaky is safe, she might start eating again and get her strength back. Then they'll be able to proceed with the operation."

"Speaking of operations, I hope Pamela's surgery goes well. She's putting up a strong front, but that's how my sister is. I know she's relieved I'll be there for her. I can't tell Dad about it, though, or he would run to New York, too. It would be very stressful for him."

"He has a right to know about his daughter," Alicia said, "but I can understand your concern, John. I won't say a word."

***

Later that day, Laura called to tell Alicia that Patty had driven Angelina to her house to see Sneaky. The reunion had been heartwarming, and the girl ate every bite of the lunch Laura's mother prepared for her. Alicia was as relieved and excited as Laura at hearing this news.

A short while after that, as Alicia was still feeling good about Angelina, the phone rang again. This time it was Gilly.

"Ali, can you come by the inn now? I need to talk with you." She didn't seem upset, but Alicia wondered what she wanted to say that she couldn't over the phone.

"Yes. I'll let John know. Give me a few minutes."

John was upstairs watching cartoons with the twins. Sitting with them between his legs on the floor of the nursery, he was giggling along with them at the antics on the large TV they'd recently added to the room.

"Hey, honey, what's up?" he asked as she entered.

"Sorry to disturb your show, John, but Gilly called and asked me over to the inn."

"Sure. You go ahead. I'm enjoying these as much as I did Bugs Bunny and Loony Tunes when I was a kid."

Alicia gave him the thumbs-up sign, kissed both kids whose eyes were still glued to the screen, and headed downstairs. As she left the house, she noticed the patrol car that had been stationed by it was gone. She wondered if Ramsay had told Stryder it was no longer necessary or if Stryder had pulled his men off to deal with other crimes in Carlsville. She'd have to break the news to Gilly that the cute cop on patrol had left his post. She still felt wary as she checked the back of her car as she got in. She could walk to the inn, but she'd rather drive. Walking there didn't feel safe while Mary Beth's murderer and possibly the person who left John those threatening messages on her life still hadn't been caught.

Chapter Eighteen

Gilly was alone on the inn's porch when Alicia arrived. She was sitting on the swing, writing on a pad. As Alicia parked and got out of her car, Gilly waved but remained seated. "Hi, Ali. Thanks for coming so fast. Come join me."

Alicia did. "You had good timing. If you'd called earlier, I might've slammed the phone down on you."

Gilly raised an eyebrow. "Why? Were you and John in the middle of something hot and heavy?"

Alicia laughed. "Oh, yes, it was hot and heavy but not what you think. I came home to find him with his old girlfriend."

Her friend's eyes widened. "No. I don't believe it. John would never … "

"Wrong again. They were with the twins. Nothing was going on, but it was the fact she was there in our house with our children." Alicia began to get revved up again.

"Calm down, honey. I'm sure it's not what you imagined. I've got something to take your mind off things." She turned her pad around for Alicia to see. There were two columns written across the Cobble Cove Inn stationary. One had a list of names; the other was labelled "motive."

"Does Ramsay know you're playing detective, Gilly?"

Her smile gave Alicia the answer. "Nope. He's gone off to Carlsville to check out that room. I wanted to go with him, but he refused. The boys went over their friends' houses, and Edith and Rose are working inside. I took the opportunity to jot down a few notes about the case." She handed Alicia the pad.

Alicia took a breath when she saw the names listed. "Gilly, are these the people you're listing as suspects? What is Donald doing on this list?"

"I've listed all the men who might be masquerading as Mark Marks. Donald had a run-in with Mary Beth the night of your release party, and do you really know what he thinks of you?"

Alicia laughed. "Donald lives with Roger. I'm sure he can vouch for the fact that Donald hasn't gone anywhere near the Carlsville Hilton. As far as the run-in with Mary Beth, Donald wouldn't commit murder because of it, and he and I get along well."

"We can't rule him out. What do you think of the other names?"

"We? Gilly, John is right about us leaving this investigation up to the authorities." Despite her words, Alicia recalled sitting in a hotel room with John as he created timelines and connections to a crime and asked for her help in completing them. Now they only worked together on their books.

She glanced at the pad again. There were five names and a question mark. The first one listed was Dominic Carr, Mary Beth's ex. Then came Donald, followed by Marvin and Kyle, the two men she had autographed books for at her release party. The last name before the question mark was Cooper Halliday, the writer who had spoken emotionally at Mary Beth's memorial service.

"I nearly added the hotel manager as the question mark," Gilly explained, "but he wouldn't book a room in his own hotel, and his son seemed nice enough."

"I think you can cross out Donald. Now what motives do you have for these other people?"

"I've been thinking." Gilly took back the pad and tapped the cap of her pen on it. "The ex might've wanted to come back and was rejected, but that doesn't explain what he has against you, and I can't see him wanting a reunion with that woman. He surely must've been relieved to have her out of his life. I have no idea about Marvin or Kyle, but Cooper Halliday was you and John's rival as well as one of Mary Beth's clients." She turned her pen around and put a line through Donald's name. "I'll eliminate Donald for the time being, but I'm not convinced he's innocent yet."

"Gilly, this is all conjecture, and why am I in the equation or Mary Beth for that matter? How do you know which of us was actually the murderer's target?"

"I don't, so I have to consider both of you as targets." She scribbled two other names on the pad. "I'm also listing Mary Lou and Lindsey Harrington even though they're women because they could've been working with someone. Oh, and what about the mother? She looked husky enough to pass for a man in disguise."

Alicia remembered what happened with Gloria Langley, so she couldn't disagree. "That's quite a list, Gilly, and I almost hope Lindsey's guilty, so I can put her behind bars far away from John."

Gilly laughed, but Alicia was half-serious. "Now what do you intend to do to narrow down that list?"

The glee in Gilly's eyes almost frightened her friend. "What else? We're going to question people. Not to take any fire from under Ron and Steve, but the cops don't always ask the right questions. Something else for you to consider, Ali, that those guys totally overlooked." She paused waiting for Alicia to ask her what, but when she didn't, she continued. "Who would have access to John's email and cell phone number and be familiar with your books?"

The first person Alicia could think of was already dead. Mary Beth.

***

Alicia listened apprehensively to Gilly's plan. She wanted to gather information from Ramsay using her feminine wiles, so she could locate the people on her list and then seek them out with Alicia's help.

"Who should we start with?" she asked, tapping her pad.

"Well, Dominic Carr is first on your list, even though I'm sure Ramsay battered him with questions because the husband is always the first suspect."

"That means a trip into the City. It's a bit far. Maybe we can do a phone conversation. If I get his number, I can call from my cell and put it on speaker, so you can hear. What do you think?"

"I think you're crazy, Gilly, and the sheriff will not appreciate your meddling."

She grinned. "He won't mind at all after I show him some of the scenes I learned from my bodice-ripper books."

"Are you really that desperate?"

"Actually, it's a lot of fun." Gilly turned serious suddenly. "Honey, I'm worried about you. If the person who killed Mary Beth is actually after you, I want to find him before he kills again."

Alicia sighed. "I'll help, but I can't let John know I'm involved in this." She got off the swing, sending it moving gently. "I should get back home. Things are better between us now, and I've agreed to go to dinner at Mac's house tomorrow night with John and the twins. Lindsey's invited. She's leaving the next day, and it can't be soon enough."

Gilly got up to see Alicia off. "Don't worry, sweetie. John loves you, but he probably has fond memories with Lindsey. Let him get that out of his system. Once she goes, she'll return to a memory. You're the one he'll be living with the rest of his life."

Alicia nodded. "If I didn't know you were a year younger than me, I'd think you were a wise old woman."

"After raising three boys alone, I'd say I am. I'll keep you posted to my progress, Ali. I have a date with Ron tonight and some bottles of the inn's best whiskey for the occasion."

"I thought you didn't drink."

"I don't, but Ron does. I need to loosen him up and that'll help. That and all I've learned from my romance reading."

"Good luck." Alicia smiled. "And thanks, Gilly. I know you mean well. I just don't want you to risk your safety."

"That's my choice, Ali. I'm your friend."

They hugged a minute and then Alicia got in her car and drove back home.

***

"Everything okay with Gilly?" John asked when Alicia came into the kitchen where he was preparing dinner. The twins sat in their high chairs playing with their plastic baby utensils.

"She's fine. Uhm, that smells good, John. What do you have in the oven?" Alicia peeked through the glass screen. A casserole bubbled over with cheese.

"Not as good as the mac'n'cheese Dad makes, but the twins should enjoy it. I'm adding green beans as a side, and you can have a salad with it if you like." He stirred the sauce pan on the stove.

Alicia waited for him to pursue the topic of her visit with Gilly, but was relieved that he didn't. He also avoided speaking about Lindsey. Things seemed to have returned to normal in his world, even if chaos still reigned in Alicia's.

The rest of the night was uneventful. After putting the twins to sleep, they went next door to their own room. Alicia wasn't upset when John brought his laptop to bed.

She wasn't much in the mood for lovemaking but imagined Gilly was having a very different night with Ramsay. She wondered if the sheriff visited her in the top room of the inn where she and her sons lived away from the guests, or if she'd slipped out and visited him at his house, asking Edith or Rose to babysit for a few hours.

"Even though we don't have a new editor yet," John said, switching on the computer, "I thought I'd continue writing our next book. I have some ideas." He paused. "You don't mind, do you?"

"No. I have some reading to do, John. I think it's important we get on with the manuscript. Have you been in touch with anyone from Prime Crime since the murder?"

"You remember I spoke to Lucille. She was Mary Beth's boss. She hasn't contacted me about a new editor yet. I did hear from Mary Lou, though."

"When did you hear from her?"

"While you were at the inn. She called and asked if we might be interested in submitting our next project to her."

Alicia hadn't expected Mary Lou's sister to make good on her offer of representation and definitely not the day after Mary Beth's memorial service. "What did you tell her?"

John looked at her over the top of his screen. "I said we'll send her a synopsis and the first three chapters when we have them. I think it's a good opportunity, Ali. We could end up with a large publishing contract. It could be the break we've been waiting for."

"I don't know, John. Mary Lou doesn't seem much nicer than her twin. Do we really want to go through that type of stress again?"

John smiled. "Now you're falling back on your worrisome nature, Alicia. We only spoke to the woman once and during an emotional time. Try to be open-minded. We can at least consider her offer."

"I guess you're right, at least I hope you are." She turned over and reached for the book she was halfway through reading as John went back to writing.

***

The call from Gilly came early the next morning. They had just finished breakfast and were planning their day. John wanted to take the kids to the park again, but rain was in the forecast. Alicia suggested they stay at home, and the twins could watch cartoons or they could break out some of their toddler toys and play with them.

Then the phone rang. As John took the kids out of their high chairs to let them walk around the house while he supervised, Alicia picked it up.

"Good morning, sweetie." Gilly's voice sounded cheerful.

"Hi, Gilly. I gather you had a nice night last night."

"Exceptional. Not only was it utterly romantic, but I hit pay dirt about the backgrounds of our suspects."

"Our suspects? Gilly, you forget that we're not officially on this case."

"Never mind. Do you want to hear what I have to say?"

"Can you tell me over the phone, or should I come over?"

"I'll come there. Give me a few minutes. The boys are going to their friends' again, and Edith and Rose will be here soon."

***

When Gilly arrived, Alicia took her into the room at the end of the hall that had been turned into her private office and shut the door. John knew Gilly would be visiting and took the twins upstairs to play.

"So, what did you find out, Ms. Marple?"

Gilly laughed, but her eyes were shining. "Okay, here's the rundown, Alicia. Marvin's full name is Marvin Schultz. He's a bookseller in Carlsville, married with a few kids. Kyle Washington is an English professor at Long Island University on Long Island. Your new PR person happens to have been one of his friends." She paused, letting her words sink in. Alicia wondered if Washington had taught at Post when she'd been a student there. She also wondered what type of friends he and Nancy were.

"Go on," she prompted Gilly, who didn't need much encouragement to continue. Her friend had been thorough in her "interrogation" of the sheriff.

"Let's see now. Who else?" Gilly seemed to be trying to recall the rest of the information she'd gathered. "Oh, yes. Dominic Carr, Mary Beth's ex-husband. He doesn't have much of an alibi for the day she was murdered. He wasn't at work because it was a Saturday. However, he lives alone in his apartment. Ron said there's no indication of a girlfriend, so either Mary Beth put him off women or he's very discreet about his relationships. The other possibility, as slim as it is, is that he may have wanted her back."

"How long were they divorced?"

"Ron said it's been about ten years. They were married for nearly twelve, so he put up with her for a long time."

"What broke them up?"

"Good question, Ali." Gilly's smile widened. "Mary Beth was seeing someone."

"Hmm. So she cheated on him. Do you know who her boyfriend was?"

"No, but Ron thinks Mary Beth has been with several other guys since then."

Alicia thought about the woman's caked makeup and her careless flirtation with John.

"Who was she seeing currently?"

"That's what we need to determine, but back to Dominic. He didn't own a car. He used public transportation in the City. However, he had big bucks and was able to afford a town car whenever he left the City."

"What are you getting at, Gilly?"

"He hired one Friday night and used it to return to the City Saturday afternoon. Ron thinks he was in the Cobble Cove area on Saturday morning."

"What did Carr tell the police? Why was he out of town?"

"He said it was a personal matter, but Ron and Steve can't track down any relatives nearby. Even though his excuse is flimsy, they don't have any evidence linking him to his ex-wife's murder."

"What do you think?"

Gilly considered the question and then said, "I'm not convinced he's guilty. I find it odd that he would wait this long after their divorce to kill her. Also, I don't see his motive for sending strange notes about you to John."

"Those notes could've just been to throw the police off his trail," Alicia explained. "But if Carr was the man who was booked into the room next to his wife, she should've recognized him, disguised or not."

Gilly nodded. "Good point. Then there's Cooper Halliday, the author."

"He was the man at her memorial service," Alicia recalled.

"That's right."

"If he killed her, why would he have gone there?"

"Ron says that isn't unusual. Killers often return to the scene of their crimes or attend the funerals of their victims."

"Hmmm. What did you find out about him?"

"He's married, with a son, and has a home in Carlsville. He writes a mystery series, like you and John, and Mary Beth was also his editor."

"I'll have to ask John about him. He didn't attend our release party, but maybe they know one another. Did he have an alibi for Saturday morning?"

"Here's the thing." Gilly lowered her voice even though the door was closed. "His wife said he'd been away since Friday night with their son at a writer's conference at the Mohonk Mountain House. They both returned Saturday night."

"How old is his son, and did the conference check out?"

"Indeed. The son is nineteen and enrolled in a journalism program at Carlsville U. He's trying to follow in his dad's footsteps like Joe Hill is following in Stephen Kings'."

"That rules him out, right?"

"Not necessarily. Ron said that, although father and son registered for the conference Friday night, they attended different programs on Saturday morning."

"So neither one can corroborate the other's story?"

"Yep. It's interesting and maybe worth pursuing, but I'm still thinking about Mary Lou and Lindsey. Something tells me they're involved in this murder somehow."

"Do Ramsay or Stryder share those suspicions?"

"Ron won't commit to anything. The weapon hasn't shown up yet. Mary Beth was killed in a public place which makes it a little more difficult. I wanted to ask him about Donald, but you made me cross him off the list."

Alicia was suddenly reminded of her experience with a friend who turned out to be one of her children's kidnappers and realized that even someone familiar could be a suspect.

"Put him back on your list, Gilly. I'll try to help you find information about him and if there was any connection with Mary Beth. I mean to call and check in with Sheila today, anyway."

"Thanks. Keep me posted, honey, and I'll do the same."

"Are you going to be calling or visiting any of these people?"

"Not without you. I have some numbers. I'll let you know what I arrange."

"I'm still not totally on board with this, Gilly, but I'll help if I can. There's one thing that really bugs me, though."

Alicia had Gilly's total attention. "Please tell." Her friend's eyes widened again in anticipation.

"It's Sneaky. How did he get in Mary Beth's car, and why was he so interested in her room? Animals know things. I realize the murder didn't occur at the hotel, but maybe something else did."

***

As it turned out, Ramsay had followed Alicia's thoughts. While she and Gilly were summing up their ideas about the murder, Gilly's cell phone rang.

"Hello, Ronnie."

Ronnie? Alicia had to suppress a laugh at the nickname her friend gave the sheriff. She listened to Gilly's replies and tried to figure out what Ramsay was saying from the other side of the line.

"He what? Oh, I forgot about that. What about Sneaky? He was the one who was curious about her room." She glanced over at Alicia and, after a pause, said, "Okay. We'll be there in a little bit. I'll call Laura."

As Gilly hung up the phone, Alicia said, "What was that all about, and where are we going?"

"Back to the Carlsville Hilton."

Gilly had that scary gleam in her eye again. "It seems Mac has volunteered Fido to check out Mary Beth's room. I'd forgotten he had those police dog training lessons after what happened last year. I really should consider that for Ruby one day especially since she's now the inn's guard dog. Anyway, I suggested Sneaky shouldn't be let out of the action. After all, Sneaky was there, and may have found things no one else could possibly suspect

"He agreed to let you bring Sneaky back to the hotel?"

Gilly smiled. "Yep. I'll call Laura. She'll probably want to come along, too."

***

John didn't try to stop Alicia. He just reminded her about the dinner with his father and Betty that night. He didn't mention Lindsey, but Alicia knew he was thinking about her. It still made her stomach knot. In a way, she was glad she had something to keep her mind off the upcoming meal with John's old girlfriend.

Gilly stopped at Laura's house first to pick up her and Sneaky. Laura had agreed immediately to Gilly's suggestion and had Sneaky in his cat carrier when they arrived. Alicia was thankful that that dark skies that threatened rain hadn't yet kept their promise. Matt Devlyn wasn't there, but Alicia wondered if he was back at work and what he would think about them bringing Sneaky there again.

They pulled up to the hotel just as Mac was getting out of Ramsay's patrol car with Fido. Gilly parked her car in the spot next to them and joined the sheriff as he greeted them all.

"Stryder's already inside," he said. "He wasn't happy about us bringing the cat. He's pretty sure Fido will sniff out anything that we missed."

"Haven't they brought dogs in before?" Alicia asked. "When they first investigated Mary Beth's room?"

"Yes, but they want to give it another sweep. I asked if we could bring in Fido because of how he's helped in the past."

"Fido doesn't mind a little friendly competition," Mac said his hand on Fido's leash. The dog sat obediently at his side, only a few feet from Sneaky's carrier.

Sneaky and Fido had been together several times at the library and got along well despite the stereotype of cats and dogs being enemies. Laura told them that it was a myth that cats and dogs don't get along. In fact, from her own experience, two cats were more likely to be enemies. "They don't call them cat fights for nothing." She smiled. "But animals are like people. Some get along—some don't."

"I think animals are better than people," Ramsay said. "from what I've seen out in the field. At least, most of them don't kill one another."

Fido suddenly got up and began to pull at his leash. "Why don't we go inside?" Mac asked. "Fido's eager to do his detecting work."

***

Matt was at the check-in desk again. His eyes widened in surprise as they entered, and Alicia wondered why Stryder hadn't told him they were bringing the pets.

"We're here to see Detective Stryder," Ramsay said, flashing his badge.

"Of course," the hotel manager said. "He's upstairs at the room."

They all knew which room he meant. Ramsay led them to the elevators, where they crowded in. Laura held Sneaky's carrier while Fido stood by Mac's side, his brown eyes bright with anticipation, his tongue lolling out with his excited breaths.

Gilly and Ramsay exited the elevator first. Mac followed with Fido. Alicia and Laura with Sneaky were at the end of the procession as they headed toward Mary Beth's room.

Stryder stood outside with two other officers. The yellow police tape was lifted, and another man was inside poking around.

As they approached, Stryder glanced at the cat carrier and frowned. "I only agreed to your bringing the dog, Ron."

Ramsay said, "Don't sweat it, Steve. Let the cat have a go. It can't hurt."

"I disagree. I don't want cat poops all over the murder scene, or he could rip up something."

Laura objected to Stryder's comments. "Fido can also make or tear something," she said. "I take full responsibility for Sneaky. Cats are neater than dogs."

"Whoa now," Gilly said. "Let's not get into a cat vs. dog argument here. Give them both a chance. Please, Steve."

Stryder sighed. It was obvious Gilly knew how to charm him, too.

"Very well. Let them in." Stryder moved away from the door, and Mac entered with Fido. Laura and Sneaky were right behind. Laura carried Sneaky's carrier in first and then opened it to release him. Alicia and Ramsay looked on.

After a few minutes of the animals searching their surroundings, Sneaky turned around and headed for the door. Laura scooped him up in her arms. "I guess Sneaky's not interested in anything here."

"That's strange," Alicia said. "The hotel manager's son said he was eager to get in this room when he first came."

"Maybe the scent's gone," Laura said. Alicia noticed how her face changed slightly when she'd mentioned Matt Devlyn.

"That's not it," Stryder said from behind them as Fido began pawing at something in the far corner of the room. "Looks like the dog's found something."

Mac went to see what Fido was trying to reach. "Not sure what this is," he said, handing a tiny object to Ramsay.

Ramsay looked back at Stryder. "It's a bug. Someone was using it to watch Mary Beth."

Stryder took the device and examined it. "We need to have another talk with Devlyn. If someone put this here, they had to have access to this room." Then he walked to Fido and rubbed his back. The dog wagged his tail. "Good job, boy. I guess we know who the smarter animal is now."

"Maybe not," Laura said from out in the hall. "Sneaky seems to be on another trail." No one had noticed the cat leave the room. Alicia joined the group to see what was going on next door. Sneaky was scratching the door of the adjacent room.

"We should let him in," Laura said. "Is the door open?"

Stryder, still holding the listening device, strode over to her. "We can't have that cat defacing hotel property."

"But maybe he's trying to tell us something, Steve," Ramsay said.

Stryder grinned ironically. "More likely, he's looking for his litter box. I found it very odd that they allowed him in that room in the first place. It might even be occupied now if they've cleaned it up."

"No one's in there," a voice said from behind them. They all turned to see Matt Devlyn coming down the hall. "Dad said you were up here with Sneaky. I figured I'd bring the key to the other room just in case you wanted to check it out."

Laura smiled at Matt as he slid the card key into the door slot. Sneaky raced in before the door was completely open and everyone else followed, Stryder huffing the way Ramsay used to do.

When Matt switched on the lights, the transformation awed Alicia. The room had been cleaned up. All the toys, scratching post, and other signs of cat occupancy were gone.

"I took everything back to the shelter that I'd borrowed," Matt explained. "but I gave Laura the items I purchased for her own cats."

"He's going under the bed," Laura exclaimed as Sneaky dived beneath the box spring.

"Probably looking for another catnip mouse he left under there," Stryder said.

"I don't think so." Matt had crouched down and was peeking under the bed. "There's something big down there and he's tapping at it. Hear it?"

Everyone stopped talking, and Alicia heard the noise Matt Devlyn indicated. Sneaky was batting an object around, but it wasn't a toy mouse. "Can you reach it?" Laura asked, squatting down next to Matt.

"I'll try."

"Watch out," Stryder warned. "That cat might nip you."

Alicia wondered if the detective really disliked cats or if, like Donald, he put up a show and was just teasing. Since Stryder was the one who notified her that Sneaky was at the hotel, she considered he might have a hidden soft spot for felines; but if he did, it was hidden pretty deep.

Matt reached his hand under but, before he could grasp whatever Sneaky was playing with, the cat kicked it out from under the bed. There was a collective gasp as they all realized what Sneaky had found. A gun.

Chapter Nineteen

"I don't understand," Stryder said, donning gloves and picking up the weapon. "We made a thorough search of this room.

It looked to Alicia that Ramsay was trying to hide a smile. "Not as thorough as the cat, it seems," he said.

Stryder chose not to reply. He handed the gun over to one of his men. "This needs to be dusted for prints and checked in our database." Sneaky, having lost his toy, came purring around the detective's ankles. Alicia feared he might kick the cat away and Laura probably had the same thought, so she scooped him up and put him back in his carrier.

"I've spoken to your father about the guests who stayed on this floor," Stryder said, addressing Matt. "But maybe you can shed some light on who used this room last?"

Matt shook his head. "Sorry, Detective. I didn't get a good look at him. I already told my dad everything I remember from last weekend."

"What about your hotel surveillance cameras? We need a copy of the recordings from Friday and Saturday."

"I already asked for those," Ramsay said before Matt could answer. "Devlyn says the system was down for a few days before they could have it repaired."

"Wonderful!" Stryder expressed his frustration in sarcasm. "Were any other employees on staff those days besides you and your father?"

Matt thought a moment and then said, "Amanda was here. She was helping me at the desk on Friday morning."

Stryder's eyes lit up again as they had when Fido had found the bug in Mary Beth's room. "We're going to need to contact her."

"Sure. Dad has her number."

As the group began to back out into the hall, Ramsay said, "Steve, if there was a listening device in the room next door, wouldn't there be another one in here if this is where our perp was staying?"

"Could be he took it with him, but strange he left the gun. We'll know more when we identify it and whatever prints we get off it."

Gilly, quiet until now, came up to Alicia's side and whispered in her ear, "I'll update you as soon as I get the details from Ron. I'm proud of Sneaky. He may have found the clue that solves this case. I was rooting for him all along."

Alicia wasn't as confident. Something seemed wrong, but she couldn't put her finger on it. Then it suddenly came to her. The gun that Stryder's officer had bagged resembled one she'd seen before. She wasn't familiar with guns and probably couldn't tell one from another, but she recalled being shown a similar looking one by someone she knew who had gotten it for protection after the incidents that occurred last year. She racked her brain, trying to recall who that person was and then Matt Devlyn's words came back to her when he had described the man checking into the hotel Friday morning. Even though his memory of the man's alias had been more prominent in his mind, Matt had mentioned the guest had a thin moustache. Her co-worker, Donald, had recently grown one, and the pistol that looked identical to the one Sneaky found was the weapon Donald had purchased.

***

When they were in Gilly's car, with Laura and Sneaky in the back seat, Gilly asked Alicia what was wrong. "You look upset, honey. I know it must've been a shock when Sneaky kicked that gun from under the bed, but I think it's more than that. What's on your mind? I see the wheels turning."

Alicia grinned halfheartedly. "I shouldn't tell you this, but believe I recognized that gun."

Laura gasped. She had quieted Sneaky down after they'd left the hotel. He had objected loudly to being re-caged. Matt had helped her place his carrier in the car, and Gilly had rolled her eyes knowingly when the young man offered to visit Laura the next day to check on the cat.

"Check on *her* is more likely," she'd whispered.

Now Alicia, still unsure whether to voice her suspicions to the sheriff's girlfriend, blurted out, "I might be wrong, and I hope I am, but that gun bears a striking resemblance to the one Donald showed me he'd picked up last year at Roger's urging after the gift shop burglary."

"That can't be," Laura said from the back seat. "Donald probably got rid of that gun long ago. He only purchased it to please Roger. I doubt he'd even know how to use it."

"I'm not saying it's the same one, but it looks similar."

"Well, the police will identify it," Gilly said. "However, I think you and I should go have a talk with Donald first."

"I'd like to come along, too," Laura said. "I can drop Sneaky back at my house with Lily. I'm sure she won't mind cat sitting for a little while, and Donald doesn't live far from me."

"Okay, you can join us," Gilly agreed.

"I still don't like us playing amateur detectives. Maybe we should wait until Ramsay and Stryder have more information about the weapon."

"No." Gilly started the car. "That's not a good idea. First of all, Donald knows you and Laura pretty well because you work together. He'd be more likely to open up to you than the cops. Secondly, there are some major clues that are being overlooked. I didn't mention them to Ron yet because I didn't want to embarrass him in front of Steve."

Alicia was curious. "What clues, Gilly?"

Her friend pulled out of the parking lot and made a left toward Laura's house. "The gun that was discovered did not have a silencer on it. If a silencer wasn't used, it's likely the murder wasn't committed Saturday morning or we would've heard the shot."

"Wait a minute. How would you know what a silencer looks like, Gilly?"

"I told you I don't only read romances. Besides, I've started watching a lot of crime shows since I've been dating Ron."

"Does that mean the murder didn't happen in the library?" Laura asked.

"Not necessarily." Gilly's eyes were on the road. "I was the one who found the body, and it looked pretty stiff to me. I think Mary Beth was killed earlier, before the library opened."

"How can that be?" Alicia was trying to follow her friend's train of thought. "Wouldn't they have already figured out the time of death?"

"Maybe they have. Ron doesn't tell me everything. I think he worries I would leak it to you and then it would end up in the paper because John would hear about it and scoop Andy."

"That's crazy. John knows how to keep things quiet. Anyway, let's say the murder took place earlier, how did Mary Beth get inside the library? And what about the killer? Did he just follow her in?"

"Alicia, I don't have all the answers – yet." Gilly emphasized the word "yet" as she made another turn that was sharper than Alicia felt comfortable with. Sneaky's carrier, although seat belted in, slid across the seat. Laura put her hand over the top and whispered to the cat that everything was okay.

"What I do think so far is that Mary Beth knew her killer and went to the library with him either that night or early in the morning."

"Gilly, I just remembered that Mary Beth told us she had an appointment Friday night when she was leaving our house after dinner."

"Did Mary Beth have a boyfriend?" Laura asked from the back seat. They were on her block now and Gilly was pulling up in front of her house.

"That's a good question," Gilly said parking. "What I'm considering is that the person Mary Beth had an appointment with, and we still can't rule out a woman, went to the library with her and was able to get inside somehow."

"There's really only two ways she could've done that," Alicia said. "Either they broke in, and the police would've known if there was a sign of that; or they got someone on staff to open the door and shut off the alarm."

"Only Gladys would be able to do that, although Gerald Fox might have access to the alarm code," Laura pointed out.

Alicia trusted the custodian and, although she didn't know the new guard well, her instincts told her that he was innocent. "Laura, didn't Sheila give you the access code? I thought all the librarians had it."

"No. I didn't know any other staff members had it except the custodian and guard."

"They put in a new alarm system before you were hired. Sheila gave out the codes to me, Vera, Jean, and Donald." Donald! Alicia almost bit her tongue.

Gilly voiced Alicia's fears. "It points to Donald again, doesn't it?"

Alicia couldn't deny that statement. It was also ironic that, although Sheila had updated the alarm system,

186 • Louise De Debbie

she was only now in the process of installing security cameras. Had they been added the week before, it would've been easier for the police to determine what exactly had happened Friday night or Saturday morning.

***

After Laura dropped Sneaky with her sister, Gilly drove to Donald's apartment which was only a few blocks away. Donald and Roger shared a small house on the end of a quiet street. When they pulled up, Alicia noticed Donald's car wasn't in the driveway, but she recognized Roger's. It was a little after 3 p.m., and he was probably home from work from the elementary school.

"We may have missed Donald," Alicia said, "I don't see his car."

"He may have just gone out to the store or something," Laura suggested. "We can ask Roger." She glanced toward Roger's car, what Donald termed an "old junk box." Alicia knew Roger wouldn't part with it, not only because of automobile prices but because, like Casey, he was fond of the machine after purchasing it new when he first got his license twelve years ago. At thirty, Roger was four years younger than Donald.

"He could be at the store, or he could have made his getaway," Gilly said.

Alicia didn't find the joke funny. "Okay, Detective Nostran, let's go question his partner then."

The three women exited the car and went up the walk. Alicia noticed the border of marigolds and pansies by the door and a late blooming rose tree. Donald had told her Roger enjoyed gardening while he was no green thumb. She wondered if the landscaping was done by the landlord or if Roger was allowed to plant outside the apartment.

Gilly, standing at the head of the group and donning the role of leader, tapped on the door with her fist because there was no knocker. Alicia thought they would've gotten a faster response from the bell, but Roger answered quickly.

The blond man was quite a bit shorter than Donald and, around five-foot seven, just a few inches taller than Alicia. Gilly, at five-foot two, looked up at him.

"Sorry to disturb you, Roger. I'm Gilly Nostran, Alicia's friend. Is Donald around?"

Alicia realized that Roger and Gilly had never been introduced. Roger did know Laura because he met her when he came to visit Donald at the library but that was before Gilly had been hired as a part-time clerk.

Roger pushed back a lock of his wavy hair. His hazel eyes surveyed the three women on his doorstep. Then he remembered his manners. "Don is out, but please come in. He should be home soon. He left me a note that he was stepping out for a bit. It's been tough for him since the library's been closed. He's been cooped up here while I've been working. Terrible business about that murder. You're not safe anywhere." He grimaced.

They entered as Roger walked back into the house. The place looked like the typical bachelor pad but neater. Donald joked how he and Roger were a bit like the Odd Couple characters, Felix and Oscar. Roger was the neat nut and did all the cleaning. He was the slob who left his clothes all over the floor and the leftovers of his meals in the sink. There was no sign of any of that in the tidy kitchen and living room into which they walked.

"Excuse the mess," Roger said, apologizing for what appeared spotless to Alicia. "I just got home from school and haven't had a chance to clean up."

"Your apartment looks very nice," Laura said. Alicia imagined the girl was comparing it to her cat-filled home where she, her parents, and her siblings lived comfortably but messily.

"Thank you. Have a seat." He indicated the brown Naugahyde couch. "Can I get you anything? Tea? Coffee? I just put water on. I usually have tea when I get home from work."

Gilly answered for everyone. "Please don't bother. We can't stay long. In fact, if Donald isn't back soon, we can catch him another time. But don't let us keep you from your tea."

"Okay. Be back in a minute."

When Roger left the room, Gilly whispered, "We can ask Roger a few questions about Donald's whereabouts on Friday night and Saturday morning."

Alicia knew Gilly would be the one asking all the questions. She found it somewhat funny that her friend had adopted police jargon since being around Ramsay so much.

Roger came back, holding a steaming tea cup. "Is there anything I can help you with before Donald returns?"

Alicia saw Gilly's eyes light up. "Actually, there is. We were just wondering if you can tell us where Donald was last Friday night and Saturday morning. I imagine he was here with you?"

Roger had taken a sip of tea but almost spit it out, coughing. He recovered himself quickly, grabbing a napkin and wiping his mouth. "Sorry. It went down the wrong way." He put his tea cup back on its doily and raised his eyes toward Gilly. Alicia didn't know if he realized she was dating the sheriff because the reply he gave was incriminating to his partner. "Actually, Donald wasn't here that night or morning," he said. "We had a stupid tiff, and he ran out. I don't know where he spent the night."

Gilly's eyes widened. She turned to Alicia. "Wasn't Friday the day he called in sick after your book release party?"

Alicia felt a knot form in her stomach. "Yes. He said he had a stomach virus. He wasn't feeling much better at work on Saturday either, and the, uh, incident with Mary Beth didn't help either." She hesitated to use the word "murder," although they all knew what she meant.

Roger glanced at her. "That's strange. Donald didn't complain about any stomach problems before our argument. As I said, I didn't see him until Saturday afternoon when I heard about Mary Beth. Such an awful thing." He grimaced again.

"Did you know her?" Gilly prompted.

"No, but Donald told me she wasn't such a nice person. Even so, I was sorry to learn of her death."

"What did Donald say about her?" Alicia was amazed at how good an interrogator her friend was.

"He said she bossed him around Thursday night at the library. He called her a 'shrew.'"

"Is that what you argued about?"

Roger shook his head. "No. It was a stupid fight. Friday night I'd cooked a vegetarian, gluten-free dish, and he said he was sick of my healthy meals. He told me he'd go somewhere and find food that tasted real. He threw some clothes into a bag and rushed out of the apartment."

"And you didn't see him again until after the murder?" Gilly had no problem mentioning the crime.

Roger met her gaze. "That's right," he said earnestly. Then, as if he suddenly realized why he was being questioned, he added, "I guess that means I can't give Donald an alibi in that woman's murder. But I can tell you this. Donald is no killer. He won't even swat a fly. His temper can flare at times, but it dies quickly."

Alicia noticed the expression on Gilly's face and realized she didn't quite believe Roger's words.

Roger stood up. "Why are you asking about this? The police already questioned Donald."

"Did they ask where he was Friday night and Saturday morning?" Alicia thought Gilly was pushing it. Roger's face began to darken.

"No, but he was working Saturday morning." He looked at Alicia. "You were with him. You know that."

Before Alicia could reply, he added, becoming defensive, "I think you ladies should leave. If Donald has anything else to add to what he's already told the police, I think he'd rather speak with them."

***

Gilly was quiet as she drove Laura home. Alicia assumed it was because of the way Roger had reacted; but, after Laura had been dropped off, Gilly said, "I was pretty good, wasn't I? I asked him questions Ron hadn't even thought of."

"Gilly, Ramsay didn't know about the gun until today. It might turn out to be someone else's, anyway."

"We'll see." As Gilly headed toward Cobble Cove, her cell phone buzzed. She had it mounted on her dashboard in a hands-free holder. "It's Ron." She pressed the speaker button. "Hi, hot buns, what's up?"

Hot buns? Gilly had more nicknames for the sheriff than Alicia had ever heard, but at least they were pleasant ones.

"Got a make on the gun, Abby, and you won't believe who it's registered to."

"Try me. You might be surprised."

There was a bit of static on the line, and, as Ramsay let out a breath, it muffled the reception even more, but Alicia managed to hear his reply. "Donald Davis."

Gilly gave Alicia an I-told-you-so-look as the sheriff continued. "His prints are the only ones on it, so we're going to have to take him in, but I have a feeling he's got a good explanation. He's helped me at the library, and I wouldn't take him for a killer, but you never know about the quiet ones."

Alicia expected Gilly to tell him Donald was out and that they'd been to his apartment and spoken to Roger, but she didn't. Instead she asked, "What about the silencer?

Did that turn up, and am I right that the ME listed the time of death late Friday night or early Saturday morning?"

There was a longer pause on the line this time and Ramsay voiced an expletive. "How could we have overlooked the silencer? We were keeping the time of death confidential even from you."

Gilly winked. Alicia knew it was a good thing the cell phone didn't have a visual display.

"How about the bug? Any prints on that?"

"No. It's clean, and the other one hasn't turned up. We might find it at Davis' home. Stryder is getting a warrant now. I better be going. I'll keep you updated, Abby." He clicked off quickly.

"Why didn't you tell him about our visit?" Alicia asked as Gilly headed in the direction of Stone Throw Road to take her home.

"He'll find out soon enough, but don't worry. I have ways of soothing his anger."

"That's not what I'm concerned about, Gilly. I can't believe they're going to arrest Donald."

"You seem to have faith in him. What if he's guilty?"

"What motive would he have? He barely knew Mary Beth. Just because she ordered him around during the book release party doesn't mean he shot her. Sheila orders him around all the time, and she's still alive. Also, you forget about the email and text messages John received which seemed like threats against me and that Mary Beth and I shared a similar bone structure, and she was wearing the same blouse as me on the day she was killed."

"I haven't forgotten, Alicia. Those messages sent to John may have been to lead the police off the trail, or maybe Donald had intended to kill you. Was he acting differently to you lately?"

"Gilly, that's insane. Donald and I are co-workers, friends …" Alicia's words drifted off as she remembered Casey's betrayal.

"I actually don't think it's him," Gilly said turning into Alicia's driveway. "I hope you help me prove the cops wrong."

"How do you plan to do that, Gilly?"

"First, we need to find out exactly where Donald was Friday night. Then we need to look over the remaining list of suspects and see who else was missing during the hours Mary Beth was murdered before the library opened on Saturday."

Alicia suddenly remembered her dinner at Mac's house with Mary Beth. "I'm sorry, Gilly, but you're going to have to do that on your own. I have somewhere to go tonight."

"Ah, yes, the old girlfriend's farewell party."

"It's not a farewell party. It's just a dinner."

"I'm sure you'll be glad she's leaving."

"Relieved is more the word."

Gilly smiled. "You have nothing to worry about, honey."

"Only a killer who might be striking me next."

"Not if Donald is guilty and behind bars."

"I thought you believed he was innocent."

"I do, but I don't have evidence to back that up for the police or myself. And, tell me, Ali, why are the unmarked cars gone? Aren't you still being protected?"

"I don't know. Maybe Stryder's men had other assignments."

"I'll talk to Ron about that. In the meantime, I'll finish working on this alone. You stay safe at home with John and then try to enjoy your dinner tonight. Don't think about Donald. Concentrate on getting Lindsey Harrington out of your face."

Chapter Twenty

When she joined John, he knew immediately by looking at her face that something was wrong.

"What happened, Ali? You seem upset."

She could barely hold back the tears. "It's Donald. He's going to be arrested. They found a gun at the Carlsville Hilton. It's registered to him, and his are the only fingerprints on it. The bullets match the one that killed Mary Beth."

John was shocked. "I don't believe it."

"Neither do I or Gilly, but Roger says Donald wasn't home during the time of the murder, so he may not have an alibi."

"You spoke with Roger? Why did you do that? Haven't the police questioned him and Donald already?"

Alicia couldn't lie to her husband. "It was Gilly's idea. I wasn't too thrilled about it, but she's conducting her own private investigation using information from Ramsay and her own instincts."

John wasn't pleased. He glanced across at the playpen where the twins were happily occupying themselves building a tower of alphabet blocks. "I don't think that's a good idea, and you shouldn't be involved. It could be dangerous and also affect the real investigation."

"I'll try to stay out of it, John, but Gilly's my friend. I know she's only trying to help."

John looked back at her. "I know. I hope they clear Donald, but I don't want to see Gilly make a fool of herself or, worse, get killed."

"You really think she'd be in danger?"

"When you're hunting a killer, that's always a possibility, Ali."

***

Alicia tried to push aside her thoughts about Donald and Gilly and enjoy the last meal with Lindsey Harrington. She couldn't help but notice that John was spiffing himself up more than usual as they prepared to leave. He'd even added a spritz of cologne, an old birthday gift she'd given him that hadn't even been opened until that night. He'd also chosen two of the nicest outfits for the twins. She, on the other hand, dressed casually in jeans and a sweater. She wasn't trying to impress or outdo Lindsey. After that evening, the woman would be gone from Cobble Cove and as Gilly so delicately put it, "out of her face."

Mac greeted them at the door. Betty was in the kitchen, setting the table. Alicia offered to help, but she told her to just have a seat and pulled over the two high chairs Mac kept for when the twins visited. Alicia sat the twins in them.

Lindsey hadn't yet arrived, and Alicia imagined she was planning a grand entrance.

"Has the case been closed yet?" Mac asked as Fido came bounding into the kitchen. Alicia realized he didn't know about Donald.

"I believe they're working on something, but there are no solid leads," John said, casting a glance in Alicia's direction. She was relieved he wasn't mentioning the arrest. It would be on the news soon enough.

"Seems to me they would have a good lead once they locate the weapon," Mac said. He went to the refrigerator and brought out a large bowl of salad that he placed on the table and added a serving spoon.

"It's more complicated than that," John said as Mac invited him and Alicia to sit as he joined them. "Just because a gun is registered to someone doesn't mean that it's used by that person."

Alicia was becoming a little uncomfortable with the conversation and was relieved when Betty said, "If you guys want to talk about murder, please don't do it at the dinner table."

Mac raised a white eyebrow at her. "You're right, dear. Let's talk about more pleasant things. I'm eager to see Lindsey again after all these years."

Oh, God, Alicia thought. *I'd rather talk about the murder.*

"I remember when you brought her here to visit during one of the college vacations. That was so long ago. She was lovely." He glanced over at Alicia. "But not half as pretty as your wife, of course."

Despite her father-in-law's compliment, Alicia's stomach took a turn. She wasn't sure she'd be able to eat much even though the smell of Mac's cooking was mouthwatering.

Before Mac could continue reminiscing about Lindsey, the woman was standing at the door, tapping lightly.

Betty let her in with a big smile. "So nice to meet you, my dear. Jonathan has told me so much about you."

Alicia always found it interesting how Betty preferred to call Mac by his full name.

Lindsey entered the room. She was also dressed casually, but she filled out her sweater better than Alicia, and her long, wavy tresses shone golden in the candles Betty had lit on the table.

John got up and hugged her, and she gave him two quick kisses on the cheek and another that almost touched his lips. She just nodded at Alicia and shook Betty and Mac's hands. Before taking a seat across from Alicia and John, she also kissed both babies on their foreheads. Alicia felt her jealousy flare as the twins smiled and giggled at her. She had to remind herself that this was Lindsey's last day in Cobble Cove.

"It's so nice to see you all," Lindsey said. "I've had such a wonderful time here visiting." Her eyes were on John as she spoke.

"I'm glad you could come to dinner," Mac said. "I understand you're leaving tomorrow."

Alicia noticed a bottle of wine on the table along with the pitcher of water Betty had laid down. Mac and his lady friend didn't often entertain with wine, so they must've considered this a special occasion.

Lindsey pushed back a strand of her hair. Still looking at John, she replied to his father's comment. "Actually, my plans have changed. I'm staying through the weekend."

Alicia fought to control what must've been a horrified expression on her face. She now knew for sure she wouldn't be able to touch a bite of her food.

* * *

The rest of the evening went downhill from there. The conversation centered around Lindsey who seemed to love being in the spotlight and gushed over her visit to Cobble Cove and how cute the twins were and what a charming family John had. Alicia fought down some food to show her respect for Mac and Betty, but her stomach threatened to heave it up when John began laughing at Lindsey's stories of their old college days. Then she felt bad a little while later when she saw tears glisten in his eyes when Lindsey spoke about Jenny. Alicia knew that it had taken some therapy and her to help John forget his first wife who died tragically in childbirth. Yet even though she tried to tell herself Lindsey was just a good friend, the fact that the woman shared a part of John's life that she never had, caused an ache in her heart.

The surprise came over dessert. John had asked Lindsey what she'd done after Columbia and whether she'd pursued a legal career. Since Lindsey had been in town, she'd never mentioned that she'd studied law. Alicia just assumed she'd taken journalism courses with John, but then she remembered her husband also said he'd minored in law. Lindsey was evasive with her reply. She said she decided not to become a lawyer, and Alicia figured she was embarrassed by the fact that she probably failed the bar. When Mac followed up by asking what Lindsey did now, she also replied a bit reluctantly. "I work on Long Island," she said, taking a slice of the apple pie Betty had brought over and baked from scratch. It was thick and full of cinnamon, and Alicia couldn't resist taking a piece. Her stomach was settling down, and she wondered if it was because Lindsey had started sounding uncomfortable.

"Alicia was from Long Island," John said. "It's a small world."

"I'll be sure to give you may address before I leave." Then, for the first time that night, Lindsey turned the conversation away from herself. "What's the latest on your editor's murder? I can hardly believe such a terrible thing would happen in this peaceful town."

Alicia, who'd been quiet throughout dinner, said, "When I first came here, there was a bad situation, and last year the twins were kidnapped."

"Thank goodness you have a sheriff," Lindsey remarked. "I'm sure he'll get to the bottom of this soon."

Alicia was hesitant to mention Donald's arrest and she knew John had already kept it quiet, so she added quickly, "We certainly hope so."

***

As they drove home, the twins asleep in their car seats, John said, "You still seem uncomfortable around Lindsey. I hope you aren't jealous. I already told you that she's only a friend."

"I know, and I trust you, John. It's difficult, though. She's beautiful, and the two of you share so many memories."

"We share memories, too, Ali, and we'll be sharing them the rest of our lives. Lindsey doesn't hold a candle to you in the looks department. I mean that."

"I wonder what would've happened had you stayed in New York instead of coming home to Cobble Cove with your dad when your mom was ill."

John shook his head but kept his eyes on his driving. "Dad would probably quote Robert Frost at this point – the road not taken. Remember how he always says, 'things happen for a reason.' We often think the decisions we make are in our control, but fate plays a part. I truly believe that."

"So we were meant to meet?"

"Of course." John smiled, and Alicia saw the outline of his dimple. Her heart did a tiny somersault. He was right. Lindsey was his past. She was his present and future.

***

They pulled up to their house and parked. As Alicia was helping John unbuckle the babies from their car seats and carry them in, she noticed a car parked across the street. She thought Stryder's men might be back, but then she realized a woman sat behind the wheel. Looking closer, she realized with a shock that it was Su Li, the Asian lady who'd attended her author talk and who had asked for her autograph. When the woman saw Alicia looking, she started up the car and drove away.

"Did you see that, John?" Alicia asked as she put her sleeping daughter across her shoulder.

John had Johnny on his back. "Notice what, honey?"

"One of the women who had attended our book release party was sitting in a car across from our house.

When she saw me, she drove off. What was she doing there, and why is she still in Cobble Cove?'

"Are you sure it was her?"

"Yes." They walked to the door, and John opened it.

"Maybe she's extended her time here like Lindsey."

"That's crazy. At least Lindsey knows you. That woman was alone at the library, and Cobble Cove is not exactly the tourist mecca of the world."

John grinned. "You have a point, but if you're concerned about who you saw, why don't you ask Gilly? She said some people are still staying at the inn from last week. Maybe that woman is one of them."

Alicia knew Lindsey was staying at the Cobble Inn; but if Su Li was, that still didn't explain what she was doing near their house.

**

John put the twins to bed and then said he wanted to try to do some writing. He was hopeful that they'd be hearing from Prime Crime soon with a new editor.

Alicia decided to take John's advice and call Gilly, but the phone rang before she had the chance.

She saw her friend's number on the call waiting display. "Hi, Gilly. You read my mind. I just got back from dinner and was about to call you."

"Alicia, I'm not calling about your dinner, although I'd love to hear about it." Gilly sounded excited. "I have some really good news for you."

"You found some evidence to clear Donald?"

"I didn't have to." Gilly paused. "They released him when they heard his story and a witness verified it. Ramsay also put in a good word for him."

"But I thought they proved the gun was his? What was his story?"

Gilly took a breath and then let out a jumble of words almost as quick as Mary Beth's lightening sentences had been. She told Alicia that, after Donald's fight with Roger, he spent the night at the Carlsville Hilton. Amanda, the hotel clerk, had checked him in and she corroborated his story. The room in which he stayed was on the main floor and nowhere near Mary Beth's or the room where the gun was found.

"If that's so, then what was the gun doing in the mysterious Mr. Marks' room?" Alicia asked.

"Donald told Steve that he didn't even know the gun was missing. He kept it in the glove compartment of his car. Roger had his own gun in the apartment. Donald didn't like guns at all, but Roger talked him into keeping it after the crimes that occurred last year."

"That still doesn't make sense, Gilly. Are you saying that the guest who stayed at the hotel and planted the bug in Mary Beth's room also stole Donald's gun?"

"That's what Steve and Ron think. They said Donald hadn't locked his car."

"But how would the person know the gun was there?"

"They don't know, but there are too many questions to hold Donald. They're keeping an eye on him, though."

Alicia had a sinking feeling. The only person who might know Donald kept a gun in his glove compartment was Roger. It was also plausible that Donald had given his partner the library entrance code, even though the librarians were told not to share it with their friends or family.

***

"There's something else odd, Gilly." Alicia said. "When I got home, there was a woman in a car looking at our house. It was the Asian lady from my book signing. When she saw me, she drove off. Is she still staying at your inn?"

"Yes. Sorry I didn't tell you. She and glamour girl are the remaining guests from last week, but GG is leaving soon."

If Alicia wasn't so upset by that fact, she would've laughed at her friend's nickname for Lindsey. "Unfortunately, that's wrong, Gilly. She told us at dinner she's decided to stay a few more days."

"I can tell her I'm expecting more guests when she asks for an extension."

"Don't do that. She'll just find a room elsewhere. Maybe I'm paranoid, but I think she has her sights on a reunion with John. You should've seen them at Mac's house reminiscing about their college days."

"You have bigger problems than your husband's old flame, honey. Remember, you're the one lighting his torch now."

Alicia laughed at that. Gilly could always find a way to make her smile. "You sound like John's father using quotes and euphemisms, but I get the point. What are you planning to do now that the suspect has been released?"

"Go on to Suspect Number 2, of course."

Alicia tried to recall the names Gilly had on her pad. Since Donald had been moved up on the list after the gun was found, she assumed the next person was Mary Beth's husband, Dominic Carr. Gilly confirmed that by saying, "I have Carr's number. I'm going to call him after I hang up with you. I'll let you know what he says."

"How did you get his number, Gil? Oh, wait. Maybe I don't want to know. What are you going to say to him? He might hang up on you. Roger wasn't thrilled when you approached him acting like a police officer."

"I'll be more discreet this time. I'm learning better investigative techniques."

Alicia sighed. "Just be careful, okay."

"I'm not the one in danger, honey."

"You still think the killer was after me?"

"We can't rule that out yet, even though John hasn't received any further messages. Unless he's not telling you about them."

"He wouldn't hide that, Gilly. I'm just afraid that you might push someone's buttons the wrong way. You really should leave this to the police."

Gilly ignored her warning. "Look, sweetie. I have to go. I'll keep you posted on everything, and I'll keep an eye on GG and that Asian woman, too. Maybe we can get together tomorrow, and I'll share all my notes with you."

"Sounds like a plan." Alicia regretted the words as soon as she said them. If John knew she and Gilly were still playing detectives, he wouldn't be at all happy.

Chapter Twenty-One

Alicia found it hard to sleep that night. Her mind kept going over everything. Donald was free but still not in the clear. Roger might be involved, but why? Two of the people who'd attended the book release party—Lindsey and Su Li—were still in town and acting as if they had ulterior motives. What about Chloe? She may have been the last one to see Mary Beth alive before the editor had her mysterious appointment. Then there was Mary Beth's ex who Gilly was currently investigating, although the police seemed convinced he was innocent. And what about the sister, Mary Lou? Although she'd claimed not to have seen Mary Beth for years, was that true?

Tossing and turning with her shifting thoughts, Alicia decided to get up and do something more productive. John was out like a light beside her, and there were no sounds from the twins' room, so she assumed they were also fast asleep.

Stepping into her slippers, she left the room and headed downstairs to her office. John had said he'd written another chapter in the book and sent it to her. She might be able to keep her mind off all her concerns if she looked it over and got to work composing her own scene.

Booting up her computer, she realized she hadn't checked her email in a few days. Things had been so hectic that she hadn't had time to do so. She opened Chrome and typed in her Gmail address. As usual, there was lots of spam, but her heart skipped a beat when she saw an email from M. Marks. It was dated just a few hours ago. The subject line read: "The story's not over." Her hand shook on the mouse as she clicked open the message. It was longer than any of the ones John had received, and the words struck fear up her spine:

Dearest Marjorie,
We need to meet, so I can write you a proper ending. Gabby doesn't have to be in it or any of the other characters. Midnight Sunday at the place where you set the climax to Written in Stone. Let's re-edit the scene.
M.

Alicia just sat there stunned, staring at the screen. She knew the place he meant and so would John. She had to tell him and alert Ramsay. The reference to Gilly, the character Gabby in their books who was the best friend of Marjorie, bothered her because it seemed to indicate that the author of the email knew that her friend was asking questions.

When she was finally able to pull herself away from the screen, she left the email up and went back upstairs. As she passed the nursery, she heard only the light snores of her children. John was still sound asleep in bed as she slipped in next to him. Her first impulse was to wake him and tell him about the message, but it was 2 a.m. If the person who'd sent her the email was planning something the following night, they would have all day to speak with Ramsay and figure out what to do about it. She knew it would be useless for her to get to sleep now, but what was the point of disturbing John?

She lay her head against the pillow and spent the remaining hours going over all that had happened in the last week and the words she'd read on the computer. By 7, her mind still had not come up with any answers. All she had were questions. Who was impersonating the fictional detective in her and John's books? Who had lured Mary Beth to the library and shot her with Donald's gun? Why was Lindsey still in town? What was Su Li doing watching their house? How did the email sender know Gilly was investigating the murder? How did that person have her and John's emails and John's cell number in the first place? Last, but not least, why was she being summoned to meet with him at the climactic setting of their book, *Written in Stone*?

***

John found her making breakfast in the kitchen. Since he cooked most nights during the week, Alicia often prepared meals on the weekends. And since the library was still closed and she hadn't been able to sleep, she'd occupied herself by putting together John's favorite morning dish, scrambled eggs with cheddar cheese, peppers, and onions.

"Smells delicious," John said, entering the room and sniffing the air. "What did I do right last night? As I remember, I fell asleep before I could ravage your beautiful body."

Alicia placed a heapful of eggs on a plate. Instead of answering him, she said, "I'll make something else for the twins later. Let them sleep. I wanted to have a few minutes to talk with you."

John raised an eyebrow as he took a seat at the table. Alicia brought over both their plates of food, but she knew she wouldn't eat much. The coffee would be helpful, though, so she poured them both a cup.

"What's wrong, Ali? You look tired. Did you have trouble sleeping?"

She sat across from him. "I didn't sleep all night. That's what I want to talk to you about."

"Hmm." John glanced at her. "This isn't still about Lindsey, is it?"

She shook her head. "No, John. Lindsey is the least of my concerns right now. I received an email last night. It was from M. Marks."

John's eyes grew serious. He dropped his fork on his plate. "He wrote to you? What did he say?"

"I have the email up in my office. You can look at it later. We need to speak to Ramsay. Marks wants to meet with me at midnight tonight at the place we featured at the end of *Written in Stone*."

"You mean that deserted area near Cove Point?"

Alicia nodded. "In the book, we refer to it as Bay Bridge."

"That's where Marjorie Meyers rescued the woman who was being hunted by the killer."

Alicia looked up into his troubled eyes. "Yes, John, but M. Marks says he wants to give me a different ending."

John's face turned angry. He stood up quickly. "Why didn't you wake me up last night and tell me about this? Let me see that email." As he rushed from the room, Alicia followed him down the hall.

In the office, John switched on the lights and then hit a keyboard key to wake up the computer. Staring at the words on the screen, he muttered, "This is crazy. Once we tell Ramsay about it, he'll have his men surround the area. How does this guy expect to escape?"

Alicia tried to remain calm even though her insides were shaking. "John, I thought about it all night. It's obvious whoever is doing this is not sane. Maybe he wants to be caught. Maybe he wants to die, but he might want to bring me down with him."

"That won't happen." John turned to her. "You're not going anywhere, but the police will be there."

"He'll probably know that and just try another time. Remember what happened with the twins? We were both prepared to meet the kidnappers on Cove Point when we found the dead body. He might be up to something else, but it looks like I've been the target all along."

"We don't know that for sure, Ali. You stay here, and I'm going to the sheriff's office. Better yet, let me call

Kim or Dad and have someone watch the twins while we go together. I need to know exactly what Ramsay has uncovered so far."

Alicia knew there was no sense arguing with John, and he was right that they needed to get as much information as possible before they made any decisions on their next move. She picked up the phone and called Mac.

***

Her father-in-law, a morning person, was there within minutes. Alicia grabbed her coat and John helped her put it on.

"We shouldn't be gone long, Dad. Thanks for coming over."

Mac didn't question where they were going or why the urgency. He simply nodded. "No problem, John. I love to babysit. You know that. I would've brought Betty with me, but she's already gone to her yoga class this morning."

It was no secret Betty spent most nights with Mac, even though she kept her own house, now much brighter and more inviting than it had been in the days she'd been a recluse.

"Pamela practices yoga, too," Alicia said. "Maybe I should try it. Where does Betty go?"

"There's a yoga center in Carlsville. They have early Sunday morning classes. Betty usually comes home, changes, and we go to church afterwards."

Alicia had forgotten about church. Lately, she and John had not attended as often as they should. "Sorry about that, Mac. Maybe you two can go later. I know there are several services."

"No worries. Betty usually drags me along, but I don't always need to go there to speak with God. I talk to him daily. In fact, I think he's rather sick of me." Mac grinned, and Alicia caught the outline of the dimple John had inherited from him.

"Thanks, Dad. The twins are still sleeping upstairs. Alicia made some great scrambled eggs this morning, but something came up, and we didn't get to eat them."

Alicia wondered if John's explanation about the food gave Mac the wrong impression because his grin widened. "I remember those days, Son. Your mother and I used to let a lot of dishes go to waste when the urge hit us. I'll just make up another batch of eggs for my grandchildren. You just go and do what you need to take care of."

"We appreciate that, Dad. If you need us, just call us on our cells."

"Will do. Now scoot." Mac walked toward the stairway, balancing on his cane.

"I can bring them down to you," Alicia offered. "The playpen is still set up in the living room, so you don't have to chase them."

"No need. I can handle them. They're being quiet, but that's not always a good thing."

"They may still be sleeping."

Mac gave Alicia a doubtful look. "We'll see about that. Now go. Everything will be fine."

John signaled to Alicia as he put on his own coat. She knew there was no arguing with Mac either, so she followed her husband out the door.

***

When they arrived at the sheriff's office, Alicia was surprised but not shocked to see Gilly there. A few officers were making phone calls and working at desks when they entered. Gilly, seeing Alicia and John, came over to them. "Ron's in his office. I was just coming out to get him some coffee. I was going to call you later. What brings you both here? Where are the twins?" She appeared a bit anxious, so Alicia put her at ease by saying, "Carol and Johnny are home with their grandfather. John and I are here to speak with Ramsay. Can he see us?"

"Certainly." Gilly's alarm turned to curiosity. "I'll take you back to him with his coffee. Do you want any, too?"

Alicia shook her head, but John said, "I can definitely use another cup. I'll make it myself, though. Thank you."

Gilly filled Ramsay's cup and took a munchkin from a Dunkin Donuts box along with a napkin. "I feel bad for Ron. He can't eat regular donuts anymore, but at least he can get a taste of them with a munchkin."

"Might be just as many calories," John said, grabbing a powdered jelly. Alicia couldn't help but take the Boston Crème. She excused herself by thinking of it as the breakfast she missed, even though she knew it had less nutrition than the scrambled eggs.

Ramsay was sitting behind his desk. Gilly placed the coffee and donut in front of him and took the chair to his right. "Alicia and John are here, Ron. They have something to discuss with you. They said I could stay."

The sheriff nodded, glancing down at his munchkin with disappointment and at John and Alicia's donuts with barely concealed desire. "Have a seat. Nice to see you both. The kids okay?"

"They're home with my father," John said. "This isn't about them."

"Oh, good." Ramsay ate the munchkin whole and washed it down with a sip of his coffee. "I guess it's about Mary Beth then."

"Yes," Alicia said. "but me more than her."

"Fill us in," Ramsay said, including Gilly in the discussion.

John proceeded to tell Ramsay about Alicia's email. He also included the parts about Gilly and their books and what he and Alicia thought the sender meant. When he was finished, Ramsay said, "I hate to admit it, but we're not getting anywhere on this case. If this person is really the man who occupied the room next to Mary Beth and shot her in the library and he's willing to meet with you," he looked over at Alicia, "our job will be that much easier."

"Not at the price of her life," John said. "Our book has a happy ending, but he's intent on changing the story."

"She'll be fully protected. I'll get Stryder and his men to provide backup."

"What if we can find out who he is before then?" Gilly suggested. "I told you about the calls I made to Carr and Halliday. You still haven't spoken with Roger again or that hotel clerk who checked Donald into the Carlsville Hilton that night."

Ramsay looked annoyed. "I told you to stop playing Miss Marple, Abby, and you have no right to tell me or any of my officers how to do our jobs."

Alicia expected Gilly to back down. Instead, her friend said in an even, controlled voice, "And may I ask who figured out that Mary Beth's time of death was earlier than was reported? Who knew the silencer was missing from the room where the gun was found? Who thought it was a great idea to have Fido and Sneaky search the hotel?"

Ramsay sighed, but he was calmer. "I admit you've had some insights into this case, but I can't allow you to pursue it any further. One thing is talking with me about it; another is actually questioning suspects." His voice lowered, and Alicia realized he was concerned for Gilly's safety.

"If you have a suggestion on what we should do next, I will consider it."

"I do, Fuzzykins," Gilly said with a smile. "Carr seems to be a dead end. Excuse the pun, but I'm practicing my detective speak. He had no problems talking with me, and I learned where he was at the time of Mary Beth's death."

Ramsay raised a gray eyebrow. Alicia thought it was a response to the nickname as well as the statement. "What did Carr tell you that he wouldn't tell the police and how did you get it out of him?"

Gilly flashed her eyelashes. "It was over the phone, so all I could use was my voice, but took full advantage. Anyhow, I guess it was easier talking with a woman. He said that, since the divorce, he'd found it hard to, uhm, make love with another woman. He'd discovered a side of himself he never realized was there. He'd met someone at his job who he had a rendezvous with the night of the murder. They'd taken a trip together to a cabin he owns not far from Cobble Cove. They stayed there together until Saturday afternoon."

"I assume this person you're referring to was a man?"

Gilly nodded.

"Did you get his name?"

"No. Carr wants to protect him. He's not out of the closet, even though in these days it's easier to tell people."

Alicia thought of Roger, but he worked at the school and not on Wall Street.

"I'm not sure that story is true," Ramsay said.

"I believe him." Gilly sounded confident.

"What about your other call? The one you placed to that writer, Cooper Halliday?"

"No luck, Ron. He didn't answer his phone, but I left a message with my cell number. I'll let you know if he calls back."

"You said you had some ideas on what we should do next," John said, entering the conversation as he finished his donut and wiped the white powder from his mouth. Alicia recalled the white beard he'd donned for the Christmas Fair last year after the horror of the kidnapping. In a few months, he'd play the part again.

Gilly took a breath. "I'd really like to talk with Amanda, the girl at the hotel. It seems to me an odd coincidence that Donald, Mr. M, and Mary Beth were all staying there last week. There's something else that's really bothering me." She paused as if for effect to add weight to her words and looked toward Alicia. "Mr. M left the gun for a reason – to place the guilt on Donald, but he must have another gun. The one I think he plans to use tonight."

Chapter Twenty-Two

"That doesn't make sense," Alicia said, breaking her silence. "Why did he leave Donald's gun at the hotel if he meant to use his own gun on me?" Her stomach was twisting at the thought that they were talking about the killer planning to shoot her.

"Maybe because he thought he'd killed you the first time," Gilly replied. "Remember that text that John received."

"But he had to know it was Mary Beth if he took her to the library before or after hours," Ramsay pointed out.

"You think Ali and Mary Beth were both his targets?" John asked. Without waiting for an answer, he added, "That means he had a motive against both of them."

"It still doesn't explain the gun switch," Gilly pointed out.

"Don't you know that not everything is tied up even in a mystery novel?" John said, "and the killer seems to be going by the book, our book, if you know what I mean."

"Then the answer must be in your book." Gilly's eyes lit up. "I have the autographed copy you gave me, but I haven't read it yet. Is there anything in the book that might help us figure out who Mr. M. is?"

John shook his head, but Alicia had a thought. "If he's acting like the killer in our book, asking me to go to Bay Bridge which is actually that small drawbridge across Cobble Point, maybe he's planning the same scenario as that which the killer used on his first victim before Marjorie Meyers saved the second?"

"But the stories are different," John said. "In the one he seems to be creating, Marjorie Meyers is the victim, and Detective Marks is the killer."

"He's using our work like a blueprint but mapping out different plotlines," Alicia said.

Before any of them could voice further hypotheses, one of Ramsay's men rushed in. "Sorry to interrupt, Sheriff, but there's been a report of a break-in at one of the shops in Cobble Corner and the store owner and a few customers are being held at gunpoint."

Alicia was reminded of the gift shop burglary last December, but that had occurred when no one was in the store. A hostage situation could be deadly.

Ramsay jumped up. "I've got to go," he said. "Alicia, John. I'll call you at home later, and we can work out a plan for tonight. Gilly, you go back to the inn. I may be a while."

"Be careful, Ron." Gilly moved out of the way as Ramsay headed to the door.

"Which store is it?" John asked as he joined Gilly and Alicia out in the hall.

"Chloe's Closet," the sheriff replied.

***

After Ramsay and a few officers left, Gilly, Alicia, and John headed to their cars. Gilly said, "Can you come back to the inn with me, Ali? We can talk a bit."

Alicia was surprised that Gilly didn't mention the irony of Chloe's Closet being the target of the burglars. She looked toward John to see if he thought it was a good idea for her to go with Gilly and was surprised when he gave her the go ahead.

"It might be a good break for you, Ali. I'll watch the kids until you get home." He glanced at Gilly. "Don't get her into any trouble, and make sure you bring her back."

Gilly smiled. "Don't worry. I'll make sure your wife is safe. Ron will let me know as soon as the situation at Cobble Corner is resolved. There's no sense in her hanging around at home worrying about this until then."

John nodded, gave Alicia a kiss, and drove off in his pickup. As Alicia joined Gilly in her car, her friend said, "Don't be alarmed, honey, but I told a little white lie. We're not going to the inn. We're going to the Carlsville Hilton to talk with Amanda."

Alicia should've known Gilly didn't give up so easily. "I thought Ramsay gave you orders to stay out of this case."

"The clock is ticking. I think I can get to the bottom of this before you have to meet Mr. Marks. Ron is preoccupied with this break-in, so it gives us the perfect opportunity to solve things on our own."

Alicia sighed. Gilly could be as stubborn as John when she'd made up her mind. "Okay, I'll go with you, but as soon as we speak with this woman, we leave and go back to the inn. Got it?"

Gilly smiled. "Yes, ma'am. I give you my word."

***

A wind had picked up and nearly blown them into the hotel. Alicia's hair whipped across her face and Gilly's hat nearly flew off. "Boy, that wind is strong, Ali. The weather's changing."

"It's nearly October, but unexpected weather can hit at any time." Alicia recalled the Thanksgiving snowstorm three years ago that changed her life.

Matt Devlyn was at the desk when they entered. He smiled at them. "Mrs. McKinney, Ms. Nostran. What can I help you with today?"

Alicia smiled back, but Gilly's face remained neutral. "Where is your clerk, Amanda?"

The young man hesitated. His smile faded. "Amanda's at the hospital. She's visiting her mother. Mrs. Halliday is quite ill and Amanda sees her every day, but she should be back soon if you care to wait." He indicated the couches in the lobby.

Alicia knew Halliday wasn't an uncommon name, but it seemed too much of a coincidence that one of the suspects had the same name. Gilly voiced her thoughts. "Is Amanda's mother any relation to the author, Cooper Halliday?" she asked.

Matt nodded. "Yes. She's his mother. Amanda is his sister."

"Oh, my God!" Gilly turned to Alicia. "How did Ron and Stryder miss that?" She glanced back at Matt. "We'll wait, but would it be a problem to meet with her upstairs in the room that Mrs. Simmons occupied?"

What was Gilly planning? Alicia was sure the hotel owner's son would turn her down. Instead, looking a bit perplexed, he said, "No. The room is still unoccupied. I don't think they want anyone in there, but you're free to wait outside it if you'd like. I'll send Amanda up when she arrives."

"Thank you." Gilly strode toward the elevators, indicating that Alicia should join her.

As they rode up to the top floor, Alicia asked, "What are you up to, Gilly?"

"It's obvious Amanda is involved in what happened. She must be helping her older brother."

"If she's an accomplice, she'll probably face jail time. We need to inform the police. Since Ramsay's occupied, we could call Stryder. He's in charge of Carlsville arrests, anyway."

"Not yet, Ali. I'm pretty sure Amanda knew what went on that night, but I'd like to confirm it first. Halliday might be Mr. M. or it might be someone he or Amanda knows. I promise I'll call Steve as soon as we get that information from her."

As the elevator came to a stop, they alighted. The hall was dark. It seemed that the whole floor was being kept closed. Alicia remembered the crazy competition between Sneaky and Fido and how the pets had turned up evidence in Mary Beth's murder that had pointed to Donald but was dismissed. So many questions still filled her mind. She doubted the young hotel clerk could or would answer all of them.

The yellow tape still hung on the doorknob of Mary Beth's room, but Alicia noted it was slightly ajar. "Gilly, it's open," she whispered, wondering why she was keeping her voice low. They were the only ones up there. Someone had just forgotten to close the door.

"Let's go in then," Gilly said in her normal voice. "Maybe we'll find some more evidence."

"Are you crazy? We can't tamper with anything."

"We won't touch anything. We'll just go in and look. C'mon, Ali."

Alicia had her hand on her cell phone ready to dial John. She reluctantly followed her friend into the dark room. The shades must've all been pulled down because not a hint of outside light shone through.

"I think the light switch is over here," Gilly said.

Just as Alicia moved forward, a hand clamped her mouth shut as someone stepped out of the shadows and grabbed her. Her muffled scream alerted Gilly. "Alicia, what's …?"

"You sure made it easy for me," the man holding Alicia said. "I wasn't going to wait until tonight, anyway, but I had plotted this scene with only one murder. Now I'm forced to commit two. Oh, well. That's a great twist."

Alicia felt the strong arm around her throat. She struggled to reach her phone, but it dropped to the floor.

The man kicked it out of the way. "Yours, too, Gabby." He called Gilly by the name of Marjorie Meyers' friend.

"My boyfriend is the sheriff," Gilly said. "He'll be here any minute."

Alicia knew she was bluffing, and so did the man who waved a gun at Gilly. "He's back in Cobble Cove, and my son is taking care of that. Chloe's Closet certainly came in handy in our plans."

"You killed Mary Beth," Gilly said. Alicia was surprised she sounded so composed.

The man laughed, and it was an eerie sound bouncing off the walls. "You catch on quick. She was no mistake. I wanted her dead and Marjorie, too."

Gilly ignored the way the killer referred to Alicia as her main character. "Why? Was it because your books weren't doing as well as John and Alicia's?" she ventured.

Another laugh. "I'm a superior writer. Reviewers have referred to me as a 'master of suspense.' I've had bestsellers; but when Mary Beth approached me about the movie, I knew I would way surpass the Groucho Marx series."

"The movie?" Alicia managed to ask, although her voice came out weak against the stranglehold.

"Yes, she said she would arrange it with her sister who was the best agent in New York. All I had to do was be nice to her. So I was. My marriage was a sham, anyway. My wife just kept pushing me to write more books. She was more of a shrew than Mary Beth." He laughed again. "When I asked about the movie, she kept stalling. She said her sister was busy. I don't think she ever intended to speak with her sister about me. Then she asked me to come along with her to Cobble Cove for the book release party. That took nerve. I haven't released a new book in two years."

Alicia watched Gilly take small steps toward the door. It was a good idea to keep Halliday talking, so he might not notice her make a run for it. But he had a gun and would use it. Only one of them might be able to escape. Alicia knew her friend would risk her life for her, and she would do the same.

"Why did you come to our party then?" She had to keep him talking.

"I didn't intend to go. I booked myself in the room next to Mary Beth. We had worked that out in case my wife discovered where I'd gone."

"But you bugged her room," Gilly said, inching toward the wall.

"Stop right there. I see what you're doing," Halliday snapped. "If you move any further, I'll shoot both of you and not tell you the rest of the story."

Gilly froze in her tracks.

"Yes, I bugged the room. That's how I found out Mary Beth had no intention of talking to Mary Lou about having my books turned into a movie. She was actually trying to get a deal for your books."

Alicia caught her breath. She was becoming dizzy, and she didn't know if it was the tightness of the man's hand on her throat or because of what he was saying.

"So Mary Lou lied about not talking with her sister?" Gilly asked mirroring Alicia's thoughts.

"She lied about everything." The man spit out the words, and a stray fleck hit Alicia's cheek. "I was just good enough for her in bed. That's the only reason she kept my books with Prime Crime. I heard what she said to Mary Lou about how much better the McKinney's books were. That's a joke. I decided to show her that I knew how to stage a murder scene." His voice grew evil, and Alicia recognized the same tone that Tina had used on the audio device she'd tried to blackmail John with. Gloria had sounded the same last year. She and Gilly were dealing with a madman.

"How did you do that?" Gilly asked, still trying to keep him talking, but not moving from her spot.

"I asked her to join me at the library after she came back from her dinner. I told her I wanted to show her some crime books that would help me with my next mystery. I knew she would find that strange, so I added that it would be romantic for us to get cozy in the stacks with no one around."

"But how did you get in?" Gilly asked. Alicia wanted to voice the same question, but she could barely breathe. His grip had gotten tighter as he'd talked, and she prayed he'd loosen it a bit with his reply.

"Research. I've learned a lot through the crimes I've committed in my books. I think Mary Beth was impressed."

Alicia still didn't understand how the police hadn't been able to tell Halliday had broken in, but then she remembered that Gilly had theorized that some of the details had been kept from the public.

"Why didn't you just kill her here?" Gilly asked. Alicia noticed her composure was starting to crack. Her voice sounded shaky. She was probably wondering how much longer they could keep Halliday talking.

"I wanted to follow the book as closely as possible." Alicia realized he meant the library murder scene she and John had included in *Written in Stone*.

Suddenly, the grip around Alicia's neck loosened. She was relieved until Halliday pushed her forward toward Gilly. She rammed into the wall, but now both of Halliday's hands were free.

"I don't need to tell you the rest. Some things are best left up to the reader's imaginations." He pointed the gun at a spot between them. The faces of John and the twins flashed before Alicia as he clicked back the trigger.

Chapter Twenty-Three

Alicia shut her eyes as the shot rang out. She felt nothing. Why wasn't there any pain? Why only one shot? Maybe she was spared, and Gilly was dead. The horror of that thought made her open her eyes and then she saw him on the floor, shot in the leg, and rolling toward the gun that had fallen from his hand. A high-heeled shoe kicked it away as Lindsey Harrington entered the room, pointing her pistol at Halliday. Alicia thought she must really be dead because what was John's ex-girlfriend doing there?

"Don't move, or I'll shoot you again." Lindsey waved the gun as she inched forward. Su Li followed behind, also holding a gun. "Stryder's men are downstairs and will be up shortly." She turned to Alicia and Gilly, whose face also held an expression of astonishment mixed with relief.

"It's a good thing I followed you ladies. Do you always ignore your men?"

"I don't understand," Alicia muttered. She was trying to figure out what was going on as Lindsey walked behind Halliday and handcuffed him. "You're under arrest for the murder of Mary Beth Simmons and the attempted murders of Alicia McKinney and Abigail Nostran."

Through teeth gritted from pain, Halliday laughed. "What a great twist. You must be an undercover agent."

Lindsey never answered the question because Stryder rushed in at that point and took over. She relinquished Halliday with a shove and walked over to Alicia and Gilly.

"Sorry for the theatrics. We've been following Halliday from Long Island since the day of your book release party. We had a feeling he'd cause some trouble here, but we had no idea he was planning to murder you and Ms. Simmons."

Gilly's voice still shook as she asked, "Are you with the FBI?"

Lindsey smiled. "No. I'm Michael Faraday's partner. He sends his regards, by the way."

Alicia was shocked. "Did Ramsay know?" she asked.

"He didn't. We kept it quiet from everyone. I'll fill you in later. In the meantime, it's best we get out of here." She turned to Su Li. "Officer Li, why don't you follow Ms. Nostran back to the inn? She seems a little shaky."

Alicia still wasn't certain she was alive or awake. It all seemed unreal. She watched as Stryder and his men took the handcuffed Halliday to the elevator. As she and Gilly followed Lindsey and Su Li downstairs, she saw Matt Devlyn standing next to a tearful young woman. One of Stryder's officers approached them, said some words, and Amanda joined them as they brought both her and her brother to a police car.

"She's being arrested for her role as an accomplice," Lindsey explained. "They also have Halliday's son in custody. Believe it or not, the gun he was using at Chloe's Corner wasn't loaded. He's only 19. He said his father talked him into the whole thing as a diversion for the sheriff, so he could stalk you out before the midnight meeting."

As they passed Matt Devlyn, he called to them, "I'm so sorry about everything. I had no idea what was going on. Thank goodness you're both okay."

Alicia smiled weakly at him. She was still dazed. Lindsey offered to drive her home in her car. She said she wanted to speak to John, anyway. Alicia felt no jealousy at this statement. She was thankful Lindsey had saved her and Gilly's lives.

When John opened the door, Alicia's heart flooded with joy at the sound of the kids babbling in their playpens. She fell into his arms. "They've caught him, John," she whispered.

"Ali," he murmured and then, glancing at Lindsey. "What happened? Where's Gilly? What are you doing here, Lindsey?"

They walked into the house. "She saved my life, John. She's Faraday's new partner. Gilly is fine. She's being escorted back to the inn by the woman who was watching our house. She was an undercover officer, too."

John looked shocked but relieved. "You were tailing Ali, not me," he said to Lindsey. Just like John to make a joke out of the situation.

Lindsey met his smile. "Why don't we all sit down, and I'll explain everything?"

***

Although there were a lot of things Lindsey couldn't explain because only Halliday knew them, she was able to fill John and Alicia in on some things they didn't know and Ramsay and Stryder probably didn't either.

"Halliday was a petty thief. His books weren't selling well, but he had dreams of becoming the next James Patterson. Mary Beth cultivated those dreams. Unfortunately, she made him too many promises she couldn't keep."

"He mentioned a movie," Alicia said. "He told us that her sister was going to set it up for him. Was it true that Mary Beth had spoken to Mary Lou before her murder?"

Lindsey sat forward in her chair facing John and Alicia on the couch. She held a cup of coffee in her hand that John had brought out along with tea to calm him and Alicia. When he'd heard that she and Gilly had faced Halliday's gun, his face had turned white.

"I can't say for sure, but it's possible. All I know is that Halliday and his son were breaking into cars on Long Island last year. He was arrested by Faraday, but released on bail and seemed to have a good record after that, but his finances were in poor shape. He owed a ton of money in gambling debts. We thought he saw his opportunity to pay them off by writing a bestseller, but he had writer's block and couldn't produce anything. It must've frustrated him greatly."

"I can understand that," John said. Alicia knew how he'd suffered last year when he found himself unable to write their second mystery until a trip away had helped but also endangered their children.

"How did he think killing Mary Beth or me would help?" Alicia asked as she took a sip of tea. The shaking inside had finally begun to subside.

"We assume he wanted revenge on Mary Beth when he discovered she was playing him. He wanted to kill you because he was angry that your books were doing so well. He figured, with you gone, John would not be able to continue them."

"I don't understand how you got involved," John said. "How did you know to follow Alicia, that she was in danger, and why such secrecy? Wouldn't Ramsay and Stryder have helped you if they'd known?"

Lindsey considered a moment and then shook her head. "That was all Faraday's idea. He knew about your book release party, and he also knew that you and I had gone to school with one another. He talks about you often, and I mentioned our history to him once."

Alicia might've flinched in the past at those words, but she was now glad for them.

Lindsey continued. "Su Li, having just passed her police exam and given notice at her parent's restaurant, had just joined us, and he knew I needed some sort of backup.

He had his eyes on Halliday because of a message that had been sent to his office prior to the book talk."

"Message?" This was news to Alicia. "You mean Halliday mentioned his plans?"

Lindsey nodded. "At that point, I doubt the plans included killing Mary Beth, but he was pretty set on taking you out of the picture."

"What type of message?" John asked. "Did Faraday get an email or something?"

"It was a note that was left at the station. It wasn't addressed to Faraday. It said, "Marjorie Meyers must die.""

"Faraday reads our books," John put in. "I send him a copy every time one is released."

Alicia knew John still kept in touch with the detective who helped them when she went back to Long Island after her house fire. Ramsay also got copies of the book, and she imagined he took no offense to the reference to the detective they based on his old persona.

"That's how he knew the note referred to a death threat to Alicia. He sent me and Su Li to the book release party. When all went well, we were going to chalk the note up to a prank and return to Long Island. I wanted to visit with John, though, without telling him why I was actually in Cobble Cove. But before I could make those arrangements, Mary Beth was murdered."

"So you came to dinner with us to learn more about that," Alicia said.

"Not entirely. I still wanted to see John and Mac and your beautiful children; but, yes, that was my second purpose."

"The police stopped sending men to watch me," Alicia added. "Is that when you took over?"

"Yes, but I think I was a bit more discreet than they were. I didn't always park my car across the street."

"Why did Ramsay take the men off patrol if he didn't know who you were?"

"He probably had a shortage of officers at that point. I would've kept watching, anyway. I had a feeling you and not Mary Beth was the main target, but I now know both of you were part of Halliday's revenge scheme."

"What about Donald?" Alicia asked. "Did Halliday break into his car at the hotel and take his gun?"

"Yes. Amanda admitted that she knew her brother was breaking into cars that night. She thought he was only looking for money. She knew what dire straits he was in financially but couldn't help him."

"But why did he need Donald's gun when he obviously had others?" John asked.

"It must've been a coincidence that he found the gun in Donald's glove box. He was wearing gloves as he searched the cars in the lot. When he came across the gun, he thought of that scene in *Written in Stone* where the killer blackmailed someone by leaving a gun behind in his rented room."

Alicia recalled how she and John had discussed that scene. "So he really was going by our book? He probably didn't even know whose gun it was."

Lindsey nodded. "Nope. You'd be surprised how many people leave guns in their glove compartments, but he wasn't even looking for one. He had two others. The one he gave his son for the store debacle and the one he brought back to the hotel and which he planned to use on you and Gilly because she accompanied you."

"But that one was loaded," Alicia said, lowering her voice as the horror hit her again.

"Why did he bother to go back to the hotel?" John asked. "And how did he know Ali would go there again?"

"Another lucky or, maybe we should say unlucky, coincidence. He went back to talk to Amanda, but she wasn't there, so he decided to wait for her upstairs. Their mother is really ill and that's why she couldn't lend him any of the money he needed."

"So Devlyn knew someone was upstairs? Why didn't he say anything?"

"He didn't know," Lindsey said. "When we got to the hotel, he told us he stepped away from the desk for a few minutes to use the rest room before you came in. He thought he heard the elevator behind him when he got back. It's probable that Halliday sneaked in, didn't see Amanda at the desk, and went upstairs on his own. Your arriving there was another break for him, but it turned out not to be lucky either."

"He told us he was planning to find me before the midnight meeting, but that I'd ended up coming to him."

"Thank God it all turned out well," John said, putting his arm around Alicia.

"Yes. I don't know how to thank you for saving my life and Gilly's," Alicia told Lindsey.

Lindsey stood up and went over to the twins who had quieted down while the grownups talked. Bending down and giving each a kiss on the head, she replied, "I was just doing my job and helping out an old friend. Now it's time to go. Both of you take care and enjoy your precious family."

John and Alicia walked with Lindsey to the front door.

"Are you leaving town right away?" John asked.

"As soon as this is all tied up. I can't leave Faraday alone too long or he'll eat all the donuts in the station." She smiled.

Alicia recalled the thin detective's ability to finish a box of donuts without gaining an ounce. "I think we'll be fine in Ramsay's hands and, once he's filled in, he'll be as grateful as we are for your help."

"Anytime." As John watched Lindsey walk to her car, he turned to Alicia. "Those donuts certainly don't look bad on her."

Alicia tapped him on the arm. "It's a good thing she saved me because I was close to killing both of you."

John's smile deepened. "Sorry if we made you jealous, but even if Lindsey's mission hadn't only been to protect you, my story with her ended years ago. Our story is forever." He closed the door and took Alicia in his arms. They kissed as the twins giggled happily in their playpen, unaware of how close they'd come to losing their mother.

Chapter Twenty-Four

The next few days were filled with answers, but not all of them were complete. It was obvious that Cooper Halliday was insane, and Ramsay said that he might plea insanity. His sister and son, however, would serve some jail time. Stryder had broken the news to Halliday's wife who he said had taken it without remorse but with some surprise. It seemed they had been far from the happy couple, and she was already in the process of filing for divorce. She'd suspected his affair with Mary Beth for a long time but had nothing to do with the editor's murder.

The library had reopened a few days after Halliday's capture. When Alicia returned to work, she'd faced Donald and apologized to him for the questions she and Gilly had posed to Roger. He told her he understood and that he had been stupid to leave his car unlocked with a gun in it. He had turned it in when they'd tried to return it to him and even persuaded Roger to give up his. "It's safe in Cobble Cove now with Sheriff Ramsay in charge," he said. "Even though Detective Harrington solved the case, Ramsay and Stryder were doing a great job."

Alicia laughed. "Leave it to a woman to get the real work done."

***

A few days later, Alicia and John visited Gilly at the inn and brought the babies along. Gilly's sons were around and had fun playing with the twins. While John supervised, Alicia and Gilly sat talking over tea and some of the brownies Gilly baked earlier. Only a few were left because the boys were intent on ruining their appetites; and John, a kid himself, grabbed a handful on the way in.

Gilly gently swayed in the porch rocker next to Alicia. "It's so hard to believe that your rival was actually your savior."

Alicia smiled as she reflected. "Our saviors, Gilly. I thought we were doomed. I guess that cuts short your career as an amateur sleuth."

Gilly rolled her eyes. "I wouldn't say that. If it was up to Ron, it would be over, but I think he actually welcomed our help. I wonder what would've happened if I hadn't brought you back to the hotel?"

Alicia had to admit that Gilly had a point. Halliday was surprised by their arrival and hadn't had the time to fully prepare.

"To change the subject because, to tell the truth, I'm sick of it," Alicia said, taking the next to last brownie in the basket. "Sneaky is back at his post upstairs in the library, but Sheila has put up a sign in the lounge for staff members to be sure to close any windows they open there. We don't want that sneaky cat, excuse the pun, escaping again."

Gilly laughed. "I think Sneaky is actually a good amateur sleuth himself. How is Laura doing? Has she hooked up with Matt?"

"Let's just say she's gone to lunch with him a few times since coming back to work."

Gilly winked. "I knew it. They have so much in common. It's nice to see young love."

"What about middle-aged love like you and Ramsay and me and John?"

"Even better. Old age love isn't bad either. I wonder if Mac and Betty will be going skiing again this year."

Alicia recalled how her father-in-law and the Director of the library board had gone to a ski resort at the same time she and John had been in New York City last December. Both of them had to return early because of the kidnapping. "Believe it or not, Mac mentioned to John that they might try skydiving this year."

"Good for them." Gilly raised her cup of tea as if in a salute.

"Did Ramsay say anything about Mary Lou? How she took the news of Halliday's arrest?" Alicia asked.

Gilly took a sip of tea, put down her cup and said, "She admitted to having spoken to Mary Beth the night before the book release party. She said she was afraid to say anything because she might be considered a suspect. Ron told me she regrets that she and her mom were estranged from Mary Beth for so long. Both of them aren't easy to know, but I think the face they showed the world was not what lived inside them."

"That's very insightful, Gilly. Do you really believe that? I mean the way Mary Beth pestered me and John, drove us harder than was productive. Look what she did to Halliday."

"What Halliday did to her, you mean. There's always two sides to a story, Alicia. He was crazy, and I think he initiated their affair and imagined the movie deal. She probably only kept him on for company. She must've been lonely."

Alicia hadn't considered that. "Maybe that's why she called us so much, why she took on more work than any editor for a small publisher. I never looked at it that way, Gilly."

"You learn to look at things a multitude of ways when you're raising three boys," Gilly explained. "And, speak of the devils, here they come."

Gilly's sons came rushing out on the porch with John trailing behind.

"No more brownies?" Danny said, seeing only crumbs in the basket. Gilly had eaten the last one.

"I'll make another batch tomorrow. It's way too close to dinnertime."

Danny's other two brothers both frowned.

"I was telling your boys about the two detectives you had boarding here," John said, also looking a bit disappointed that the brownies were gone. "They didn't believe me at first because the officers were women."

"I'm surprised at that," Gilly said. "I've been reading them the law for eight years now."

"But you're not a woman," John said with a grin. "You're their mother."

"Watch it, mister, or I'll tell the sheriff on you. Worse, I'll never let you have another brownie again," Gilly teased.

John mimicked a pout to match the boys who had gone running across the front lawn to play catch in a circle with their dog Ruby running after them. "Want to join us, Mr. McKinney?" Billy called.

"Not now. I want to talk with your Mom a minute." He took a seat between Alicia and Gilly. "I have some interesting news that I thought I'd share with both of you."

"The newspaper publisher sharing news. It must be juicy," Gilly said leaning forward.

"I'm not in the newspaper business much anymore, but this does have to do with my writing. Actually, our writing." He looked toward Alicia.

"What is it, John? Do we have a new editor finally?"

He gave her his boyish grin. "Better than that, Mrs. McKinney. We have an agent."

"Don't tell me. Mary Lou called you."

"Yes. She called on my cell while I was inside with the boys. You definitely are good at solving mysteries or at least of reading me."

Alicia laughed. "Well, maybe we should give her a shot. Is she sending a contract?"

"It's already been emailed to me."

"How did she know you would accept?"

"She didn't. I told her I'd need to speak with you, of course. We can look over the contract together later, but there's more."

"More?" John could drive Alicia crazy when he drew things out, but she knew she was even more guilty of doing that sometimes.

"I think I know what John is holding back," Gilly said before he could continue. "There really was a movie, wasn't there?"

"What are you talking about?"

"Gilly's got it," John said. "Halliday didn't lie. When Mary Beth called Mary Lou from the Carlsville Hilton, she asked her to consider *Written in Stone* for a movie deal. She's offering it to us now."

"Oh, my God!" Alicia exclaimed.

Gilly was on her feet, and her excited scream brought her sons running back to the porch. "What did we do, Mom? We kept the ball away from the windows like you always ask," Danny said.

Gilly was jumping up and down. "Not you, boys. It's the McKinneys, they're going to be in the movies."

Alicia just sat there stunned as John smiled slyly and covered her hand with his.

Chapter Twenty-Five

Alicia felt as though she was living a flashback with even the rain providing backdrop to the memory. She was back on Long Island with John, Gilly, and Ramsay for Mary Beth's funeral in the small cemetery behind Trinity-St. John's Church. Their previous editor's body had finally been released for cremation after Halliday, his son, and Amanda had been brought to justice. Stryder had not accompanied them this time, but Lindsey was there with Faraday. Alicia was surprised at how much older he looked; and, in some ways, in worse shape than Ramsay. It was interesting to see the previous partners together again.

The six of them were huddled close not far from Mary Beth's family. Mary Lou, her mother, and Mary Beth's ex, Dominic Carr, made up the rest of the guests attending the brief ceremony. Gilly held her large umbrella over Ramsay. Lindsey held hers over Faraday, while Alicia and John stood under Alicia's umbrella. Although she tried concentrating on the conversation of those around her, the heavy rain seemed to drown out most of the words. She noticed Gilly looked intent on what Mary Beth and Mrs. Simmons were discussing. She overheard something about a movie and a contract and knew that they were talking about the plans they'd also mentioned when they'd met up in the church's vestibule. The atmosphere among them was much different this time. It was as though the weight of suspicion and guilt had lifted, and the group could genuinely mourn the person whom they'd lost.

"I'm surprised Mary Beth's ex-husband came," Alicia whispered to John as she took her attention away from her friend and glanced toward Carr. Standing near the niche which would soon hold her ashes, he hugged Mary Beth's urn against his chest.

John, following Alicia's gaze, said, "He probably loved her once. This is his way of saying goodbye. It's sad when relatives never get the chance to bury their hatchets before it's too late." He grinned wryly as he realized his poor choice of words. Alicia knew Pamela probably felt the same way after Peter's murder.

The minister walked up to the wall where a blank slate would be engraved with Mary Beth's name, birth, and death dates in the near future. He also held an umbrella, and she noticed his shoes were caked with mud after accidentally stepping into a large puddle as he walked through the graveyard toward the mausoleum.

After saying a short prayer that everyone joined in for, the bald minister raised his eyes toward the small gathering. "I know Mary Beth touched you all in a different way. She wasn't the most personable lady, but she had strong convictions and the determination to see them through. She may have had difficulty in showing her affections, but I believe she cared more than her friends and family knew. It is with sadness yet relief that we bid farewell to Mary Beth Simmons. The crime that took her from us too early has been solved." He glanced in the direction of Ramsay and Lindsey. "We should be thankful that the Lord has welcomed her into heaven where she probably has issued him a full agenda." A smile cracked the side of his face.

Alicia thought she heard a few muffled laughs.

"Does anyone have some words to add before we end this service?" the minister asked over the crack of lightning. It looked as though he was hoping to wrap it up fast.

Dominic Carr stepped forward. Without an umbrella, he was getting drenched. He placed the urn into the small slot in the wall that was reserved for it and turned to face forward. "I have something to say. I was married to Mary Beth, but I wasn't the best husband. She wasn't easy to live with, but neither was I. We all have faults, and we all make mistakes. I wish I could tell her now that I'm sorry for how I hurt her." He lowered his head, his rain-flattened hair dripping drops down his face mixing with what Alicia saw were tears.

John took the stage next walking up to the Minister and standing next to Carr. "Alicia and I knew Mary Beth since she became the editor for our mystery series two years ago. She expected a lot of us, but she also helped turn our writing into saleable books. We owe her our gratitude, and it's our pleasure we have now signed with Ms. Simmons." He turned toward Mary Lou with a quick smile. "We recently learned that was Mary Beth's wish. She was always looking out for us." He walked back to Alicia.

The minister waited a pause, but no one else stepped forward, although Alicia saw that Mary Lou and her mother were both sniffling into handkerchiefs. They were finally able to release the tears they'd held back at the memorial service. The minister said a few more words, closed the small door on Mary Beth's remains, and then the group headed toward the cemetery gates and out to their cars.

Alicia, John, Gilly, and Ramsay were not staying overnight this time. They were headed back directly to Cobble Cove from the funeral.

The car Lindsey and Faraday came in was parked next to Alicia's. John had left his pickup home again. Ramsay and Gilly had taken Ramsay's squad car. Alicia could imagine her friend might think the sheriff's vehicle an interesting setting for a romantic interlude, and smiled at the thought.

Lindsey walked over to John, and Faraday had a few words for Alicia. Ramsay and Gilly had already said their goodbyes and were driving away, Gilly meeting Alicia's eyes with a smile and a thumbs-up sign.

"It was nice to see you again, Alicia. You look great," Faraday said. "John showed me the photos of your kids. I must visit and meet them one day."

"That would be wonderful." Seeing the deep lines that were now etched across the detective's face as the rain slowed down and a bit of sun touched the wrinkles, Alicia wondered if he, like Ramsay, would be retiring from the force soon.

"You have a very smart partner," Alicia added. "She really saved the day."

He nodded. "I hear she and John were once close. I hope it didn't cause any issues between you."

Alicia paused. "Not after she saved my life. How is your family?"

"They're fine, but the wife still complains I don't spend enough time at home."

"You need a vacation. Why don't you leave Lindsey and Su in charge and take your wife on another honeymoon?"

Faraday laughed. "I heard what happened when you and John did that last year. Nah, I think I'll just hold off until retirement and then sit home and watch crime shows on TV while Daniella cooks my favorite meals." He winked. Alicia knew Faraday, like John, was the main cook in the family.

"Talking of Su Li, I notice she didn't come with you guys."

"She was on another case. We have to get back, too." Faraday put out his hand. "Be safe, Alicia, and don't let that friend of yours lead you into trouble." Faraday had teased Ramsay about his relationship with Gilly, but Alicia knew that Faraday approved of his old partner's choice in women.

"I'll make sure of that," John said stepping next to Alicia. "Gilly has a strange influence on my wife. I don't mind it when she shares her seductive techniques, but when she talks murder, I draw the line."

Alicia tapped his arm gently with the tip of her folded up umbrella.

"Ouch, you could hurt me, and there are two cops here as witnesses."

Lindsey tossed back her hair and laughed. "You always were such a teaser, John. You're lucky Ali puts up with you."

John put his arm around Alicia. "I sure am, and I plan to put up with her for the rest of our lives."

Epilogue

One Month Later

Alicia sat in the waiting room of Sloan Kettering Memorial Hospital, gazing out the windows as red, gold, and orange leaves drifted to the ground. It was a sunny October day. Looking next to her at John who was speaking with Gary and Patty, she reflected how life was full of so many coincidences. A few weeks ago, she'd been surprised to learn that Pamela's mastectomy had been scheduled on the same day as Angelina's bone marrow transplant. John, keeping his word to his sister, had not mentioned anything about Pamela's surgery to Mac when he'd asked him to watch the twins while he and Alicia went to New York to visit Angelina in the hospital. John had also kept his promise to hold his sister's hand as she went into surgery.

Now the four of them were waiting together trying to pass the time until they received word about their loved ones. Alicia and Patty sat quietly, lost in their own thoughts, while John and Gary talked together about a variety of meaningless topics from sports to politics. When their conversation turned closer to home, they avoided talk of Mary Beth's murder or the reason they were both at the hospital, focusing instead on the happy news about John and Alicia's movie deal. "I've been meaning to congratulate you both," Gary said, including Alicia as he glanced in her direction. "I just had so many other things on my mind."

"No need to apologize," Alicia said. "I know how worried you've been about Angelina. We're both praying for her."

Gary nodded. She could see the dark circles under his eyes that matched his wife's. She kept staring ahead as if in a trance.

"Thank you," Patty said in a low voice. She'd been following the conversation all along. Gary put his arm around her. "It's going to be fine, honey."

A short time later, the Millburns were told they could go in to see their daughter, and John and Alicia followed a nurse to see Pam in recovery.

John walked to his sister's side as Alicia stood back giving them some privacy. Pamela's short blonde hair was feathered against the white hospital pillow. She wore no makeup but still looked younger than a woman in her sixties.

"I didn't get a chance to bring you that PB&J sandwich," John said. "Sorry about that."

Pamela smiled, showing her perfect, white teeth. "Silly brother. Your being here is enough for me." She looked over at Alicia. "You, too, sister."

Alicia was touched. Pamela had never had a sister. Peter, Alicia's first husband had been Pamela's step brother, as was John.

"I did as you asked," John said. "Mac and your daughters don't know that you're here."

"Thank you." She looked relieved.

"The doctors told me they got everything, Pam. You should be fine."

Pamela glanced down at her breasts, covered by the hospital sheet, and then back at John and Alicia. "How about Angelina? How is she?"

"Her procedure's over. Her parents were just allowed in to see her," Alicia said. "We're going to visit her as soon as they let us."

"Give her my regards and Patty and Gary, too."

"It's because of you that the bone marrow transplant was even possible," John said as Alicia recalled the money

Pamela had gifted the Millburns last Christmas after it was not needed for the kidnapping ransom.

Pamela smiled. "If I've learned anything in my life, John, it's that money can do wonderful things if spent in the right direction, but it can also cause a great deal of pain."

Alicia knew Pamela was referring to what happened between her and Peter, but she also realized that Cooper Halliday was another example of the damage greed could do.

***

When Patty and Gary told Alicia and John that they could have a turn speaking with Angelina, John suggested Alicia go herself. "You shouldn't tire the girl out with too many visitors," he said, "but please tell her I hope she feels better soon."

Alicia smiled. "I will, John."

Angelina was sitting up in bed when Alicia entered. She'd already been moved to her own room, and Patty told her that she and Gary could stay the night. Angelina would be released the following day.

"Hi, there," Alicia said stepping into the room.

Angelina smiled. She looked pale but happy. Her mother had brushed out her hair, which had already grown in thicker than it had been before the chemo. "Mrs. Mac. Thanks for coming. Mom said your sister-in-law is in the hospital, too. Is she okay?"

"She's fine, Angie, and I'm so glad to hear that you are, too."

"I heard about the bad man who killed your editor. Is he in jail now?"

Alicia was hesitant to talk about unpleasant things, but the girl had been through so much herself. She knew she could handle it. "He's actually put away in a place where he can do no harm to anyone. It's a place where people who have problems in their mind are sent."

"It's sad." The girl's eyes were watery. "He was a writer like you and Mr. Mac, right?"

"Yes."

"What happened to him? Why did he get sick in the mind?"

"No one knows the answer to that, Angie. It happens." She paused, then said in a cheerful voice, "Don't worry about him. Just get well, sweetie." Alicia wanted to kiss the girl, but she was wearing a mask the nurse had her put on before entering the room and was warned about passing any germs to Angelina.

"Mom says I won't be able to go anywhere until I'm all better, not even school. She says she'll tutor me at home, so I don't miss too much."

"That's a great idea." Alicia knew Patty, as a Kindergarten teacher, was well equipped to instruct her daughter.

"When I can go out, can I visit Sneaky at the library? I'm so glad he was found."

"Of course," Alicia said. "Laura is keeping a close eye on him, so he won't be running away again."

"I don't think he will. He just wanted to catch the killer."

Alicia laughed. Out of the mouth of babes. "You need to rest, Angie. I'll visit you when you're back home."

The girl waved as Alicia walked out into the hall. John was standing there.

"How is she?"

"A little weak, but she's a fighter."

He smiled. "Like my sister and you."

"I'm no fighter. Lindsey had to save me."

"I'd like to think I saved you, and you saved me, too."

She looked into his blue eyes and realized what he said was true. They'd faced big battles and overcome small fights to create the life they now shared. They'd survived because of their faith in one another and the strength of their love. As they walked down the hospital corridor hand in hand, Alicia understood that there were no coincidences. Mac had been right that things happen for a reason. It was all part of their story, the one that had the happy ending after the characters confronted their crisis and the author wrote the wrap-up scene.

"That's true, John," Alicia said, squeezing his hand. "We've saved one another."

About Debbie De Louise

Debbie De Louise is an award-winning author and a reference librarian at a public library on Long Island. She is a member of Sisters-in-Crime, International Thriller Writers, and the Cat Writer's Association. She has a BA in English and an MLS in Library Science from Long Island University. Her three published novels include *Cloudy Rainbow*, *A Stone's Throw*, and *Between a Rock and a Hard Place* (Solstice Publishing, 2016) that has been on the Amazon bestseller list for cozy mysteries and was named the #2 mystery of 2016 in the P&E Reader's Poll. Debbie has also written articles and short stories for several anthologies of various genres and a romantic comedy novella, *When Jack Trumps Ace* (February 2017). She lives on Long Island with her husband, daughter, and two cats.

Social Media Links:

Facebook: https://www.facebook.com/debbie.delouise.author/

Twitter: https://twitter.com/Deblibrarian

Goodreads: https://www.goodreads.com/author/show/2750133.Debbie_De_Louise

Amazon Author Page: http://amzn.to/2bIHdaQ

Website/Blog/Newsletter Sign-Up:
https://debbiedelouise.wordpress.com

Acknowledgements:

I'd like to thank the fine staff at Solstice Publishing especially Kathi Sprayberry, Melissa Miller, and Kate Collins for all their hard work on behalf of their authors. They are truly an amazing publisher, and I am very lucky to be part of this group.

I would also like to acknowledge my fellow Solstice authors and other author friends as well as my family and all those who have supported me on my publishing journey.

To my newsletter subscribers who entered and won my character naming contest last November before I began *Written in Stone*, thanks for providing the great monikers for Nancy Haines (Nancy Haines); Lindsey Harrington (Jackie Tansky); Dominic Carr (Rose Foster); Cooper Halliday (Mary Preston); and Matt Devlyn (Melanie Bracco).

Last but not least, I give my heartfelt thanks to my readers for their interest and encouragement. I love writing for all of you. Thanks for reading.

If you enjoyed this story, check out these other Solstice Publishing books by Debbie De Louise:

A Stone's Throw (Cobble Cove Mystery #1)

Widowed librarian Alicia Fairmont needs answers...
After her husband is killed in a hit and run accident, Alicia travels upstate to his hometown of Cobble Cove, New York, hoping to locate his estranged family and shed light on his mysterious past. Anticipating staying only a weekend, her visit is extended when she accepts a job at the town's library.

Secrets stretch decades into the past...

Assisted by handsome newspaper publisher and aspiring novelist, John McKinney, Alicia discovers a connection between her absent in-laws and a secret John's father has kept for over sixty years. But her investigation is interrupted when she receives word her house has burned and arson is suspected, sending her rushing back to Long Island, accompanied by John.

Back in Cobble Cove, cryptic clues are uncovered...

When Alicia returns, she finds a strange diary, confiscated letters, and a digital audio device containing a recording made the day her husband was killed. Anonymous notes warn Alicia to leave town, but she can't turn her back on the mystery—or her attraction to John. As the pieces begin to fall into place, evidence points to John's involvement in her husband's accident. The past and present threaten to collide, and Alicia confronts her fears…

Has she fallen in love with her husband's killer?

https://bookgoodies.com/a/B06XGNXQCS

Between a Rock and a Hard Place (Cobble Cove Mystery #2)

Librarian Alicia McKinney has put the past behind her…

Two years ago, Alicia discovered both a terrible truth and lasting love with John McKinney in the small town of Cobble Cove, New York. Now a busy mother of twin babies and co-author of a mystery series, Alicia couldn't be happier.

Alicia's contentment and safety are challenged…

Walking home alone from the library, Alicia senses someone following her, and on more than one occasion, she believes she is being watched. Does she have a stalker? When the local gift shop is burglarized, the troubling event causes unrest among Alicia and the residents of the quiet town.

John and Alicia receive an offer they can't refuse…

When John's sister offers to babysit while she and John take a much-needed vacation in New York City, Alicia is reluctant to leave her children because of the disturbances in Cobble Cove. John assures her the town is safe in the hands of Sheriff-elect Ramsay. Although Alicia's experience with and dislike of the former Long Island detective don't alleviate her concern, she and John take their trip.

Alicia faces her worst nightmare…

The McKinneys' vacation is cut short when they learn their babies have been kidnapped and John's sister shot. Alicia and John's situation puts them between a rock and a hard place when the main suspect is found dead before the ransom is paid. In order to save their children, the McKinneys race against the clock to solve a mystery more puzzling than those found in their own books. Can they do it before time runs out?

http://bookgoodies.com/a/B01M59PPBY

Celebrating Christmas with My Characters

The characters from Debbie De Louise's Cobble Cove cozy mysteries gather in the Cobble Cove library to celebrate the holidays. Each character receives a gift from the author, and Alicia, the main character, reads some excerpts from the first book, A Stone's Throw, and the new release, Between a Rock and a Hard Place.

http://bookgoodies.com/a/B01N2QYML8

When Jack Trumps Ace

Jackie Riordan's in trouble . . .

When her jewel-thief father is caught in the middle of a heist, Jackie makes her getaway to his ex-jail pal's apartment. a man called Ace, who lives in an upscale neighborhood of Chicago. What she doesn't count on is falling in love with him and becoming his partner in crime. She also doesn't expect to compete with Ace's old flame or deal with his cat Roxie who causes her allergy attacks.

All bets are off . . .

After Jackie discovers clues left by her father which lead her to a treasure that Ace may have stolen, she contemplates her next move. Should she trust Ace and believe her father gave him the money, or head home to her mother, a religious hypocrite who would have no qualms about ratting out her own daughter to the cops?

Things that sparkle aren't always Diamonds . . .

Before Jackie can decide who the good guys really are, she finds herself atop the Willis Tower carrying her father's ashes in her pocket and aiding Ace in the largest jewelry heist of his life. Things go terribly wrong, and Jackie's only choice seems to be to walk away from Ace or face imprisonment.

https://bookgoodies.com/a/B06X8ZZCTH

The Path To Rainbow Bridge

A familiar poem for many pet lovers describes a place called Rainbow Bridge where pets go when they pass on and where their beloved human eventually joins them. If you have ever lost a special animal companion and wondered if Rainbow Bridge actually exists and what it's like, the answer is imagined in The Path to Rainbow Bridge.

This story, told from the cats' point of view, takes place during preparations for an incoming resident—a woman named Kate's elderly Siamese. The cats Kate has bonded with throughout her life also reside on Rainbow Bridge and are happy to welcome the new member of their fur family. However, a big surprise awaits one of them after the new cat arrives.

http://bookgoodies.com/a/B01LX0QRY0